## Praise for

# LAURA ANNE
# GILMAN

"Do you believe in magic?
You will when Gilman's done with you."
—*New York Times* bestselling author Dana Stabenow

"Readers will love the *Mythbusters*-style fun of smart, sassy people
solving mysteries through experimentation, failure and blowing stuff up."
—*Publishers Weekly* (starred review) on **Hard Magic**

"Layers of mystery, science, politics, romance, and old-fashioned
investigative work mixed with high-tech spellcraft."
—*Publishers Weekly* (starred review) on **Pack of Lies**

"Innovative world building coupled with rich characterization
continues to improve as we enter the third book of this series."
—*Smexy Books Romance Reviews* on **Tricks of the Trade**

"Gilman spends a good deal of time exploring—
and subverting—the trope of the fated-to-happen relationship.
Readers will find this to be an engaging and fast-paced read."
—*RT Book Reviews* on **Dragon Justice**

"Gilman delivers an exciting, fast-paced, unpredictable story
that never lets up until the very end. There's just enough twists and turns
to keep even a jaded reader guessing."
—*SF Site* on **Staying Dead**

**Also available from**

# LAURA ANNE GILMAN

**and Harlequin LUNA**

### Retrievers

*Staying Dead*

*Curse the Dark*

*Bring It On*

*Burning Bridges*

*Free Fall*

*Blood from Stone*

### Paranormal Scene Investigations

*Hard Magic*

*Pack of Lies*

*Tricks of the Trade*

*Dragon Justice*

### The Portals

*Heart of Briar*

*Soul of Fire*

# soul of fire

## LAURA ANNE GILMAN

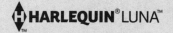

Recycling programs
for this product may
not exist in your area.

SOUL OF FIRE

ISBN-13: 978-0-373-80357-6

**Printed in U.S.A.**

For Josepha. For Danny. For Big Pete.
I hope you knew how much you meant to me.

*"You may go, human, and take your beast with you. Safe across our borders and safe for…"* He pretended to contemplate, but she knew he had planned what he would say before he opened his mouth. *"Ten weeks and ten days and ten hours, you may have, for your audacity and your honor."*

Jan frowned. Something wasn't right. *"Ten weeks and ten days… and ten hours,"* she repeated slowly.

*"You wish it shorter, human?"*

She had thought—She didn't know much, but everything she had read told her that seven was the magical number. But as odd as that seemed, that wasn't what…

They said she could go and take her beast. That meant Martin. But…

*"And Ty,"* she said. *"I fought to bring Tyler home. Those were our terms."*

# Chapter 1

In the middle of the chaos, the constant hum of conversation, the noise of chairs and feet, Jan could hear the clock.

"Shut up," she told it. "Shut up."

Lisbet, at the other side of the desk, looked at her with sympathy and then—clearly deciding against saying anything—went back to work.

Jan should do the same. But this morning, her thoughts wouldn't settle.

It had been ten weeks, five days, and seven hours since she had made her desperate bargain with the preternaturals of the Court Under the Hill, forced them to hold off on their raids, to stop whatever plans they had to invade the natural world. Ten weeks, five days, and a few hours less since she, boyfriend and kelpie in tow, had come back through the portal, battered and exhausted.

The supernatural defense had gathered—regathered—here in this off-the-track property to begin their race against time. And in the main room, a grandfather clock that had probably been installed when the farmhouse had first been built back in the eighteenth century ticked off those moments, as if any of them might forget.

Jan looked around the room, crowded with half a dozen battered metal desks similar to her own, and was painfully aware that she was the only human there, the only one who probably didn't have some sort of supernatural time-of-day awareness hard-coded into her wetware. She didn't need it; she could feel the hours passing like her own heartbeat. Every morning, she watched the sun rise into the sky, so different from the ever-present gloom of the preternatural realm, and felt time slipping away from them.

Being the only human didn't make her special, though. None of them could forget. Everyone here lived and breathed with the knowledge that every moment pushed against them, straining the atmosphere, making even the most patient of the them—and few of them were patient to begin with—snap at each other over the smallest of things.

Ten weeks, five days, and seven hours had gone by. They had four days and, what, seventeen hours left before the truce ended, and the preternaturals—the elves of lore, lovely and deadly—were free once again to open portals between the worlds. And once that happened...

Jan's skin prickled unpleasantly. She knew too well what would happen.

"Jan?" A voice broke into her thoughts. "You want some more coffee?"

"Oh, Roj, thank you, yes, please," she said, holding up her mug for a refill. The slender, blue-skinned supernatural filled it, then moved on to the next desk, where mugs were already raised, proof that no matter the species, caffeine was the productivity drug of popular choice.

Jan looked around the room again, rather than go back to staring at notes and graphs that weren't telling her anything new. Twelve weeks ago, Jan had thought that fairies, elves, werewolves were all myths, stories, legends. Then elves had stolen her boyfriend—lured him away via an internet hookup site—and she had been caught up in a chase that had partnered her with a sweet-tempered if homicidal kelpie, and sent her through a transdimensional portal into the heart of the preternatural world, where she had challenged the preternatural court to win back her love and managed to bring everyone back safe, if not sound.

No. Jan shook her head. Not sound. And not safe, either.

Before, she had learned, there had been certain times, certain places the preters could come through to this realm and vice versa. You either knew and waited, or you stumbled on them, and that was it. Now, somehow, the preters were using humans to open and maintain portals between the worlds. The preters didn't need to wait anymore for a seasonal event or random alignment.

They—the rightful residents of this world, humans and supernatural alike—were racing a clock to prevent an invasion. And the tick-tick-tick wouldn't stop—until the clock ran out.

Jan couldn't stand it anymore. She got up from her desk, pushing her chair back and making a harsh scraping noise against the wooden floor. Lisbet looked up again with a frown, and Jan smiled an apology at the *jötunndotter,* who just shook her head and went back to scowling at a printed report, marking notes with a red pen. Jan left the room, leaving her coffee there to cool.

The farmhouse was a sprawling structure, added onto over generations. Each room had been given over to another facet of their operations, nothing left to idle loitering. But one of the renovations had given the main house a porch that ran along the entire length of the back side, where residents went to steal a cigarette or a moment of silence, away from the ever-present hum of activity inside. Jan found herself there, inevitably, unconsciously, breathing in the cool morning air, searching for the calm she needed to keep working.

And then, equally inevitably, she looked across the yard to the source of her unease and disquiet. Along with the other outbuildings that came with the farm, there was a small shack that had been repurposed as an apartment. It looked harmless enough. The door was open, and she could see movement within. If she wanted to, she could walk across the grass, go up the two shallow steps, and go inside.

She wanted to. She wouldn't.

Tyler was there.

Tyler. The reason she had gone Under the Hill. The reason she was caught up in all of this. Her boyfriend—the man who had been her boyfriend—had been brought into that shack when they'd returned, and had refused to come out ever since. The damage—both physical and psychological— that had been done to him by the preters…they were still trying to unravel it. His memories were coming back, but they seemed…empty, like something he'd read and remembered, not lived. Even when he smiled at her, something was missing.

She had been warned about this, warned that there would be changes, but she hadn't believed. Hadn't understood. All the reading she'd done since then, crammed into half an hour every night before she fell over from exhaustion, had only gone partially toward explaining it. This was more than PTSD, more than Stockholm syndrome.

What the fairie world took, they kept.

Jan wanted her lover, her leman, back. She had fought magic to reclaim him, damn it, gone into the heart of the preter court and won him back by sheer human stubbornness, but that had only done half the job. The man he had been…was gone.

She felt the now-usual tightness in her chest rise, and breathed out through her mouth, then in again through her mouth, letting the tension slide away just a little. The last thing she needed was a stress-triggered asthma attack.

Tyler was safe. That was what mattered. Safe for now, anyway.

None of them would be safe for much longer if they couldn't stop what was coming.

There was a faint noise behind her, the squeak of a door and the soft sound of footsteps. AJ, she identified, not even questioning that she could identify the *lupin*'s steps now.

"Hey," he said, less in greeting than warning, so she wouldn't spook. They were all a little on edge, yeah. Even AJ. Maybe especially AJ.

Jan didn't turn, didn't acknowledge the noise until the *lupin*—the leader of this ragtag and motley resistance—reached around her with a small plate that looked as if it had been stolen from a back-roads diner, the white surface chipped a little at the rim. But it was holding a thick slice of toast covered with cheese, and her stomach rumbled in reaction, reminding her that she hadn't eaten anything all morning, and four cups of coffee wasn't enough to keep a human going.

Ironic, that supernaturals remembered that, when she couldn't.

"You okay?" AJ asked.

Her mouth twitched in a grin, even as she picked up the toast and bit into it. She was living in a farmhouse in western Connecticut, surrounded by supernatural creatures out of a fairy tale, while her boyfriend was being deprogrammed, and the rest of them tried to find a way to stave off an invasion from another...world? Universe? Reality? An invasion of bloody-minded elves, according to her friend Glory, who— when Jan had finally admitted what was going on and asked for help—had taken the news with terrifying aplomb.

"Oh, good," Glory had said, her voice scratchy over transatlantic phone lines. "Because when you disappeared for a week without a word, I thought you might've had a nervous breakdown or something. Elves are much better."

The memory of that conversation was almost enough to make Jan smile now. "Yeah, I'm fine," she said to AJ.

The *lupin* snorted at that, clearly not believing her. She turned to face him, wiping toast crumbs off her mouth with the back of her hand. The heavy monobrow and elongated nose that was almost a muzzle she barely noticed now; instead Jan saw the worry in those dark brown eyes and the way his mouth was trying not to snarl. Their fearless leader was upset.

"What happened?"

The snarl turned into an annoyed twist. "The Toledo lead didn't pan out. Team just reported in. There's an enclave of supers who've been behaving badly, but no queen." She was almost afraid to ask what the *lupin* considered "behaving badly" for supernaturals. Her research suggested that could be anything from pranking humans to eating them.

She was pretty sure AJ would put a stop to any eating. Pretty sure. But not sure enough to ask. There were reasons why humans and supernaturals didn't cross paths on a regular basis. But they had no choice now, not with a preternatural queen somewhere on the loose and her court hell-bent on reclaiming her—and claiming this world as their own. Better they find the queen first. Find her and use her to force the preters back through the portals, once and for all.

"So it's back to the drawing board for Operation Queen Search?" she asked, turning her back on the shed and whatever was going on there to face the problem she could maybe do something about.

"There are a few other teams still out, checking into leads," he said. "But—"

"But we're running out of time," she finished for him. The cold pricking feeling on her arms increased, a feeling not even a sweater would stop. She knew; she'd tried.

Ten weeks, ten days. The numbers ran through her head

like code, her brain trying to solve it the way she would have solved a problem in her previous life, when the worst problem she'd faced was a website going live with an error somewhere in it, and a client screaming at her boss, who would then scream at her.

There were only four and a half days left before the truce she had brokered ran out, before the preternatural court resumed their attempts to steal this world for their own. Not much time left for them to find a way to stop it.

"We're fucked, aren't we?"

AJ laughed, the low chuckle still as disturbing a sound as the first time she'd heard it. "We've been fucked since day one," he said.

"You know, boss, as a morale builder, you are beyond crap." But she didn't have anything better to add. They'd been working both sides of the problem, AJ's team searching for the queen, her team trying to find a way to break down the new magic, stop the portals from opening. They weren't making much progress on either. And every day, her skin felt colder, her lungs a little tighter, and she couldn't blame it on her asthma or the increasingly colder weather.

The *lupin* looked as if he needed a mug of coffee, too, but it was toxic for him. His dark brown eyes were rimmed with a faint pink from lack of sleep, and it made him look slightly rabid.

"The preters have kept their word, have stayed on their side," he said. "Definite downtick on reported disappearances." She knew that; she'd been watching the same reports he had. "But the minute the truce is over, yeah, they'll be back. And they know we're onto them, so they're not going to bother being subtle."

Considering that the most recent preternatural idea of subtle—hooking up with gullible humans via internet dating sites and then using glamour to steal them away, an updating of the old legends—that was a terrifying thought.

"Should we be expecting violence? I mean…warlike violence?" Jan still had nightmares about the assault on her apartment, the memory of too-fluid limbs, gray-green fingers reaching for her, feathers and blood splattered on the walls, her friend Toba dying, to save her…

"It's not the way they've done things traditionally," AJ said, "and preters are all about tradition."

Tradition being the dark of the moon creating natural connections between the two realms, wooing humans by song and dance, or whatever the fairy tales claimed, not sexy chatroom profiles and hauling their prey through portals forced into existence by some unknown magic.

"But from the reports," AJ went on, "and your leman's memories, such as they are, I think we can't rule it out. Whatever new magic they're using to create these new portals, it's changing them."

"And not for the better," Jan said with feeling.

"They were never all that great to begin with," the *lupin* said, monobrow raised slightly. "We just knew what to expect from them."

"I've become a big fan of predictability," Jan said, even as her cell phone, stashed in her jeans pocket, vibrated and let out a small chime. Crap signal, but her alarms still worked. "My group should be getting ready to log in for the morning meeting. You want me to mention this or not?" She might have been—nominally—leading that side of their operation, but AJ made the decisions. He was their pack leader, literally as well as figuratively.

"No," he said, then added, "no point to it, is there?"

She'd learned how to recognize the twitch of his face that meant a real, if ironic, smile, and grimaced in return. He was right. Since nothing had changed, there was no point wasting time talking about it. "If we actually come up with anything, I'll let you know."

Jan paused in the hallway before going inside, doing a quick personal inventory. Shirt, not coffee-stained. Hair, reasonably combed. Face, presumably clean, or at least AJ hadn't mentioned anything, and he would have.

"Oh, god, I hate this," she muttered.

Jan had lasted exactly one year in a traditional job before finding one that allowed her to telecommute. Most of her day had been spent working in front of monitors, interacting with people via text or the occasional vid conference. Jan hadn't been required to attend meetings in person, much less expected to lead those meetings. Fortunately, Ops—*her* team—was easy enough to manage, once she had all her geeks pointed in the same direction.

She took a deep breath and said her mantra, the same one she had been saying for weeks now: *You are Jan Coughlin, who was chosen out of how many others to save the world; you have survived gnome attacks and the preter court, being attacked by creatures you can't identify, and this briefing is by comparison a piece of cake. Damn it.*

The communications room had taken over what had been the front parlor in the original farmhouse. The rest of the main floor had been given over to the work space she'd been using earlier, the constant flow of people making it unworkable for conferences of any size and impractical for any kind of privacy. So they'd kicked out the supers who had been nesting in the parlor, cleared all the furniture out, and replaced it with a narrow trestle table that could seat six with room for paperwork and coffee mugs, and hung a massive monitor on the far wall. When the brand-new communications system—

ordered and installed by Jan herself—wasn't in use, the rest of the room was taken over for smaller meetings. But right now, it was filled with people, all waiting for her.

Jan was the only human in the room. She'd almost gotten used to that by now, shoving her way past Lisbet and Meredith, the *lupin* who had found them and brought them here after they'd come back through the portal, to get to her chair. They both looked up and nodded as she passed. Despite AJ's original claim that supernaturals didn't use tech, it had turned out that there were a number of them who not only did, but understood it better than their alleged human expert. Jan was a geek, but her skills were testing and repairing, not creating. There were ten members of her team, including Jan herself, and four of them could blow her out of the water when it came to figuring out *how* things worked.

Five if you counted the person on the screen.

"Hey, Janny-girl. You look like shite."

Jan gave the speaker a finger and sat down, placing her reclaimed coffee on the table within easy reach. "Morning to you, too, Glory." It was afternoon in the U.K. where the other woman was, actually, but Jan held that at eight in the morning she didn't have to make allowances for anyone else.

The other woman raised her own mug in counter-salute, even as the display split, her image taking up the left-hand side, while another face appeared on the right.

"Hey, y'all." The man in the new display waggled his fingers, and another hand reached in from offscreen to wave, as well. Kit and Laurie, out in Portland. It was oh-fuck-early out there, but the two of them had probably been up all night.

Glory, Kit, and Laurie: three of the five people Jan had dared contact after escaping the preters. The three of the five who had actually listened—*believed*. Or at least, not immedi-

ately assumed that she had lost her mind or that she was pulling the monster of all pranks.

Jan winced a little, thinking of the reaction of the other
two, people she'd thought she could trust, could count on to
have her back. One of them had been her boss—had been,
since he'd fired her on the spot. Her only consolation was that
if they failed and the preters overran this world, she'd be able
to say *I told you so*. As consolation went, it sucked.

"All right, people, let's get this show on the road," Jan said,
speaking louder to be heard over the chatter of voices, trying
to project confidence and get-it-done-ness. She barely recognized her own voice. She wasn't Linda Hamilton, *Termi-
nator*-style quality, but there was grit in her that hadn't been
there a few months ago. And it wasn't just the lack of sleep.

Nearly everyone on the Farm was part of the hunt for the
preter queen or watching for some sign of renewed kidnap-
pings. She—and her team—needed to figure out how to *stop*
the new incursions, once and for all.

"Do we even *have* a show? Or a road, for that matter?" Meredith asked. The *lupin* would much rather have been part of
the hunt; she had loudly regretted ever admitting that she'd
once run a computer help desk, once it stuck her on the team.

"Meredith, please." Jan raised a hand, and the *lupin* ducked
her head in apology. Jan wasn't even close to alpha, but AJ,
who was, had told Meredith to obey the human, and so she
would. "Do we have *anything* coming in, from any source?"

They had to shut this down. For now, the portals were
few and far between, but the fact that they existed at all,
outside the traditional connections between worlds, was bad
enough. Nobody knew what the preternaturals could do if
they succeeded in opening enough portals to come here en
masse. Even discounting three-quarters of every fairy tale

ever, Jan knew firsthand that they weren't going to leave humanity alone.

Jan had seen what his preternatural seducer had done to Tyler. She had seen what became of the Greensleeves, the abandoned human slaves. She had looked into the eyes of the preter consort and seen nothing of compassion or kindness.

A world where preters could come and go freely, not bound by anything save their own whim, was not a good thing. Not for anything born to this world, human or supernatural.

That was why they were here. Four days and counting.

"Talk to me," she said now, trying desperately to channel some of AJ's natural take-charge-and-inspire leadership into her voice "Somebody tell me something good, something exciting, something that will make me giddy like a schoolgirl."

There was a hesitant silence, and Jan wished that she'd gone back to get her coffee before coming in here. Then Kit started talking.

"Well, if nobody else wants to go first, I will. I'm pleased to report that our little rumor-string has hit critical mass and gone fucking viral." He was clearly running on caffeine fumes at this point, red eyed and rumple haired, but his voice was certain. "Every person who's ever even thought about using a dating site is going to hear the rumor about the slave-trade ring scouting for likelies."

AJ hadn't wanted them to focus any energy on that problem, but Jan had insisted. They didn't know what sort of magic the preters were using to create the portals—before, portals had appeared at the whim of the seasons, or the stars, or something even more random, but Tyler's experience with the preter-bitch Stjerne had made it clear that humans were at the heart of it now.

That had been the argument that Jan had used, that had made AJ agree, but Jan would have pushed for this no matter what her pack leader said. These were people being taken. Humans like Tyler. Taken, abused, broken...and, unlike Tyler, not rescued.

Jan might not be able to save everyone, but she would do her damnedest to make sure no more were lost.

"I still say we should have just taken down the dating sites altogether and been done with it weeks ago," Lisbet said from the other side of the table. *Jötunndotter* were slow to move, their stonelike bodies heavy and stiff, but they had no patience with doing things slowly otherwise.

"Where's the skill in that?" Kit was...enthusiastic. Preters or prototypes, he didn't really care, so long as it was a challenge. Finding a way to warn potential victims without getting laughed off the internet, and making sure that it went viral, had been his personal side project, and he wasn't paying attention to the bigger picture. Everyone kept sane in their own way, Jan supposed.

"You really think that will work?" Andy asked, dubious. "Human males are not known to be cautious." Coming from a *splyushka*—a cousin to Koba, who had died to protect her, back when this all started—that was almost funny. The owl-eyed supernaturals were, she had learned, noted for their impulsive behavior. They were also the ones most comfortable with tech, so she had two of them on the team: Andy and his nest-sib, Beth, who was leaning against the wall at the back of the room, silent but alert.

"True enough," Laurie leaned into the frame to say, "but they tend to bull in when they think they can handle something. The risk of ending up...well, we made it unpleasant enough to put most folk off risking an easy lay for a lifetime of that."

"And the rest of them are on their own, and good riddance to idiots," Glory said, her accent intentionally heavy in a room, however virtual, of Americans, human and otherwise. "Now, can we get down to the important things? Like figuring out how these pointy-eared bastards are even getting connectivity on their side? Because if we can't figure out how to counter it, then we need to know the bloody power source in order to pull the plug."

One of the things they'd learned was that the new portals "felt" the same to supernaturals as major human laboratories like Livermore and CERN did, a weird sort of electrical buzz. Somehow, the preters had merged their magic to human technology, using computers and brainwashed humans—*like Tyler,* her brain whispered—to create and hold these new portals. But they didn't have the knowledge to figure out *why,* or how to stop them. That was supposed to be Jan's job

"I'm telling you," Glory said, "you need to get someone inside some of those labs."

This, like everything else, was an ongoing argument. AJ had sent scouts to the perimeter, as close as they could get without being caught. But just lurking, looking, and sniffing hadn't given them enough information.

"Yeah, you're right," Andy said, "and we're going to get that access…how? It's not like we go for the hard sciences, generally, so unless you've got someone who can turn invisible and sneak in and, oh, by the way, once he's there knows what he's looking for and how to explain it to us when he gets back…"

"Are there no humans who would help us?" Beth said. "Laurie, what about your friend from MIT?"

Laurie shook her head. "He hasn't gotten back to me yet, no matter how many urgent stickers I leave on my messages. I'm hopeful—Larry's actually the kind of guy where 'Hey, my buddy the fairy says you guys might be sourcing a tunnel between worlds, want to check that out for me?' might work. But I haven't heard anything."

"Well, we haven't had any midnight visits from the Men in Black, so he hasn't said anything to anyone else, either," Kit added. "Unless they're monitoring us even now, in which case, get off your asses and do something, NSA!"

"Focus, please," Jan said amid the laughter. She looked across the table to where Galilia, her nominal second in command, was sitting. Gali wasn't technically inclined, but she'd been working on some possible inroads among the scientific community. The *jiniri* shook her head slightly: nothing new to report there, either.

Jan sighed and let the back-and-forth flow over her, listening with one ear. If someone came up with something new or even probable, she would jump in. For now, she wished again for her coffee and tried not to think about her heartbeat ticking off the time.

Nearly an hour later, the meeting ended with nothing to show except a headache and a bunch of dead ends. Jan waited until they'd all left, then looked up at the screen where only Glory remained.

"You still look like shite," the other woman said, her normal over-the-top gestures muted with concern. "Are you sleeping at all?"

"Not much," Jan admitted, leaning back in her chair. It was nice to drop the leader mask; Glory was never fooled by it, anyway.

"I told you staying out there was a bad idea."

"And where else was I supposed to go, Glory?" After the gnome attack on her apartment, the landlord had revoked her lease. It wasn't exactly a surprise—apparently the entire apartment had smelled of smoke and meat, and the door had been busted open as if a bull had gone through it—but it had left her effectively homeless, especially since there was no way Tyler could return to his old life right then, and she didn't want to stay alone in his apartment...even assuming it was safe to do so. If the gnomes could track her on a bus, to her apartment... Well, she wasn't going to put others in danger—or risk pulling more supers from the Farm to guard her.

So she had packed up her tech and as much stuff as she could fit in a suitcase, put the rest into storage, and gone back to the Farm. Unlike the rest of the troops, who were mostly bedding down in tents or trees or whatever places they preferred, she had a room in the farmhouse proper, in the half floor upstairs. It was small but comfortable, with a window that gave her a clear view over the property and enough sunlight to feel as if she was in a tree house. If anything came over the property lines, either by ground or air, she could see it coming.

It didn't help.

Glory tsked, her painted fingernails flicking at the air. Even now, Gloriana was as flamboyant as her name, thick black curls glossy as a raven's feathers, and makeup perfectly applied. Jan envied her the bright red lipstick she wore. Glory's skin was darker than Tyler's; if Jan tried to wear that shade, she'd look like a clown.

Jan rubbed at her own face, aware that exhaustion made her look even more sallow, and wished she could end this conversation.

"And I don't suppose you're getting any, either, to help rock you to sleep or make you not care," Glory went on.

Jan's headache took a sudden right turn to migraine. That did it. Glory might think getting her itch scratched was the solution to most stress, but talking about her nonexistent sex life—especially given that there were no other humans on the Farm except for Ty—was below pretty much every other topic of conversation on Jan's to-do list. She just smiled at her friend, making sure to show as many teeth as possible, said "Talk to you tomorrow," and hit the disconnect tab.

"Ixnay on the sexnay," she muttered. "That's the least of my problems right now."

There was a cough, and she looked up to see a slender, scaled figure lounging in the doorway, a reminder that space was at a premium and other people needed to use the room, too.

"Sorry," she said and left.

Midday, the farmhouse was humming with activity. Not all the supers were diurnal, but the nocturnal ones also tended to be more solitary and, therefore, quieter. Plus, Jan noted as she worked her way through the kitchen, grabbing a sandwich off a platter as she went, it looked as if a lot of them were working double shifts, making the main floor even more crowded than usual.

The urge to go to the shed and check on Tyler hit her again, and she pushed it down. He had a routine, a routine that was helping him heal, and she had other things to do.

"Has anyone seen—" she started to ask, and a handful of voices called out "At the gazebo."

"Thanks." She shook her head as she left the house; apparently she was predictable.

She found Martin where she'd been told to look, out in the gazebo—really just a wooden platform with a canvas tarp stretched overhead to make a roof—lecturing to another group of supers.

"Greensleeves are arrogant but desperate," he was saying, leaning against the railing and letting his voice project over the space. Broad chested, with shaggy brown hair framing a long, squared-off face, and wearing jeans and a flannel shirt, he looked as ordinary as any guy on the street. Even his black nails could be a goth affectation, except she knew that it wasn't polish, that the wide-set brown eyes flickered with gold fire if you stared into them too long, and his other form was a cold-blooded murderer.

Martin was probably her best friend now, even more than Glory.

There were seven other supers listening to him talk, and she couldn't identify any of their species, other than absolutely not human. "They will try to establish their superiority over you, because they have none of their own in that land," the kelpie went on. "Don't assume that means they're harmless. They're anything but—they have nothing to lose."

Greensleeves were humans who had been taken by the preters and then abandoned, left to fend for themselves in that cruel, unfamiliar realm.

She and Martin were the only ones on the Farm who had ever gone through a portal—at least, the only ones still living who had done so and come back to talk about it. With her expertise needed on the tech side, he had been tasked with telling the others what to expect, not so much from the portals themselves as the preternaturals on the other side.

"Why don't they rebel?" one of the supers asked. "Humans are supposed to be the wild card, the ones who aren't bound by tradition. Why aren't any of them—"

"What? Charging in and biting off the head of the preter queen? Leading the thralls and changelings in revolt?"

"Yes?"

"You're an idiot," Martin said, neither kindly nor with any venom, simply stating an obvious fact.

Jan listened to him talking and felt an odd disconnect. She had told so many people, so many times, every detail she could remember of their time in the other realm, their experiences didn't quite feel real anymore. It was more as if she'd read it somewhere, read it so many times that she'd internalized it somehow.

But in her nightmares, it was all very real. That was probably why she wasn't sleeping.

She caught the kelpie's eye, and he nodded slightly; they were almost finished. Jan kept walking; he'd catch up with her when he was done.

She finally sat—and then lay down—on the grassy slope by the retaining pond, a green-slicked pool that was home to a dozen or so ducks and a handful of cranky water-sprites. They stayed on their side, and Jan was careful to keep at least a dozen yards away from the edge of the pond. Water-based supernaturals were just as likely to lie, cheat, and otherwise mess with humans as their land-based cousins, but their games were often more lethal. Jan remembered their near-deadly encounter with the troll-bridge in the preter's world and shuddered.

The irony that she was waiting for a water-sprite was not lost on her. Martin was a kelpie, and kelpies lured humans into riding them, then drowned them. It was, as Martin said, "a thing."

Jan couldn't help it—she laughed. Her best friend was not only not human but a borderline sociopath serial killer. Somewhere, her life had gotten seriously off track.

"I don't even know who's in the play-offs," she said to the squirrel that had paused, midscurry, to stare at her. "We spent all that money on the tech, and I didn't even get a TV." Or a new laptop, for that matter. Fairy gold was a myth, and AJ held his checkbook tighter than her worst client.

Not that she had any clients right now. Or a job. Or anything in the way of a future if they didn't figure a solution out, or find some weapon, or do *something*.

The squirrel's beady black eyes held her gaze and then it scurried off without giving her any advice.

"And at this point, I'm just sad enough that I'd take it."

"Take what?"

"Nothing. Never mind."

Martin dropped to the ground next to her, heedless of the dirt he'd get on his jeans, and groaned as if he'd been hauling bricks all morning rather than lecturing. There was a splash from the pond as someone raised their head to see who had arrived, then disappeared again.

With nothing new to update him on, they lay there in silence for a few minutes, just breathing. If she were going to "get some" as Glory suggested, Martin made the most sense. He had certainly flirted enough to suggest he'd be open to it if she asked. But every time she thought about asking, something stopped her. Jan didn't love him, not in that way, and some days she wasn't even sure that she liked him—Martin was amoral in the real sense of the word, and how could you call someone like that a friend?—but they'd been through enough together, seen each other clearly, and that had created a bond that was somehow more than love or friendship.

Some days, Jan thought that bond was all that got her through each new bit of insanity. She wasn't willing to risk it just for sex.

And besides, a small, smart voice in her head reminded her Martin was a hopeless flirt, yes, but one who tended to drown his partners. He'd warned her often enough.

Without anything new to talk about from the briefing and not wanting to talk about Tyler, Jan said the first thing that came into her head. "All your lectures, the lessons...does AJ really think they're needed? I mean, that anyone is going to have to go back there?" The thought sent a cold tremor down her spine. The preters' home was beautiful in a terrifying way.

Massive trees and sunless skies, dragon-sized snakes, and endlessly rolling plains that had led them to the vaguely familiar mountain that housed the preternatural court. No human, no mortal supernatural should ever have to see it, not in real time and not in their dreams.

"No." Martin plucked a strand of grass and let it flutter out of his fingers, falling to the ground, as he studied the pond where the ripples were slowly fading. "Not unless we have some crazy-brave leman who wants to rescue her lover."

"Or some crazy-dumb kelpie who thinks he can just march into the preter court and demand answers."

He looked away from the pond long enough to give her a wry, self-mocking little grin.

"No, AJ doesn't want to send anyone back there," he said. "But he doesn't want what we learned to be forgotten, either. You know that. They've been quiet for so long, trapped by the old restrictions, the difficulties in luring people into their grasp, that all we had were folk songs and legends. We need actual information to protect ourselves. Ourselves and humans. Firsthand reporting should last us another couple of generations before it's out-of-date again," Jan couldn't argue with that. Humans only knew preternaturals and supernaturals as fairy tales, children's stories, not real. They hadn't been prepared, weren't prepared for the truth. The weight of *knowing* kept her from sleeping, filling her dreams with worst-case scenarios and crushing guilt.

He rolled onto his side and studied her. "What's wrong?"

"I don't know. It's just… This morning I woke up, and it was the same as it had been every morning since we got back. That first rush of energy, when everything seemed like it was finally making sense, that we knew what to do, do you remember? It's gone. I can hear the clock ticking in my head, and we're getting nowhere."

Martin started to say something, a faint noise of protest, and let it trail off, unable to muster an argument, because she was right.

"No matter what we do to warn people, there are still going to be idiots who say sure, let's run off with a stranger, give over our free will—" and she hated the bitterness, the anger that was in her voice but she didn't have to pretend here "—there will always be enough idiots that they'll be able to keep opening portals. And we don't know how they're doing it or how to close them. I don't think we can figure it out."

"Your team…"

"Good people. Smart people." And never mind that most of them weren't people at all, not in the human sense, but she'd gotten past that weeks ago. "But this is so far beyond us, it's like…" Her hands waved in the air, signifying her frustration. "We've got theories, but that's all. And AJ's plan to find the runaway queen, use her to force them to leave us alone…it was a good idea, but they've gotten nowhere, too. AJ said the most recent tip didn't pan out. We're out of time, Martin."

If this new magic the preters were using to open the portals *was* based on tech, or somehow influenced by it, they needed to understand *how* in order to stop it. And this morning's meeting had once again established that they didn't and couldn't. Maybe it was a thing only preters could see, could understand. At this point, Jan wasn't ruling anything out.

The portals were the means, but they weren't the cause. Preters had always stolen humans, had always meddled, but they'd never *hated* before, not like this. Jan remembered her contest of wills back Under the Hill, in the other realm, and shivered a little. The preter queen had used knowledge of the portals to flee into this world and disappear, leaving her court and consort behind. That had been what had triggered this new behavior, their anger at this realm—their anger at *humans.*

The portals were the means, but the queen was the missing piece, the trigger and the solution.

"We need to find her," Jan said. "And we need to find her *now*."

Martin rolled over onto his back, looking up at the sky, but his hand reached out and gathered hers, fingers folding together. "So we will," he said, his confidence unshakeable. "You just have to come up with a clever plan."

Despite herself, despite or maybe because of the tension stretching her almost too tight to breathe, Jan laughed. And that was why she loved him, because he said things like that and meant them. "Right. I'll get right on that, then."

# Chapter 2

The Lady Nalith, once queen of the Court Under the Hill and now in chosen exile, was satisfied—finally—with the workman's efforts. She ran her fingers over the tangle of cords, then along the gleaming rim of the screen, careful not to touch the screen itself; she had no desire to interfere with the display, and even the faintest ghost of her fingertips could do that, she had been told.

"Remarkable," she said, her voice almost a satisfied purr. "Not even in my old court was there magic of this quality."

"It's a plasma display, millions of these tiny cells between the glass," the human began to say before being cut off by a sharp gesture with her other hand. She did not care what means the creature used. Her concern was not with the conveyance, but what it conveyed.

She stepped away from the screen and seated herself on the love seat, reclining back as though it were a throne, if one far more comfortable than any she had occupied before. On the newly installed screen in front of her, the figures moved and spoke, breaking into music and dance in seemingly random and yet perfect moments.

Opera, one of her new courtiers had told her. This was called opera. She did not understand the things the figures said, the clothes they wore, or the story that was being told, even after all these months of watching, but it did not matter. She could sit and watch and be enthralled by the display on the screen.

It amazed her, still, that in a world where so many were unaware of magic, unable to touch it, they could still create such things, almost carelessly, without notion of what they did. To pull wonder from nothing, beauty from despair, agony from mere thought...

Her consort would have scoffed to call this magic. Her former consort, she amended, eyes narrowing. Unworthy of her. He—all of them, those she'd left behind—had been blind, trapped. Only she could see. This new world, the wonders it provided. All hers now. And she would not share.

She rested her hand, fingers splayed across her chest, feeling the odd flare within. She had been cold for so long, she had almost not recognized the change when it came, had not understood what it was. Had not realized how much she longed for it, she who had longed for nothing before.

Her hold on this world was slight for now, still, but it would grow. Slowly, carefully, her presence a beacon for those who would fill her court, serve her whims. And the fire within her would grow, until it warmed her entirely.

"This is connected to the internetting?" she asked, tilting her head to follow the wires that disappeared into a hole drilled in the wall and from there she knew not where.

"It is." The human opened his mouth to say something else and then reconsidered, properly gauging her mood. He was enthralled but no fool.

Two human-creatures had come to install this internetting the first day she'd taken possession of the house. She had thought this one amusing and useful, and cast a glamour that he would return. Once he did, she had tightened her hold, binding him to her. He was old but strong, and his eyes were a pale, pale blue that made his skin seem ever paler. His graying hair and lined face should have repelled her, but this, too, in this world, instead fascinated her. Age and weakness...humans accepted them so casually, fought them so fiercely. It fascinated her as much as their creativity did.

In the old days Under the Hill, creative humans had been prized slaves, gems jealously hoarded. They were so fragile, their brilliance so brief, wasted on such short-lived, short-sighted creatures. Still, they were useful, then and now.

"You may sit," she told the human, noticing that he was still standing by the screen, awaiting her next comment. He nodded, arranging himself on the low cushions by her feet, still tense from her reprimand. Nalith sighed. Fragile and far too sensitive. She let one hand rest on his shoulder to tell him that she was pleased with his work and there was no need to be afraid.

When she was displeased, there would be no question in the matter.

The display on the screen continued, the characters moving about the stage. Their garb was elaborate, even by her standards, their motions large, their voices exquisite. Nalith did not know the story they told but felt herself caught up in their passion to tell it, something inside her twisting and shifting as the action twisted and shifted.

The sensation of being at the whim and control of another disturbed her, even as she craved it, and a frown touched her perfect features. Why was such ability to create given to humans, this power over her moods? How dare they think to move her, to manipulate her in such a way, against her will?

She had come to this world because she thought the skill would come to her here, away from that barren hill. But even here, in this fecund place, the final spark eluded her still, and that fact kindled her irritation once again.

"My lady?"

The hesitant, piping voice came from the doorway. The slight, rough-skinned figure kowtowed from where it lingered in the doorway, attempting to gain her attention but put off by her frown. She did not even bother to glare, trusting that someone else would remove it, and went back to contemplating the screen.

A faint noise confirmed her trust as another of the creatures came by, grabbing the brownie by the elbow and hauling him off down the hallway, their bare feet scuffing on the burgundy-and-blue rug. This time, her morning time, her observation of the gifts this world had to offer, was not to be interrupted. The court knew this.

Once distracted, however, her attention could not quite return to the performance, the beauty in front of her marred by her thoughts.

Perhaps she was surrounding herself with the wrong sorts. The thought occurred to her, glistening like a diamond. She called this a court, yes, but it was still a paltry shadow of what she once commanded; how could it expect to inspire? How could she burn brightly without the proper fuel?

Nalith considered that, the faint lines of her face easing. Yes. Of course. She had called the miserable little gnomes to her first, playing on their sense of dissatisfaction, the rumble of rebellion in their bellies, but while she used them, she did not trust them—they were too similar to the courtiers she had known, miserable, conniving creatures, too eager to consider their needs rather than her own.

And then the brownies had come. Wiser than gnomes, more civilized, understanding that their role was to serve and hers to reward. They had been the ones to find the first house, establishing the household, while she'd taken the pulse of this world, settled herself more comfortably and set out her lures, slowly drawing in others.

Once made aware of her presence, the creatures who lived here, the supernaturals, fell to her glamour, wooed by the magics inherent in her skin, her voice, her touch. She made them no promises. She *was* the promise: a way to break from the bonds that had held them down for so long, a chance to change the stagnant ordering of their world and become something more. She saw their ambitions and used them.

There were her human toys, yes, but supernaturals made up the bulk of her court. That had seemed proper, at first. She had thought it was the world itself, the too-bright sun and trees that did not speak. But now, now Nalith understood with a sharp clarity that *humans* were what made this world different from her own. Fierce and hot as the sun, as dumb as the trees, but powerful in their own way. Filled with a magic that Under the Hill had only been borrowing, for too long.

Just as they could be used to open portals, they could open this door for her, too. Be the soil in which her own ambitions could grow.

Nalith narrowed her eyes, staring at the display on the screen without truly seeing it. This world would give her what she wanted, or she would *take* it.

"Are you mad?" the second supernatural seethed, still pulling his companion away from where Herself rested. His fingers dug into the thin, muscled arm, not letting the other shake free.

"Cam, let me go. She needs to know—"

"She needs to know whatever she chooses to know. Learn your place, Alex, or you'll lose it. And more besides."

They were speaking in low voices, having learned already that whispers carried through the house and to Her ears. Brownies were used to moving silently through the world, doing what needed to be done, but they had no experience with the likes of Her before this.

Alex still thought it was important to share his news, but Cam was right: you learned how to deal with the queen, or you lost everything. Alex stopped trying to go back and let the other brownie drag him through the kitchen, down the bare wooden stairs to the basement.

The court's House wasn't anything particularly grand— a nine-room, three-story Colonial set on the rise of the hill overlooking the center of town, which meant that they were within steps of the main street, such as it was. Brownies tended to like small towns, but this one was tiny even by their standards. Still, it had suited Herself's demands: large enough space, few neighbors to intrude, access to cable television and the internet, and owners who could be easily driven away, so that Herself could take possession without fuss.

The building had been run-down when they'd found it. Now the walls were freshly painted, the kitchen updated, and hand-woven rugs laid in every room under exquisite furniture delivered by workers who'd entered cautiously and left with a glazed look in their eyes. The newest, most shiny tech kept Nalith well entertained with music, movies, and television, while the walls were lined with bookcases—some of which had been there when she'd arrived and the others added on. There was no pattern or rationale to the collections; whatever caught her attention or fancy was added, glanced at, and then either devoured or ignored.

The basement, however, had been left alone, and it was there that the two brownies fled, closing the door softly behind them. The cool stone walls and cement floor were bare and soothing, the lights dim enough to ease their eyes, and the furnishings comfortable and patched as brownies preferred.

The basement belonged to the lower court; it was known

to their lady but never entered by her, the one place where they could relax, discuss, and decompress from the pressure of waiting upon their queen.

The gnomes were not allowed in the basement, by common decision.

Other than their nine-member troop and the gnomes, there were eleven supernaturals serving in this court at the moment, not including those she had sent out into the world to scout for and protect her interests. Three of those others were taking their ease in the basement already: a *lupin* whose eyes Cam didn't trust and two six-legged *yōkai* who rarely spoke but were hard workers and fierce fighters. The *yōkai* were settled in the corner, their legs tucked under them, while the *lupin* was sprawled on the sofa, an open beer can in one hand.

"Seriously? What were you thinking, to interrupt her?" The argument between the two brownies had continued all the way down the stairs "Have you lost your mind?"

"All right, you made your point." They came when she called, not the other way around. "But word's come in from the old house, from the ones who stayed behind," Alex said, his voice agitated. "They came, the Wolf's pack, and tossed everything, looking for her. Looking for *her*. She needs to know!"

The Wolf had cost them the first House they had established for Herself. He had sent his people into the area, sniffing around, asking questions, raising suspicions. Making it too dangerous to stay, although none of them would dare gainsay Herself's claim that she was simply bored of the surroundings. If he were heading this way…

This house was more secure, isolated, more her Herself's liking. But they needed other options, orbiting courts to enhance her standing in the eyes of others, places where Herself could go if there was trouble. That was the plan they had laid out carefully, one strand at a time, as only brownies knew how to plan. Here, then elsewhere, building in Her name.

Brownies kept house; that was what they did. That was not, however, *all* they did, and it did not mean they thought small—or that they were always subservient.

"Court opens at noon," the *lupin* said, his gaze more alert than his body language would suggest. "You'll tell her then, and be able to tell her that we have it dealt with. Do we have it dealt with?"

Alex drew himself up as far as his slight frame was capable, and his tasseled ears twitched indignantly. "Of course. All they found was an enclave of supers, bonded together against the cold, cruel world." A brownie wasn't good at sarcasm, but he gave it his best shot. "There was no way the Wolf's sniffers could follow us here."

The *lupin* bared its teeth at the nickname but did not contradict the name. There were many *lupin,* running with many different packs; there was only one Wolf. Even before this, he'd had a reputation.

The Wolf had a reputation, but he did not have power. None of them did.

No one in this court had any illusions; the preter queen was not kind, she was not gentle, and she in no way loved them. But it was their nature to survive, all of them, and she radiated power the likes of which had not walked this world in ages. The supernaturals gathered there had cast their lot with hers, wherever it led, and if that meant turning on their kin…it would not be the first time in their history.

Most of their kind could not be bothered to lift their heads from the daily drudge, intent on holding whatever remained of their past glory or merely trying not to fade away entirely. Meanwhile, the humans, as humans were prone, saw nothing of what happened under their noses. Even the few in the lady's court, pampered pets who did nothing to serve, had been claimed by her rather than coming of their own accord.

The Wolf alone had resisted, rousing others, attempting to marshal a defense. It was doomed to fail but could cause problems until then. They would not doubt Nalith, but the court would be wary of challengers, wary of dangers to her rule.

"If he found that, he could find this house, too," Alex said, still worried. "It was one thing when they were hunting down the others—that served our purposes, as well. But he's sniffing for her now, and if his claws reach here..."

"She is stronger now," Cam said. "She had been in residence there only a few weeks, not long enough to sink her magic into the walls, set up defenses. This court grows, her power grows, and strengthens.

"But the Wolf—" Alex started to say.

"The Wolf will come to her the same as we did, drawn to her strength, and she will decide then what to do with him." The thought made Cam's ears twitch again, although this time his mouth shaped into a smirk. Their lady did not take kindly to those who challenged her.

"She's already thought of it," one of the *yōkai* said, finally entering the conversation. "Herself don't leave a thing to chance. She wants this world, so she has a plan. We work it right, we play smart, we're there when she wins. If we don't screw it up."

On that, all five could agree. Nalith had a plan; all they had to do was follow her decrees and be rewarded for it.

Above, in her courtroom, Nalith smiled. The longer she stayed in one place, the more it became hers, stretching her awareness into the very structure. The wood and stone, the water rushing through the pipes, even the wiring that hummed, but most of all Nalith felt the creatures moving through her court, doing her bidding and anticipating her needs, from the kitchen to the upstairs chambers, out into the yard where the ragged, raging gnomes built their nests, down into the cool earth of the cellar. They were odd and ragtag, these creatures, kin and yet not her own, but they contained the spark she had been searching for, each one of them. Hunger, a desire to be more than they were, to *achieve* more.

Even in this world, that spark was too rare, too useful a thing to be dismissed, even in lesser creatures. Her fingers stretched out as though to touch that warmth and then curled against the arm of her chair, reminded once again that it was not a thing she could hold.

Not yet, anyway. What might not be possible, here and now, to one such as her, now that Nalith knew what she had been lacking?

Letting awareness of her creatures fade, she watched the figures on the screen, but her thoughts were sidetracked, remembering.

*Her consort, not beloved but familiar, combed the hair of his pet and then sent it off to fetch breakfast. He stretched, content with himself, his position, his place within the universe.*

*She studied him, the too-familiar lines of his face and body, then turned away, hungry for something other than food. She did not understand it. A restlessness possessed her, turning her from her usual pleasures and satisfactions. Perhaps if she had a pet of her own, it would ease this mood. There were humans in the court, of course, but none of them were hers, none had been hers for years, since…she could not remember when. It had sung. She remembered that. Long ago. Too long, perhaps. Since long before this restlessness had taken hold of her, the sense that something had changed, without her knowing, without her permission. She resented it, but she could not resist it.*

*The antechamber had a window that opened to the air, looking out over the plains. A storm moved across the distance, blue-black clouds filled with occasional flashes of silver. Rare but not unheard of, not so unusual as to warrant note. The distant rumble of thunder carried across empty space, and she felt it again, that sense that something was different, changed. It had begun nearly two seasons past, a shake and a click inside her, like doors opening and shutting.*

*None of the others felt it. She alone—she, who was queen.*

*It had to do with humans, she thought for the first time. Humans, and the spark they carried, that made the court crave their presence. But how or why… Humans had no place in this realm, save what she gave them. They were nothing. How could they influence her so?*

*And then the storm came, rare lightning striking the windowsill where she rested her fingers, making her jerk back in surprise, she who was never surprised, never taken off guard. The touch shivered through her, and an answer came as though drawn by her own will, that touch of power spanning two worlds, spanning and binding them in her hands.*

*She hadn't understood then. But she had known the answer rested elsewhere—in the land of humans.*

*She had begun planning, that moment.*

The display in front of her ended, the words at the end scrolling too quickly to read. Nalith tried to hold the emotions the story had stirred in her, keeping them close. It was no use. No matter how she immersed herself, how much she took in, the feelings never lasted, leaving her aware of the emptiness once again.

*She had not been queen when last they made incursions to the other realm. In truth, she barely remembered it save for the busy flow of adults through the court and new pets after. There had been a girl child who'd sung sweetly, until the notes went flat and the words faded, leaving the girl silent. No matter how Nalith had ordered the girl to sing, the human could not remember the tunes. Too long Under the Hill, too long to remember.*

*That had been when Nalith had begun to understand that ter-*

*rible delicacy, that human gift. The court created nothing. No dance, no music, no songs or stories. They stole from the lips of lesser creatures, made them perform over and over until the color faded and the sounds fled, and all that remained was rote and routine. Dead sounds, dull movements.*

Humans could create, but only here, in this realm. Taken too long from it, they faded. And so it must be this place, this realm and not humans themselves, that was so filled with creation; if she owned it, she would own that, too. The desire drove her, beyond all reason. And then the storm had come and shown her the way.

A noise broke her from her reverie. Annoyed, she turned to glare at the doorway. The figure there—scrawny, with a red cap pulled close around its head, and fingers twitching as though it never knew quite what to pick up next—was showing signs of having been there awhile.

Once it saw that she had seen it, the brownie bucked and groveled until she sighed with irritation. And yet, the film had ended, and there were things that required her attention. And it had tried to speak with her before; she remembered that. She picked up the remote controlling device and muted the sound. "Go on, Cam." She was reasonably sure it was Cam.

"My lady?"

"Do not try my patience. Speak."

"There is news, my lady. The others have begun searching for you again, in the places where you have been."

This it interrupted her for? "Let them," she said negligently. "What care I if others nose about my leavings, like scavengers after the feast? They are no threat to me."

The locals—supernaturals, they called themselves—might not wish her here; she was aware enough of that, but they would not drive her out. Nalith had no intention of returning through the portal. They would simply have to accept that fact.

She would never go back. Never.

"My lady, there is more." Cam had perfected the art of the sideways reproach, the voice that said he of course could think of nothing more perfect than my lady; however, it was entirely possible she was testing him to see if he, too, knew what needed to be done.

Nalith knew herself to be arrogant, prideful, and selfish, but she could also recognize when a retainer did its job well and with a certain style. And telling her unpleasant things, without fear, was part of its responsibilities, however little either of them liked it.

That was, perhaps, why she remembered Cam's name among all the others scurrying about. It had style.

"Approach me," she said, using the remote controller to end the display on the screen. The human at her side stirred slightly; she had forgotten he was there. The brownie came into the room, its tasseled ears twitching only slightly, and made a deep bow as it came to the sofa, stopping just out of reach.

She noted that, and it amused her. She had never harmed any of her creatures, but it was good that they were aware she could.

"My lady, the loss of our previous House, while certainly insignificant, raises a point. Your court does not do you justice. This structure, while suiting your personal needs, cannot alone hold the fullness of those who wish to follow and serve you. We would extend your hold, with your permission, and secure your position."

"And how would you do this, o ambitious one?" She smiled lazily, content to have him flatter but aware that even such a creature could move to its own whims and try to cozen her. In that, this realm was no different than the one she had abandoned.

"This town suits your desires. You do not wish to leave it. And so we have been scouting new structures to replace those lost. Structures that, once emptied, would serve as an antecourt for those who may not remain within your glorious presence but serve nonetheless. Not for your own self, but to extend your hold, even where you may not reside, that all will know who rules them."

Nalith was definitely amused now. It had anticipated her desires, and that was to be applauded…but also to be watched carefully. Such an antecourt could easily be filled with those of their choosing, not hers. She had been queen too long, in a court ripe with challenges and intrigues, not to consider such a thing. "Where and when did such a lowly thing as yourself learn to twist words to your bidding so well?"

"My lady, I evolve but to serve."

Its response made her laugh. It might even have been true; these creatures had a reputation of such.

"And how would you arrange to empty and then acquire these structures?" She leaned forward slightly, not enough to alarm the creature but to indicate that it had her full attention.

"We have ways of making humans…uncomfortable," the brownie said. "What is done can be undone, and what was well-done becomes ill."

That had the sound of something it had said before or heard often. Still, that made it no less appealing for being old. There was, she was seeing, a certain *creativity* in reusing things that had gone before in new ways. Like two versions of the same play, where the ending was the same but the motivations might be in doubt, results shifting minutely with new decisions.

Nalith considered the proposal and then decided in favor. No matter the ending, it would be something *different*.

"You have my permission."

Permission had been all Cam was waiting for. Herself had plans, and so did he.

"I don't like this." Wallingford scowled out the window, his arms crossed against his chest. He was the oldest of the pack and least happy with anything they were doing

"It's necessary."

"I still don't like it. Gnomes can't be trusted."

"They can be trusted to do what they're set to," Cam replied, masking his own unease, focused on the plan, the plans, hers and his, twining together, each needing the other to achieve, although she did not know that, of course; she could not know that. She would flatten him, flatten them all, if she suspected. Nalith might use ambition, but ambition must not use her.

"And after that?" Wallingford persisted. "They tend to get... overly focused on their goals. And carried away with enthusiasm."

They both studied the group of gnomes huddled around a tent set up outside the house, at the far end of the oversized lot. There was a small campfire going, and half a dozen forms gathered around it—although there might have been less, or more, since the shadows kept changing shape slightly, making it impossible to count.

In theory, the supernatural creatures were all equal to each other, at least in their own minds. In practice...there were some species that did not play well with others. Gnomes, with ego matched only by paranoia and all that trumped by truly noxious eating habits, didn't play well with anyone except themselves. The Wolf's brigade wasn't wrong in calling them turncoats, even if the Unseelie Court could fall under that same epithet themselves.

"They have done the job so far," Cam said finally. "They fear her as none other. They will not cross her."

"And if that fear is not enough, once they start? If they go too far, out of control? That will bring the Wolf's eye to us here." The other super shuddered. They had no fear of *lupin* in and of themselves—even a pack was merely a nuisance, in the normal course of events—but the Wolf was developing into an irritating sort of nuisance, the sort that combined violence and tactics and was becoming very good at removing threats.

The gnomes had tried to take him down once already—if on Nalith's orders or another's, none of them knew, and none dared ask. The point was that the gnomes had attacked en masse—and failed.

"Eventually," Cam said, "my lady will have to deal with the Wolf, and she will do so in her own way. But for now, all gossip says they think the gnomes work for the old court, the portal-users. We will use that in our favor. By the time they realize otherwise, it will be too late, and we will be the only ones left standing."

## Chapter 3

They had been out by the pond for an hour at least. Maybe more. Jan knew that she should go back to the farmhouse, should check in with someone, should see if there was anything that she could do, anything she should do. Instead, she lay back on the grass, stared up at the pale blue sky, and tried to remember when life had been normal.

She couldn't.

"You all right?"

She smiled, a slight turn of her lips, less humor than appreciation. Martin had learned to ask that. Had learned that Jan's silences sometimes meant something *wasn't* all right.

Had it only been that morning she'd been on the porch with AJ, had talked with Glory? It felt as if it had happened the day before, or even weeks ago, the sense of urgency pounding in her veins muddling with the lack of sleep and the stress. Adding injury to insult, Jan was developing a headache that was settling in for the long haul. She probably needed to cut down on the coffee. Yeah, good luck with that.

"Another day, another lack of a dollar," she said now in response to his question, not an answer but as much of one she could give him.

"Are you still stressing over not having a job?"

Jan laughed; she couldn't help it. He sounded so puzzled. "No. I'm stressing over the fact that I'm not stressing over a job because we have so many other things to stress about."

Martin watched the way she was rubbing at her forehead, and sat up, turning so that he faced her. "Turn around," he ordered, his hands already positioning her so that she was now facing away from him, her legs crossed, her butt up against his own crossed legs. She obeyed, knowing what was coming even before his blunt-fingered hands started working on her neck and shoulders. His hands were strong but sure, moving over muscles like a trained masseuse.

"I don't suppose you did this for a living?" she asked, her body starting to relax a little.

"What, back rubs? No."

He didn't say anything more, and Jan felt her curiosity pique a little. Most of the other supers she had met were perfectly happy to talk about their jobs, the things they did to make a living, just like humans. Martin never did. But she was afraid if she prodded, he might stop, and the quiet was actually kind of nice, so she just leaned into his hands and tried to relax.

They were still sitting on the grassy bank when an air-sprite buzzed them, flying low and fast over the grass until it pulled up in front of Jan's face.

"Come!" it demanded, its voice way too imperious for something the size of a hummingbird. "Come now!"

Anyone could ask a sprite to do something; getting them to do it and right away? That meant AJ.

"We're summoned," she said to Martin, feeling the headache start to creep back. "Good news or bad?"

"Bad," he said morosely, standing up and then reaching down a hand to help her up, as well. "Probably very bad."

"More searchers back," the air-sprite said. "Come!"

That got them moving, if not as fast as the winged supernatural, who zoomed off well ahead of them. As far as either one of them knew, none of the search teams had been expected back today.

This might be good news, the news they had all been hoping for—that Operation Queen Search had finally found them the location of the AWOL preter or even, better yet, already taken her into custody. There had been rumors and hints and at least one close call when they'd been pretty sure they'd found where the queen had been staying, but she'd fled by the time they'd arrived. So maybe this time... But on top of the morning's non-news, she suspected that Martin was right.

Inside the main building, AJ was pacing across the braided rug, while other supers scurried about, trying to keep working while still trying to eavesdrop. Not that anyone was saying anything just then.

"We're here," Martin said, practically flinging himself into the room and landing almost by chance in an empty armchair. "What?"

"Go on," AJ said to a thin, red-skinned creature Jan didn't recognize and nobody introduced. "Report."

The super had obviously been waiting for that order, because he picked up smoothly. "Remember when we caught the scent of something in a little town in North Carolina? We stuck around to see if we could sweet-talk someone into telling us what had been going on there."

"And?"

"And it took a while, had to let them calm the fuck down, but the local humans finally started to talk. Seemed the most recent resident had been a tall, somewhat odd woman who, in the words of the only neighbor willing to talk to us, had her some weird-ass eyes. Nobody liked to look into them if they could help it."

Jan, who had remained by the door, shivered when she heard that, remembering the eyes of the preter she had challenged here, the ones she had faced to win Tyler's freedom. She knew what the woman had been talking about.

Supernaturals like AJ had unnerving eyes, too—the *lupin*'s pupils reflected red even when he wore his human shape, while Martin's golden flicker came and went—but even the unease you felt looking at an apex predator couldn't match looking into a preternatural's eyes and knowing that this was nothing you should ever be seeing, nothing that should exist here. The fact that the form was attractive made it no less wrong.

"I hadn't expected humans to be much help," AJ said. "What about the supers?"

The leader of the search team shook his head. "The local supers in that location were no help, mainly because there were no local supers to ask."

"In the Carolinas?"

"Not every region of the Carolinas has an enclave, AJ," Martin said, but Jan thought that he looked a little worried, while Elsa, AJ's right-hand woman, shuffled through papers as though an answer was hiding in an older report. *Jötunndotters* didn't have much expression on their craggy faces, but Elsa didn't look happy at the news, either.

"Show me a single county down there that doesn't have an enclave," AJ shot back. "More, one that's been there at least a hundred years."

"Well, if they had one ever, they're gone now," the team's leader said flatly. "Every super in a ten mile radius up and went, either months before or just before our team arrived. We found where they'd been, but none of them remained."

"Dead?" AJ's muzzle twitched, and Jan saw his hand clench in his lap, as though he had the urge to switch form and sink his claws into something. The thought occurred to her that she had never seen AJ's four-legged form, never seen any *lupin* change, but she put that thought aside when the team leader answered.

"No. No bodies, no stink of death, no stories. They merely left." He shook his head again and rested one long-fingered hand palm-down on the table, as though only that kept it upright. "They sensed the coming fire and took cover."

Not a storm metaphor, she noted absently, but fire. Supers seemed perfectly ordinary once you got past the shapes and colors, but every now and again she was reminded that there were deep cultural differences, both small and huge.

AJ stopped his pacing and stared at the ceiling, thinking. "And none of them came to us. Are we not reaching them, or do they not understand what's at stake?"

"They're scared, AJ." She hadn't meant to speak up, aware still that although they had needed her to deal with the portals, most of the supers here didn't like or trust humans much, either. "They don't care about what's at stake, only that *they* don't end up on the stake."

The team leader chuckled, a sound like rain against leaves, and nodded. "The human is right. They remember what has happened other times when the preters look at us, and they run to hide. But at least if they hide, they are not joining her."

Jan nodded, seeing his logic. Supers that were afraid would stay out of the battle and could be left out of the equation.

"Is she soliciting them?" AJ said, although it wasn't clear— to Jan at least—if he was asking or merely thinking out loud. "We had been going on the theory that supers were going to her on their own, but if she's actively building a new court…"

The tension in the room increased until Jan could practically feel it, pressing against her the way the sense of time passing pressed from within. If this odd-eyed stranger was the preter queen and she was building her own court, then their theory was right. This wasn't a visit; she was digging in and planning to stay. Worst-case scenario.

"Boss?" The air-sprite—Jan thought it was the one that had

summoned them, but she wasn't sure—buzzed down from the ceiling where it had been hovering. "I don't want to play Tinker Bell, but maybe that's not all bad?"

"Are you insane, feather-brain?" Martin asked, but AJ raised a hand, silencing them both.

"You think she could she be used as a possible ally—or weapon—to fend the preters off? That she wouldn't let them poach what she considers her territory?"

The air-sprite shrugged, wings fluttering. "Maybe?"

"Pointless," AJ decided. "Even if she were willing, or manageable, she's still as much of a danger. But... keep it in mind, yeah? Work that angle just in case."

And that seemed to be that as Jan watched the others begin to talk among themselves, picking up threads that had been abandoned when the team leader had returned, when Martin and Jan had joined them.

"All right, people," Elsa said. "Let's take five, get some coffee, and come back to look at the inventory reports."

Martin turned to AJ, speaking in low tones, and a few of the other supers gathered in to listen. Jan, not involved in the day-to-day running of the Farm, took the chance to slip out, but not before someone handed her a slim notebook from a pile, "For later reading, when you have some time." Time. She felt it pulse in her veins again, the words of the preter consort, giving them only so long and no longer before they would be on the move again.

She flipped open the cover and thumbed through a few pages as she walked: it was an agenda of the meeting, complete with index and footnotes. Jan wasn't sure if she should laugh or cry. Who knew partisan movements had perfect-bound agendas?

Elsa, she decided. Elsa was probably someone's P.A., when

she wasn't trying to save the world. Someone who didn't care that she looked like a rock, only that she rocked on the details.

Carrying the notebook, Jan made a quick pit stop in the bathroom—like at a concert, you went when you saw it empty in a place this crowded—and then paused in the middle of the main room, not sure what she was going to do now. Maybe go back to her desk and stare at the report, doodle useless notes on it. Or go over the notes her own team had made about how the preter court could be connecting to the internet from their realm, land, world, whatever. Maybe she could remember something else from going through the portal, not once but twice. That was the key to figuring out how the portals were being opened, and they just didn't have enough information.

Martin had given them everything he could, but Tyler… Tyler's memory of the portal, going through not twice but six times, was too jumbled to be useful, too tied up in his need for and his fears of Stjerne, the preter bitch who had taken him, screwed with him.

So that left her as the useful human viewpoint, trying to connect the magic with the science; only, she didn't know how.

Jan looked at AJ's report again and closed her eyes, rubbing the bridge of her nose. The headache was back with a vengeance.

Science and magic. That was why Laurie had joined their group. Kit and Glory were programmers, and good ones, but Laurie had a background in science, although it was chemistry, not physics. And that was what it had to be: some kind of weird physics thing, because the one thing that Jan knew, without a doubt beyond the fact that shape-shifters and elves and gnomes and everything else were real, was that the place they had been, the preter's realm, was nowhere in this universe.

Every time she lay down, in the instant before sleep claimed her, she could see the massive trees bearing an even more massive serpent, the troll-bridge trying to kill them, the bright, sunless sky overhead, and she *knew.*

"Jan." A soft voice called to her. Jan opened her eyes and turned, heading not for her desk but the small square of hassocks set in front of the fireplace at the far end of the main room. For once, there was only one person seated there, tech diagrams fanned out under one hand and a red marker in the other. The *jiniri* raised a hand without the marker and curled her fingers to indicate that, yes, she did want the human to join her.

Galilia was part of her team, not well-versed in tech or science but the only one who kept up with actual developments, who had friends in the scientific world. More, she was able to make intuitive leaps that made them feel maybe they were getting somewhere. Plus, she had a wicked sense of humor, Jan had discovered, and no hesitation about including a human in the conversation. Nobody here had been rude to her—they wouldn't dare—but Gali was one of the few Jan could consider an actual friend.

"Look what I found," the *jiniri* said, indicating the wide-mouthed bowl on the hassock next to her.

"Found? No, I don't even want to know where," Jan said, sinking onto the upholstered stool and reaching over with a sigh. Not even the world's most amazing handcrafted truffles could make things right, could stop the pressing of time, but M&M's never hurt.

"You were in AJ's meeting?" the super asked, going back to studying her work, but her head tilted in such a way as to indicate that she was still listening.

"Called in for the news, yeah. Not that it helps any, really. Knowing where she was doesn't tell us where she is. And unless one of you suddenly manifests some ability to track...?"

Gali looked up, smirking. "With some of the oversize shnozzes around here, you'd think someone could, right? But no. And if there was ever magic that could do it, we lost it long ago." She took another handful of M&M's and sorted through them with a double-jointed thumb, dropping the brown ones back into the bowl.

"We've lost a lot of magic over time. Maybe we can still do it and we just don't know how, or...I wonder if that's part of the problem, that we dropped a barrier, some kind of protective shield, and they're coming in because of that."

"Huh." Jan considered that, the report resting on her lap while she took another handful of M&M's as well, crunching them between her teeth more for the satisfaction of hearing things crunch than for the sugar rush. "Any way to know?"

"No. Not unless the Huntsman or someone who's been around forever knows, and if they did, they'd have said something already, right?"

"I guess." She'd heard about the Huntsman from Martin, one of the stories he'd told while they were hunting for Tyler. He was a human who had gotten tangled in supernatural affairs so long ago he was practically one of them now.

She wondered briefly if she'd end up like that, she and Tyler. Probably not. She hoped not.

"So, I've been wondering. If they're the Unseelie over there, does this make the one here the Seelie Court, then? Or are they both Unseelie and we're the Seelie? You, I mean, not me."

Gali put down her marker and gave her an arch look. "Defaulting to Celtic mythology, are you? Tsk. Lazy human."

"All right, then, tell me what to call them, and I will.

We're in the middle of deepest, whitest Connecticut with, what, twenty different species, including my own, fighting off one invader, and you're worried about me being politically incorrect?" Jan normally tried to be more sensitive to cultural appropriation and assumptions, but there was a time and a place, and four days before all hell broke through was not the time or the place, in her opinion.

Gali acknowledged the point, her delicate face scrunching in mock hard thought. "Exiled? Except that usually implies involuntary, and this crazy came here on purpose.... Immigrant Court? The Melting Pot? I have no idea. Crazy Court." The *jiniri* quickly bored of the topic, once she'd yanked Jan's chain. "Since it has no bearing at all on what we're doing, can we——"

"Queen's Court," Jan decided. "Because it's all about her."

"Great. Glad that's decided." The *jiniri* put her pen down again and stared at the human, long enough that Jan started to get slightly...not nervous, exactly, but apprehensive. Supers were like cats: if they were staring at you, they were either going to attack or piss on your pillow. Whatever Gali was about to say, this was the reason—not candy—she had called Jan over.

"What?"

"Jan, listen to me. You know we think the world of you——" Jan snorted at that, knowing full well that most supers had a dismal opinion of humans, herself not excepted, but Galilia talked right over her. "All right, *I* do. I consider you a teammate, and a good one. But it's obvious to everyone here that you're wasted, stuck babysitting us. Gloriana and the others are who we need, and you brought them to us, and now you should——"

"Go away?" Jan tried not to be bitter. For all that Martin had impossible faith in her cleverness, she knew as well as anyone—better, probably—that she was outclassed by the brains on her team, her skills barely keeping up with what was needed to figure out how the preters were accessing the internet, despite her own experiences on the other side. She had been Quality Assurance, mostly, on her job. She could test the hell out of things and fix what she broke, but the intuitive leaps that Glory and Galilia and Beth were making, the technical know-how that Kit and Laurie brought… She didn't need someone else telling her she was useless.

"No! Or yes, but I meant you should go somewhere you can be more useful," Galilia said, frowning.

"Yeah? And where's that?" Now the bitterness did come through. "Because I already volunteered to go out on the search teams, and AJ shot that idea down. And going back to my life like nothing ever happened? Not so much."

The memory of AJ trying to dismiss her still burned: *Go home,* he had said when they'd come back from the preternatural realm, staggered and stunned by what they'd seen. *Reassure your friends and family, your employer, that everything's under control, let them know that you're okay. The world isn't going to end tomorrow—not even next week. You need to pick up the pieces and go on.*

She had fought that, fought the idea that she could just go home, pretend none of it had ever happened. Martin had tried to send her away, too, his voice filled with sorrow and worry. *You'll never be able to go back if you don't go now. I don't know a lot, but I know that much. Nobody who chooses this, who chooses to walk among us…ever goes back. Not really.*

*I know,* she had told him. She had understood that she would be changed, had already been changed. Had known that she couldn't go back to what had been, even if Tyler suddenly completely recovered. But she hadn't thought that every way she tried to help, someone was already doing it better.

And never mind that she had brought those better people in because she *knew* they'd be better at it....

"Jan..." Gali's frown had turned into something else, something almost painful to look at. She'd thought at first that supernaturals were crap at the emotion thing—the *human* emotion thing, she'd thought. But that wasn't fair; they did care, and they did hurt, and they did...all the human things. They just did it differently. You had to learn the body language, listen for it differently for each species, and she was so tired of having to work so hard every day and—

And Galilia was right. Hadn't that been exactly what she had been saying to Martin earlier? They weren't needed *here*.

"No, it's all right. I get it. You're right." Jan was, first and foremost, a problem solver. She'd been trying to do that within the parameters of this gig, trying to think, work, like a supernatural. But she wasn't. She was a human. It might not be an advantage, as such, but it meant she had other options.

She needed to talk to Martin again.

"You're right," she repeated. "I need to...utilize my skill set better." It was straight out of an HR handbook and made the *jiniri* laugh, if ruefully. "If you do need me, though?" she said, even as she was standing up, grabbing a handful of M&M's to go. "To interpret, or break up a fight, or..."

"We'll howl your name loud enough to be heard over in Boston," Galilia promised.

Jan had spoken casually, as though she only had to think about what to do and a solution would appear. Figuring out what she was doing wrong was one thing. Finding the right thing to do? Harder.

*Be clever,* her brain whispered. *Be human, be stubborn, be clever. They brought you in because you had Tyler's heart, because only the heart could save him. So be the clever heart, damn it.*

What did a clever heart do?

Martin was still in the meeting with AJ, so Jan wandered through the farmhouse, acutely aware that everyone else had a place to be, a thing to do, either working on assignments or taking part in the chores that kept the farmhouse humming along, despite so many beings living there. Cleaning, cooking, managing the garden nestled under makeshift greenhouse walls, digging latrine trenches and covering them up again...

Jan had never thought about what it might be like to live in a military encampment until, suddenly, she was.

Trying to escape the buzz of people who had a clue and a purpose, Jan wandered outside, shivering a little in the afternoon air. Her feet kept her moving, until she found herself standing outside the shed, her toes practically touching the lower riser of the stairs. Suddenly, her throat was tight and her heart pounding, as though she was about to have another asthma attack.

She reached down to touch the inhaler in her jeans pocket, like a magical talisman. She had braved Under the Hill, had faced down the preter court. She could do this.

Jan took the steps before she could talk herself out of it, and with her free hand she knocked once on the wooden door.

It swung open immediately, almost as though they'd been expecting her. "Jan." Zan had been working with Tyler, pretty much 24/7 since they'd returned. A healer—combination medic and therapist—Zan looked almost human, with a narrow face and sharp features, but a birthmark the size and shape of a sooty quarter on the pale-skinned forehead drew the eye before anything else. "We haven't seen you for a while."

"Yeah." And now Jan felt like even more useless shit. "I'm sorry, I just..." Excuses weren't going to cut it; they both knew why she had been avoiding the shed. "How is he doing?"

"Come in."

That wasn't an answer, and they both knew it. Jan stepped into the shed, her hand still touching the inhaler, and saw her lover seated at the desk at the far end of the common space.

The supernaturals were taking good care of Tyler; she knew that. Seeing the space he was kept in reminded her of that fact. *Shed* was a misnomer; it was more of a cottage on the inside, with a kitchenette and enough room for the work area, and a living room space with a sofa and armchair, and there was a door off to the side, to a small bedroom addition. Tyler slept there, while Zan had the pullout sofa, able to respond at a moment's notice if the human needed care.

"Hi," she said when Ty turned to look at her. That so-familiar face, the dark skin and elegant fingers that were wrapped around a paintbrush now... She supposed it was therapy of a sort, the kind they had veterans and stroke victims do. She would have had him singing, not painting; Tyler didn't have the best voice, but he'd always loved to sing. There was a stereo in the shed, but she'd never actually heard music coming... Maybe she should suggest that.

"Hi," he said, and Jan's chest hurt. That wasn't Ty, not the tone he used with her, not the sharp, funny one or the sweeter, softer one when he was feeling playful or romantic. But it wasn't the cold "I don't know you" voice he'd used in the preter's world, either, so that was something, right? He wasn't as lost, as confused as he'd been when they'd come back.

She had visited enough before to know that there were good days and bad ones. And sometimes there were worse ones.

"I know you," he said now. "You..."

"This is Jan," the healer said. "You remember Jan."

Something familiar moved in his face, a tilt of his head, the way his gaze slid over her, face to body, and then back up to her face, and for a moment Jan thought that this would be the day he broke the last of the preter's bonds, came back to the man she loved.

"She's human. Like me."

"Yes," Zan said encouragingly, even as Jan tried not to feel too much disappointment.

"She was from my before." He'd split his awareness into before, there, and now, compartmentalizing to deal with the damage. "She took me away from there."

They'd been through this exchange before. Sometimes it was a good thing; sometimes it sent him into a muted fury. Jan couldn't tell from his voice if today it was a good thing or a bad thing.

"Yes," Zan said again, and Jan tried to keep her face neutral but positive, the way they'd showed her.

"Oh. I guess I should thank you, then." Tyler tilted his head the other way and stared at her, as though waiting for his next cue. That was the hardest thing to watch, how a man who'd once been socially adept, able to interact with anyone effortlessly, with charm and humor, now seemed lost in even the most basic of exchanges, always waiting for someone to tell him what to do or how to react. She could have dealt with a relationship ending, but not the loss of *person* Ty had been once.

"It was…" She couldn't say *a pleasure*. She couldn't say that. "I'm glad you're home," she finished, aware that he wasn't home, she wasn't home, this wasn't home. They'd never go back "home" again, not that way.

Her distress seemed to communicate itself to Tyler, because he pulled back physically. His face seemed to almost crumple, his arms drawing around his torso, and he rocked back and forth in his chair.

"Ty?" She couldn't help it; she stepped forward, her hand outstretched. His pain and confusion hurt her almost as badly, guilt for being the cause warring with exasperation that he seemed to blame *her.*

"Home. Home. Stjerne will punish me. Need to go home."

"Damn," Zan said quietly, moving across the room with a silent grace, cutting Jan's own approach off and placing gentle hands on Tyler's shoulder. "Tyler, it's all right. You're safe. You're here. Stjerne is gone. You control this space. Nothing can come here that hurts you."

"Make her go away. Go away."

The healer kept speaking, even-toned and calm. "You control this space, Tyler. If you don't want something or someone here, you can make them go away."

"Go away," he said.

Jan went, closing the door gently behind her.

It wasn't personal, not like that. Jan understood. Tyler had been badly abused by the preters, some kind of brainwashing that she didn't quite understand. That was why he was here, rather than getting help in the human world—the moment he started talking about what had happened, who had done this to him, they'd assume he was insane and put him away forever.

The same way they'd try to put her away if she tried to tell anyone. She had already lost her job over it, with no chance of getting a referral from her boss, who now thought she was insane, and she had probably ruined any chance of getting a new job back in her industry, as well.

Maybe she could go to work with AJ's car thieves. Or whatever it was that Martin did for a living when he wasn't fighting off preternatural invasions.

She thought about what the kelpie might possibly do for a living and shook her head. Or maybe not.

"Jobs are kind of a worry for after you save the world,"

she said, pressing the heels of her hands against her eyes. The tears had receded and, miraculously, so had the headache; Jan wouldn't have put it past Zan to have slipped a whammy on her, or whatever healing magic it was a unicorn did.

Thanking someone, though, seemed to be bad manners here. And Jan was avoiding the issue, trying to take on other people's problems instead of her own. She needed somewhere to think, somewhere nobody would bother her or summon her while she thought.

The problem with the Farm was that it was too crowded. Even the attic floor, nominally her bedroom space, had a meeting going on in the stairwell, three supers, who looked too much like praying mantises for Jan's comfort, hunched together, trying to put together a report. No matter where she turned, in the House or any of the outbuildings, things were happening, people were being *useful*. Everyone except her.

"Shut up," she told herself. "Stubborn and clever, remember?" So she didn't know what to do yet. She *would*. It was like the time immediately after Tyler had disappeared all over again, but then she'd had the insanity of suddenly discovering about supernaturals and the fact that Tyler had been elf-napped. Now she knew what she was facing. And she wasn't facing it alone.

"Hey." She accosted one of the kitchen workers, a dryad whose long green hair was tied up in a scarf, her long arms coated with flour. "When Martin gets out of his meeting, tell him to meet me back at the pond?"

"After meeting, human by the pond. Got it."

Sitting cross-legged on the grass once again, Jan ignored the occasional splashes from the pond and concentrated on breathing in and out slowly. Her asthma was triggered more by dust and stress, but stress and grass could do the trick, too.

Jan didn't know why she kept coming out here, unless maybe it was because she knew that anyone out here would ignore her, let her mope in peace. For a bunch of alleged nature-friendly beings, few of them ever came out this far.

Maybe it was because they were all too busy, AJ's orders snapping them into action, focused and intent. She was the only one without a purpose, without a plan. But she was going to come up with one.

"We've been focusing on the portals," she said, thinking out loud. "On the portals, how they're controlling them and where the queen might be hiding. Turn it around. Why here? Never mind how or why the magic changed. What do we have that they want?"

It wasn't a new question, but they'd been thinking like supers or trying to think like preters. Maybe it was time to think like a human. A stubborn, heart-driven human.

Someone was walking toward her across the grass. She knew it was Martin without looking, recognizing the weirdly heavy sound, as though his four-hooved form walked with him. She'd noticed it first when they were walking through the preternatural realm, but only identified it as being his specifically once they were on the Farm. She'd idly compared his steps to other supernaturals: some walked heavily, some barely touched the ground, but none of the others had that four-beat cadence to a two-footed walk.

"You left the meeting," he said. It wasn't an accusation, just a statement, with a hint of a question.

She kept her breathing still, her eyes closed. "Did anything useful happen?"

"Not really," he admitted. Then he paused. "You're upset."

"I'm not. I'm..." She was upset. But not the way Martin meant it. She thought. She still wasn't entirely sure she had a bead on what the kelpie meant when he said something.

Another memory: Toba looking at her with those golden owl eyes, warning her: *Do not fall into the trap of thinking that you can understand us—or that we can understand you.*

"Your leman hurt you." Martin sat next to her, and she could smell the now-familiar scent of green water and smoky moss, almost like but entirely unlike the scent of the pond in front of them, and completely unlike, say, the iron-rock-solder smell Elsa had. Jan was learning the supers by their smell now, not just their sight or sound. The thought was either really disturbing or weirdly satisfying. Maybe both. Maybe she *could* understand them, at least a little bit.

Maybe they could understand her.

"It's not Ty's fault," she said, not even asking how Martin knew it had been Tyler. Maybe he could smell it on her, too. "He can't help it. I know that. He's all sorts of fucked up and I'm the only thing that was consistent throughout." She had read up on all the syndromes and symptoms, the treatments and the stories from family members. She knew that Zan was doing the best job possible, that if they took him to a human doctor, they wouldn't understand what he'd been through, and the moment he started saying anything about the preters or… Well, she couldn't blame any human hospital for thinking he needed more than outpatient therapy if that happened. "But it hurts."

"Of course it does. Because you blame yourself."

Jan laughed, a rough exhalation that held only a little humor. "Stay away from the pop-psych websites," she told him, opening her eyes and plucking a long blade of grass, holding it between her thumb and foreginger and studying it with far more care than it deserved. "Even humans have trouble with that stuff. You'll just screw it up"

That much she did understand. Kelpies—or at least, Martin—were sweet, and funny, and affectionate…and cold-blooded killers who didn't really understand that killing people, because they suddenly felt like it, was a bad thing. He had empathy in his own way but no morality, no connection to anyone he had not learned to care about. What he might make of the five stages of grieving or some other mental-health site…

She let the blade of grass drop, watching as it fell. Emotions. Entanglement. Need. "You told me to go home. When we came back, you told me to go home and put all this behind me, both you and AJ."

Martin lay on the grass next to where she was sitting, his arms crossed behind his head, staring up at the sky. He never went closer to the water than they were sitting, never really looked at it. Kelpies were river-horses; she wondered if he had something against ponds or if it was just this pond that he didn't like. And why, if he didn't like the pond, he kept following her out there.

"We were wrong," he admitted. "AJ knew it then. He just didn't know what else to tell you. You can't go back to what and who you were. It doesn't work that way."

She held up a hand, stopping his apology in its tracks. None of them could go back. Not Tyler, not her—not even Martin. You couldn't simply walk into the preter realm, you couldn't go Under the Hill, and expect to come back the same.

"Yeah. It changes. Everything changes. So…we go forward." She wrapped her arms around her knees and thought about that, trying to weave it into what she had been thinking before.

Martin waited, maybe to see if she was going to say anything more, maybe thinking thoughts of his own. Something in the middle of the pond splashed to the surface and then disappeared. "You're thinking," he said finally, somewhere between an accusation and a hope.

"Yeah." Thinking about what they'd talked about that morning, about what Galilia had said, about what she was seeing around them. About what they had seen in the preter court. About three days left now before the truce was up.

"I have an idea," she said finally. "AJ isn't going to like it."

Martin grinned at her, his teeth blunt but the smile disturbingly sharp. "Those are my favorite kind of ideas."

# Chapter 4

AJ wanted to howl, to put his head back and let loose with a drawn-out noise that would cut through everything and bring everyone to a dead, cold stop. He didn't.

It would be satisfying, yes, but it wouldn't solve anything. The chaos of so many different supers living and working together was barely held under control, creating a constant low-level rumble. Only tightly held control allowed him to orchestrate that rumble into something like a symphony.

Having one of your remote teams drop out of sight for a week and resurface with a report that focused on the brew-pubs rather than the hunt they were *supposed* to be on…

"Pack is easier," AJ muttered almost under his breath. "I can just knock them over and they listen to me."

Elsa didn't laugh. The *jötunndotter* was a steady, steadfast second in command, but her kind weren't known for a sense of humor. "Too far to reach, too many of them."

"I can hit you and you can hit someone and they can hit the right person. That's called delegation."

"You would break your paw if you tried to knock me over."

He wasn't sure if that was an actual statement of fact or her attempt to respond in kind. He decided to take it as fact.

"Fine. If I send you out to Oregon to sit on these idiots, will you do it?"

"By the time I get there, they will have already done the damage," she responded. *Jötunndotter* did not fly. Even if she could get through security without raising eyebrows—improbable—the mass of her stony body would probably ground the plane. And the thought of her trying to fit into a narrow coach seat...

"Yeah, all right, I'll save you for a local fuckup."

AJ rubbed at his face tiredly, shoving hair away from his forehead. It felt as if he hadn't slept, really slept, in months. Maybe he hadn't. Not since all this had started, the first reports of preternaturals where and when none should be, his own curiosity drawing him to investigate, and then the sharp fear, the need to draw forces together to keep his pack, his territory safe....

AJ hadn't wanted this, the responsibility of so much, so many. He hadn't asked for it. But he had been the only one to see the danger, the only one to step up and shove people into paying attention. So he was stuck with it, apparently.

"Boss." Someone handed him a clipboard, and he signed it, noting as he did so that it was for a shipment of car parts, not anything Farm related. The old warehouse might be gone, burned to the ground during the gnome attack, but the business went on.

Somehow, that made him feel better.

AJ handed the clipboard back and looked at the larger whiteboard hung on the wall. He let his eyes scan the place names written there, all the reports that had come back of where the preters had been spotted, trying not to think of anything in particular or force a pattern on them and hoping that something would stir on its own. Instead, all he could hear, all he could sense was the never-ending swirl of bodies and voices around him.

In the weeks since Martin had brought the humans back from the preter's realm, since the turncoats had attacked the old warehouse, swarming them in an attempt to take out the ragtag defenders, nearly two dozen more supernaturals had found their way to the Farm. Some of them wanted to defend their home against a threat that had suddenly become real, some of them just wanted a fight, and some of them were bored and thought this might be some interesting mischief. AJ's job was to make use of them all.

"Mathias."

A dog-faced super looked over at him, ears pricking in anticipation. "Yah, boss?"

"Go to Oregon. Take Lurcher. Sit on whoever needs to be sat on so I'm getting regular reports. And keep them out of the blasted strip joints."

"Got it, boss." He knocked at his companion's shoulder, rousting him from his newspaper. "We're on point," he said. "Grab your bag."

"One problem. Two—" Something pinged, a soft, muted noise, and then his pocket vibrated. AJ looked at the offending pocket with the sort of loathing most saved for a worm in their meat, and reached into his jacket to retrieve the smartphone he'd finally, grudgingly, agreed to carry.

There were seven text messages from the Florida team, one after another, with the results of their hunt. Complete with photos of... He squinted and determined that, yes, that was his search team hanging out in front of a giant upright shark wearing a neon lei.

Strip joints, tourist traps... The stories that painted supernaturals as flighty, irresponsible creatures were not, regrettably, far off the mark.

AJ sighed and passed the phone over to Elsa, who glanced at the display and then passed it on to another super without comment. The third super, a juvenile *lupin* from a different pack than AJ's, scrolled through the texts and barked out information to be added to the charts.

"Teaching them how to text may not have been your best idea ever," Elsa said, her voice dry.

"Email would have been worse. Trust me," Jan said from the doorway. "More attachments, more viruses from bad-choice web surfing..." She shook her head, an odd smile twisting her face.

"You know us so well," AJ said. He liked the human female, much to his surprise, but more than that, he was learning to respect her. All the human strengths—loyalty, imagination—but without the worst of their weaknesses. More, she could make her team focus and pay attention, and that, he knew firsthand, was a daily battle.

She came into the room, and he saw that Martin was lurking behind her. Of course. Ever since the human had discovered the truth about her leman's disappearance and had—unwillingly, perhaps—joined them, even before the two of them had gone through the portal, the two had been forming a bond of some sort. Since they'd returned, that bond seemed almost unbreakable. AJ was certain that the friendship was a terrible idea and likely to get someone killed, but it wasn't as though they weren't all likely to die in the next week anyway.

"The supernatural community tends to veer wildly between deadly serious and utterly incapable of seriousness," he said now in response to her comment. "It's not really a useful life strategy."

Behind him, Elsa snorted, the way only trolls could, and Jan's eyebrows rose. She almost smiled, a real, amused smile, looking back over her shoulder at the kelpie. "You have a life strategy?"

"*Lupin* are a little more focused than most," AJ admitted, ignoring the wounded expression on Martin's face and the burst of laughter from someone in the room behind him. Everyone else was very pointedly ignoring the exchange, even as they eavesdropped as best they could without being called out for slacking. The supernatural world's reputation for gossiping like a pair of nannies was pretty accurate, too.

"Do you have a few minutes?" the human asked.

"No," AJ said. "But sit down, anyway."


"Jesus Christ," the cop said, turning his head away. But everywhere he looked, there was blood and broken furniture. But no bodies. Where were the bodies? "What the hell happened?"

"Bear," the man on his hands and knees in the kitchen said, his attention focused on the evidence in front of him more than his answer.

"Bullshit. Bears don't do this." Patek forced himself to take a better look at the damage, his expression unhappy but resigned. There were deep scars on the walls, from around waist-high, dragging down to the ground. He touched one with a gloved finger: it went at least a quarter-inch deep into drywall. "Okay, yeah, bears could do this. But inside a house? Who the fuck lets a bear inside their house?"

The first thing you learned living in the Adirondack Mountains area was to keep an eye out for bears. Make noise when you went outside in the spring, make sure your garbage was locked up and out of reach, and generally don't be an idiot, because black bears might look cute at a distance or in the zoo, but up close they were several hundred pounds of muscle, teeth, and claws. More, especially in spring, they saw nearly anything as food, and what wasn't food was easily seen as a threat.

Patek had seen a bear claw up close during training. Their instructor had used it to scare them, and it had worked. You didn't want that thing anywhere near you, not when attached to living bear muscle.

"City folk," his partner said in disgust, shifting back to his haunches. "Who the hell knows what they'll do? Feed bears. Try to pet cougars. And leave us the mess to clean up." He pulled off his now-bloody latex gloves and put them into a plastic Baggie and sealed it, then pulled on a clean pair. "Better put in a call, let the DEC know we've maybe got a mean-ass bear out there."

They tried not to say *man-eater* or *killer* anymore—the media ran with it, and while the department would want the public to use caution, too often caution turned into crazed hunting sprees that got more people damaged than the bear in question.

And god help any other bear innocently in the area.

Patek nodded, still studying the scene. Elsewhere in the house he could hear Michelle taking photographs, documenting the damage. The three of them were half the on-duty force for Little Creek. They were going to have to request outside help on this, and wasn't that going to thrill the town board?

"How many people were in the house?"

"Just Mike and David."

The couple owned the local bakery, had moved north from New York City near on four years ago. Long enough to have learned better, Patek would have thought. *Leave the damn bears alone!*

"Nobody's seen either one of them since yesterday afternoon, when the bakery closed. I'm sending samples of the blood over to County but…" His partner looked around, his expression sour. "This ain't bear blood."

"Well, it's either bear blood, human blood, or little green

Martian blood, Joe. Either way, there's enough of it that someone died here."

"Yeah, fine, so then, where's the body? Even bears don't
eat everything." Joe looked around, obviously cataloging the
broken furniture, the torn upholstery, and shattered china.
"No bits, no bones. What kind of bear eats all that?"

"Kind that's moving fast," a third voice said, and both of
them jerked upright, instinctively pulling shoulders back as
though someone were taking roll. In the doorway, a solidly
built man wearing a state trooper uniform leaned against the
frame, his hat off and sunglasses pushed up onto his forehead.
"This is the third site like this reported."

"Jesus, Saul, way to give me a heart attack. Knock next
time?" Patek scowled at the trooper, his body relaxing back
into a slouch again. "Wait—other killings, here?" If there'd
been other killings in the area, they would have heard about
it. Probably faster through gossip channels than the officials
ones, but they would have heard.

"One down in Virginia three month ago," the trooper said.
"They thought it was an isolated case at the time, but the system kicked it out when your report came through this morning. The other…" Saul Varten dropped his gaze, then looked
up again, and Patek's stomach hurt, already anticipating the
news. "There was another report as I was heading over. In
May's Creek." That was about twenty miles north, up into
the hills. "A family of five. Four, actually—the husband went
missing about a year ago."

"Jesus." Ian Patek felt his stomach clench, and he tasted that
morning's coffee in his mouth again, stale and bitter.

"That's one fast-moving bear all right," Joe said. He'd been
a lifer in the city, two dimes in uniform before he'd come
here; the man made a point not to be shocked by anything.

But his hands were fisted, as if he wanted to punch something, hard. "A bear with transport."

Patek ignored his partner and studied the trooper. "This your case now?"

"Hell, no," Varten said, sounding both annoyed and relieved. "Your bear crossed state lines. The Feds are coming."

"Send me out into the field." Jan crossed her arms across her chest and looked at AJ, waiting for his reaction.

"No. Absolutely not." The reaction was immediate. AJ's jaw was set, his eyes hooded, and his brow drawn down. Jan could see the tension practically knotting his body, and she suspected that in his other form, he would have been growling at her. Actual growls, not just low-voiced anger

Unlike Martin, who seemed to change at whim, *lupin* were either bound by the moon or had taboos against showing their furry side out to other people. So AJ didn't growl, didn't show teeth or claws. He only glared. She was okay with that—she didn't really *want* to see the *lupin* side; the human form was scary enough. But she couldn't walk away from this argument, not even if he had changed.

"Why not?" She was trying to be reasonable, practical. That was always her strong point, not to rush in with passion but lay out the reasons why something would—or wouldn't— work. With diagrams, if needed. She eyed the whiteboard off to the side of the room, then decided that would be a particularly bad idea right now. "I'm not needed here. I've done my bit, bringing you the people who are needed, who have the right skills to figure it out." It still stung, but Galilia was right. "I'm a designer, not a tech, not really. The others know what they need to do now. They can do it without me." She paused, trying to think of any other objection the *lupin* might make. "And before you say it, I'm not helping with Tyler, either."

They were inside, with walls and bodies between them, and she could still practically feel the shed, looming at her back like a personal failure.

Martin, who had been quiet throughout her entire presentation to AJ, made a noise that might have been a protest, or a laugh. "Jan, you don't know—"

"Yeah, I do. You haven't gone to see him, not once. I have. And it's never good. I'm a reminder of…of everything, and that sends him back down into a spiral. It's…it is what it is." The shrug she made seem effortless was like pushing through broken glass, tiny shards drawing tiny drops of blood, and the image was too close to her nightmares of the preter realm for comfort.

AJ didn't say anything. He'd handed Tyler over to the Farm's healers but hadn't made an effort to follow up after that, either. Jan understood; Tyler hadn't been their friend, their lover. A good manager put the right people on a problem and then moved on to the relevant battles. That was what he needed to do here. She just needed to convince him that she was the right person with the right solution.

"Let's face it, the only time I've actually been useful to all this was when I was out in the field. Where, I might add, you *sent* me." Let AJ try to wiggle out of *that*. "And because of that, Martin and I, we know preters, better than anyone else right now. We've been there, seen that, got the T-shirt and the firsthand experience."

"And that's why we need you here, to answer—"

"Bullshit." She cut AJ off with an irritated swipe of her hand, finally too exasperated to be either cautious or polite. "You've sent Martin out, and he knows as much as I do. And everything I knew, or had figured out, you know now, too. So that's bullshit. Let us find out *more*." A sudden thought occurred to her. "And if you're trying to protect me because of what happened, I... Don't."

The *lupin* scowled at her then, and she thought maybe she'd hit it. *Oh, AJ,* she thought, almost fondly. He'd dragged her into this at the start, had used her love for Tyler for his own purposes, had teamed her with a kelpie he had good reason to believe would kill her, however randomly or unintentionally, because that was what kelpies *did*. And now, for all that, AJ was feeling guilty.

As guilty as a supernatural could get, anyway.

How did you tell someone that it was okay that they'd totally used you, screwed up your life, and broken it into a thousand pieces? That you knew they'd do it again without hesitation—and you wouldn't do anything different, either?

"Seriously, AJ..." Her voice faltered, and she hesitated, trying to pick through the words that would express what she was thinking without screwing it up. "Don't. You tried to send me away once before, remember? And I wouldn't go. I'm not going to back down now, either. Stubborn human being stubborn."

He snorted, but some of the glare was fading from his eyes, and his body language was less opposed.

"I need to do this. I don't...I don't want to be protected, shielded." Supers—*friends*—had died to protect her. Her life, and Tyler's life, had been utterly upended: jobs lost, apartments lost, god knew what else. If AJ apologized, if he tried to keep her out of it now, that would make it worse, not better. "I know you think I've been through enough, but it's not enough, not until this is done." A deep breath, and then she went for the hard hit. "And I can't stay here and do nothing, watch Tyler fade, knowing that's going to happen to more people if we don't stop this, now."

AJ wasn't the type to turn away or even blink; he just

changed his attack. "You don't have the ability to detect preters, the way we do."

"Not at a range, no. But I can recognize them now." She was better at it than other humans, anyway. Experience would do that to you. She smiled now, because he'd given her the perfect opening for her final shot. "And they can't detect *me*."

That was one of the major drawbacks of both the attempt to find preters and the progress of Operation Queen Search: supernaturals could scent out preternaturals into this world, but preters were aware of supers in the same—or similar enough—way. Humans, though…they slipped right through.

It could have been insulting, but she was going to make it work for her.

"That's why you're going to send me back out into the field. Because I can do something there that your people can't." Having grabbed that opening, she was on a roll now, the way she would have been back on the job, explaining why her way of doing something would work better.

"Listen to me, all right? Just…listen. Originally, you were chasing after missing humans, because that was the link between preters and this world. Because that was how you were going to find out what the preters were up to. Right?"

He nodded once, listening.

"And that's where my team's been looking, to see what, if anything, ties them all together, how they're controlling the portals, suddenly, after generations of them being opened only at random."

Not random, exactly. Tied to seasonal effects and specific rituals. But never on call, the way the preters could open them now. They knew that it took a human—and presumably the more humans they had, the more portals they would be able to open—but not *how*. That wasn't the point she was trying to make, though.

"Meanwhile, your team's been pinpointing areas where supernaturals have been living, specifically where species that didn't respond to your call have strongholds, that kind of thing. Because your kind don't just up and move without a reason, so if they're ignoring you or gone, that means something."

She paused just long enough for him to nod acknowledgment. "Gone missing, or where there were areas of known... well, less-human-friendly enclaves." AJ was never going to be a diplomat, but he was trying; she'd give him that.

"That might potentially be preter-welcoming, where she might have set up shop. Right. My point is, you're looking for patterns, traditions, established routines. So I had a thought. Okay, I had a couple of thoughts, but they all tied up in a nice neat bow. You—everyone—keep telling me that supernaturals can't deny their nature—and that preters are all about tradition. You're all hidebound—once you get set in something, you don't leave it. Only humans zig as well as zag. Right?"

AJ just watched her, waiting for her to get to a point.

"Only, that's not true." She waited, half expecting AJ to protest or object. He didn't. Martin, lurking behind her, gave her a faint poke, encouraging her to go on.

"Okay, for example, take Martin...he's a kelpie. His entire shtick is pretty much cold-blooded murder. See human, entice human, drown human. And by the way, I have not forgiven you for not telling me all that up front."

A *lupin* smile was unnerving as hell, even when you knew what it was.

"But the thing is, I've been on his back, in his other form, a bunch of times now. Not-drowned."

Martin had refused to change form when they'd been in the preter realm, warning her that the magic there might overwhelm his control. She wasn't going to think about that right now.

"You thought he might be able to control himself because of the mission. I get that." Her life, personally—anyone's life—meant less to AJ than the success of the mission. She got that, too. He'd do it again if he had to. "But why is he still hanging around me? Waiting for another try? Or because he's actually managed to overcome enough of his basic nature to be friends with a human?"

"Or both," Martin threw in over her shoulder. "Let's not overlook that possibility."

Jan thought Martin might have been trying to help. From the look on AJ's face—and when had she learned how to read *lupin* body language so easily?—he wasn't helping. Definite hint of guilt on that muzzle, yeah, and the way his eyes tracked on her, almost sorrowfully, as if he regretted even seeing her there.

That just made Jan more certain she was on the right track.

"My point is, you—supernaturals—can change when there's a...an environmental change. Something big enough to shove against your inbred and innate whatevers. So, why are we assuming that the preters can't? I mean—" and she flailed her hands a little in exasperation "—we already know they've moved from a seven-year plan to dealing in binary terms of ten after being exposed to computers!"

Her team's conjecture, based on the fact that the preter consort had given her a binary deadline rather than one in a base of seven that preternaturals had adhered to for centuries, but it *felt* right to her.

"We don't know that for certain," AJ said. "It's a theory, based on one piece of evidence. And basing anything off what one preter does is insanity."

"It's a pretty damned good theory, thank you muchly," Jan

retorted. "But the thing is, they *did* change their magic. They changed their entire mode of hunting, from wait-and-watch to active predation. That's adaptation!"

It wasn't enough; she could see that.

"Fine, let's look at another piece of evidence—the queen came here not because she hated this world but because she was *fascinated* by it. The court confirmed this, and believe me, they were grumpy enough about that fact that it's got to be true."

"Is there a point here, human?" AJ asked, but his voice was actually curious, not annoyed. She was getting to him, finally.

"The queen came *here*. She stayed *here*. Something in this world fascinated her enough that she abandoned everything she knew, everything she had. Does that sound like a creature that can't change its nature?"

"She might simply be insane," AJ pointed out. "And what does this have to do with our plan to use her as a bargaining piece?"

"You mean other than the fact that you haven't been able to lay paw on her?

"Think about it. She came *here*. And her people are having a serious mad-on about her leaving—as in not taking any of them with her. And none of you have been able to find her, going by what *used* to be true. Might she, as insane as it sounds, and I know that to you it's going to sound seriously crazy, but might she be setting up a court of humans?"

There was a long pause, and Jan held her breath, waiting for AJ to respond so she could go on to the second part of her pitch.

"A court is a gathering of...of peers," AJ said. "Ranked peers, and none of them her equal, but peers nonetheless. You said it yourself in your report—the consort was above the others, even those on the dais with him. The queen would be even more so. Supernaturals, at least, are…lesser but of the same stuff. Humans? They think of humans as toys and pets, sometimes as tools, but never peers. I'm not sure they're even capable of that sort of a break."

His muzzle wrinkled, and Jan waited, hoping that he might be willing to consider her proposal anyway.

"You think we should be looking for more human disappearances and that those will lead us to her?" He shook his head. "You know as well as I do how difficult it was to find humans who'd been preter-napped. It's not as though the police are willing to share their records, and chasing after a maybe—"

"Not chase," Jan interrupted. "Bait. You already used me that way once before, so it's not like you can claim it's a bad idea." She wasn't going to use that as a club over him, because no matter what he might or might not regret doing, AJ didn't *do* guilt that way. But he would do what was needed, no matter who got used. She was counting on that. "And not to look for disappearances, no. Bait to see if she wants humans who understand that she *is* the queen and who don't need, I don't know, training or indoctrination."

Brainwashing. They'd tortured Tyler, played mind games on him, until he broke. But if a mortal came to her willingly, knowing what she was and wanting that, without glamour or coercion…

"You know, that would appeal to her ego," Martin said, finally joining in on the conversation usefully. "Jan's right about that. When we were over there, when she challenged them, the consort wanted Jan to give in to him, without having any claim on her obedience. They consider human servants their right, and the more interesting the human, the better. The queen is going to be worse, ego-wise. If she is building a court, having someone *looking* for her, *wanting* to serve, would be irresistible."

"No." AJ shook his head, dismissing the idea entirely.

"What?" Jan was annoyed; she'd given him a perfectly logical buildup, and he was still saying no?

"You two know too much," AJ said. "I'm willing to send you out on one of the teams, Jan, because you're right, you've proven yourself useful there. You think quickly and without the prejudices we carry, and having a human viewpoint is useful, much as our more stubborn members still want to mutter about it. But sending you out as bait like that, practically hanging a sign over you—Tasty Treat, Come and Get It? No. You have interesting theories—work on them here. Liaise with the search teams, and help us direct them."

Martin snickered. "You seriously just said *liaise?*"

Jan pivoted and hit Martin on the chest once, hard. Even she knew better than to argue—or sass—when the *lupin* used that voice. AJ was pack leader, for however a mangy pack they might be, and he had made his decision. She would have to settle for being part of a scouting team.

"Jan?" His voice was soft, but there was still a hint of a growl underneath, waiting for her to agree. Her mouth twisting in disappointment, Jan dropped her chin and let the tension leave her shoulders, as close to the "throat baring" move she'd seen other supernaturals give him when they lost an argument as she was willing to get.

AJ might be on the side of angels, so to speak, but she still wasn't going to bare her throat to a werewolf.

# Chapter 5

Martin had more experience than AJ with humans, overall. And he knew this human particularly well. He knew, despite the fact that she'd accepted AJ's decision, that this wasn't over. After Jan turned with an almost military flair and left the room, he gave one last look at AJ, despairing of his friend's stubbornness as a match to Jan's own, and followed her out to the porch. There were a few supers already there, talking quietly, but they took one look at her and Martin, hard on her heels, and left.

"Jan. No."

She turned and looked out across the yard—away from the shed, and Tyler, and into the trees that lined the far edge of the clearing.

"Jan, I can *hear* you thinking." He moved around so that he could see her face, not letting her avoid him. "No."

"Your ears aren't that good, swishtail," she said, using AJ's nickname for the kelpie.

He ran his hands through his hair, pushing it away from his face and then shaking it loose again, echoing his horse-form enough that he knew she could practically see it ghosting over him. "You're thinking that AJ is too blind or too stubborn to see straight and that you're right—and to prove it, you're going to try to infiltrate the court yourself."

She made a face at him, not willing to admit that maybe his ears were that good, after all.

"AJ isn't blind," the kelpie went on. "He's being practical. You're an asset, same as the rest of us, and he doesn't waste his assets on golden-goose hunts. And anyway, you're assuming that you'd be able to find the court to begin with, and since nobody else has, that's not exactly a reasonable assumption."

"Wait, you're lecturing me on logic? That's funny."

His answering snort was entirely equine. "I'm not entirely a creature of instinct," Martin said. "Not only, anyway. So when I bring logic and rational thought into it, you should listen."

Jan crossed her arms across her chest and stared at him. "Fine. I'm listening. This is my listening face."

She was listening, but then suddenly Martin seemed incapable of talking.

"Hello?"

He sighed and stared over her shoulder, finding it easier to speak if he didn't have to look her in the eye. "You're not wrong in that staying here is a waste of both of us. I've already told everyone everything I know, over and again, and yeah, your team outclasses you in the technical side. Even I know that."

He risked a glance back at her, in time to see satisfaction that Martin agreed with her flickering in her eyes, tempered only by the implication of "us" that he should be going with her. He was hurt at first that she'd be surprised by that. He'd saved her from the turncoats not once but twice. He'd had her back, literally, in the preter court. He had told her how to reclaim Tyler from the preter bitch who'd enslaved him. "What, you thought you were going to go out there alone?"

Jan stared at him, then blinked, emotions flickering across her face too quickly for him to identify any of them. "Actually, yes. I'm human. Whatever AJ thinks, he has no control over me. Are you ready to go against his express orders?"

Martin made a rude noise through his nose, deep, wide-set brown eyes widened in surprise and hurt. "You make me sound like a *lupin,* bound to the word of my alpha. I choose to follow AJ because I think he is the best leader, and the cause is…necessary. But I'm no herd creature, whatever you might think of my conduct."

Jan tightened her arms across her chest as though they could deflect his obvious disappointment in her. Martin waited, and finally she exhaled through her own nose, as though echoing him, and let her arms drop to her sides.

"Right." He shoved his hands into his pockets and resisted the urge to pace. "Sorry. But no, you're not doing this alone. So, maybe neither of us is being practical, or reasonable, or even smart. At least we'll have each other's backs."

"We blow off the boss, go against pretty much direct orders, and put the weirdly dynamic duo back on the road." Jan laughed, and he didn't hear any humor in it. "Okay. What's the but?" she asked, since he was clearly not finished.

"But we're out of time. We've got, what, three days left?" She nodded.

"So, once they start coming back through the portals, the bastards won't stop until they've reached saturation, or terminal velocity, or whatever it is that will allow them to keep the portals open indefinitely—or bring enough of them here that they aren't worried about this realm being a threat anymore." The sentence came out in a rush, and he stopped to gulp air. "So if we're going to do this, we have to do it right, and fast. And that means not screwing around with one of the search teams but going right to where the queen is hiding."

She frowned at him, the one serious flaw in their plan practically floating in the air in front of them, sparking with obvious-dust. "And how the hell do we do that, since as you pointed out, none of the search teams have actually reported anything useful?"

Martin stepped closer, and she leaned forward a bit, their voices lowering, even though nobody was around to overhear them or likely to think either of them worth eavesdropping on to begin with.

"If you're right about what you said to AJ, and I think you are, then the queen came here for something that didn't exist where she was. If so, if she's not only breaking patterns, she'd be building something new, not just a repeat of what she knew. Or trying to, anyway. Something human, or at least heavily human influenced. And there may be a way to track that...."

Something was happening. He could feel it. They didn't tell him anything, and he didn't ask, he didn't want to know, but he knew, anyway.

He paced, pulling his arms around himself as though he were cold. The room they had given him to sleep in was too warm, even though he couldn't find a thermostat or radiator where the heat was coming from. So he had gotten in the habit of opening the window and pulling a chair over to sleep in, rather than using the bed. He'd muss up the covers and throw the pillow back each morning. He didn't know if they were fooled, but they never said anything.

Then again, why would they? Zan kept telling him that this was *his* space, that he controlled it.

So he could just tell them to turn the heat down. But he didn't.

Maybe when he did, they'd tell him he was all better now.

He wasn't better yet. He'd gotten upset this morning, when Jan came to visit. He could remember her name now, when she wasn't in front of him. Jan. She liked her coffee with too much milk and sugar, and she snored when she had a cold, and her birthday fell when there was snow on the ground. He knew all those things and more, like the sound of her laugh, even though she had never laughed around him.

She was part of Before, too. Before, and Then, and Now.

Before had been…better. Everyone wanted him to go back to Before. If he did that, he would hear her laugh again.

So, why was it so hard? Why couldn't he get better?

He paced, unable to let go of his thoughts, unable to speak them, unwilling to leave the security of his bedchamber, even as it felt like a cage. If it was a cage, it was one that kept *him* safe, not them.

And then he heard it, recognized it, even as his body turned, his elbows leaning on the open windowsill.

Not her old laugh. This one was low, quiet, not joyful the way he remembered, but it was still amused and still filled with a sense of Jan-ness that he would recognize anywhere, anytime, no matter what else he forgot.

He found her easily. She was across the wide lawn, standing on the porch of the larger house, the building all the others went and came from all day. Her back was to him, but he recognized her, the way her hair looked, the set of her shoulders. Someone was with her: a man, square shouldered and horse faced, and he was shaking his head, raising his hands like someone giving in, but with amusement, not anger.

He recognized the man, too. He was the other one who had been with them There. Who had brought him to Now. A not-human. There were a lot of not-humans here, but they were all different. And none of them were like…

His mind shied away from remembering, but Zan said it was all right, that memory couldn't hurt him here. Like Stjerne. Stjerne had hurt him.

That was Then. Before was gone, and Then was gone. Zan said so. He was supposed to focus on Now.

Stjerne was gone, locked on the other side. She couldn't go through the portal without him. He was safe so long as he stayed here. No one here would hurt him.

His breathing calmed. This was Now. Now was Jan laughing. Having seen them, heard them, he wanted to know what she was laughing about. So, he leaned in a little more and listened. It wasn't easy, but he tuned out everything else and picked out the voices, both familiar, carried in the crisp air.

"I'm sorry, what was that you just said, again?"

"There is a spell." The non-human sounded as if he was trying not to laugh again.

"A spell. Excuse me, mister 'we don't use magic like that,' what the hell? A spell that would find a preter would have made everything a hell of a lot easier—you guys were keeping shit from me again. What the hell is with that?"

She sounded mad but not-mad. Teasing-mad. He knew that sound, too.

"We aren't. We don't. That's something humans do. Some humans. Maybe."

"Maybe? Yes or no, there's a spell? Spill it, Martin, before I braid your mane and tail with pink ribbons and start calling you My Pretty Pony."

"We don't do magic like that. But some humans can. Or they could, once."

"So, what you're saying is, we need a wizard?"

"A witch, not a wizard. Wizards are fantasy. Witches are real."

There was another choke of laughter. "Oh, yeah, I'm glad you drew that line. And you never thought to tell me about these witches, why?"

"Because I didn't think of it until now."

"And nobody else would think about asking a human for help, theoretical witch or not, right? Yeah. You guys, I swear... So, a witch should be able to find where a preter is hiding?"

"Should. Maybe. If she's willing to. But..."

"But?"

"But part of why nobody thought of it is because witches, historically, don't like us. They don't trust us."

"They've met you, in other words."

"There's history. And...we'd still have to find one, anyway. I don't even know where to begin."

Tyler watched, hidden, while Jan ran her fingers through her hair, digging into her scalp, and his own fingers flexed, remembering the feel of those soft curls under his own skin.

"Yeah. Huh. Okay, I might...I might be able to find a lead on that, if witches are actually real." Her voice dropped, and he had to focus harder, just to hear.

"Of course you might. That's what you do—you shake us up, give us new leads." There was a tone to the other's voice that he didn't like, that made his fingers curl in a different manner, digging into his palms.

"Uh-huh. It's a maybe, and a what-if, and what the hell, it's the only thing even remotely resembling a plan of action we've got. So, you think AJ will give his approval of that?"

"What, for us to go on a road trip to find a human who will just as soon hex a supernatural as talk to one, on the off chance she will cast a spell to find a preternatural queen who may or may not be collecting humans, assuming this witch even believes us?"

"Yeah." Jan's tone brightened, and now he could hear her clearly. "So, we should bypass AJ and just get in the car?"

The non-human started to laugh again, as if that was the funniest thing he had ever heard. "Probably, yeah."

Jan said something, too low for him to hear, and then she went back inside the big house. The not-human hopped over the porch railing with a peculiar grace and then headed toward the old barn.

He watched the not-human go, his thoughts whirling. The barn was where the cars were kept; he'd seen them come in and out, occasionally. Jan was looking for a preter queen and her court. Courts were not-safe. Leaving the Farm was not-safe. Everyone had told him, over and over, that the Farm was safe.

Jan was leaving the Farm.

Leaving the Farm was trouble.

Jan was going to get into trouble.

He forced his fingers to uncurl, looking at the half-moon marks left in his palms, and then he was shifting his body, pushing the window open all the way, and swinging over the sill, dropping easily onto the ground.

The air was colder here, and the lack of walls around him, keeping him safe, almost made him scramble back inside.

He set his jaw, ignored the feeling of being exposed, watched, and made his own way toward the barn.


Ian Patek normally growled like a bear himself when someone tried to horn in on his territory. In this case, though, he'd been just as glad when the Feds finally arrived, set up camp, and spread out all over the county, their "please give us everything you know and stay in touch but stay out of our way" phrased in slightly more diplomatic words. Little Creek P.D. had handed over everything they had, which wasn't much, and gone back to the daily job with a sigh of relief.

It wasn't all speed traps and pot busts, though. Part of that job—more often than any of them liked to admit—was following up on calls claiming that there was a bigfoot—or wendigo, or naked crazy man, depending on the age, gender, and sobriety of the caller—up in the woods. Patek and Hansen had been following up on one of those calls when they found the first pile of bones.

"Shit." Patek squatted back on his heels and stared at the evidence. There was no mistaking human bones once you'd seen them. Not coyote, not deer, not anything but human ribs and legs. "You think that's…?"

"Well, in the immortal words of Richard Dreyfuss, this wasn't no boat accident." Joe turned away from the pile and scanned the area. "Don't jump to conclusions. Could be a hiker who took a bad fall, never crawled out, and never got reported missing."

"Yeah." That made more sense than a mysterious killer dragging a body from a house in town all the way the hell up here. And there was only one body as far as he could tell. A hiker who got the wrong end of a bear paw, that was bad news but ordinary enough.

"There's the outcropping Missus Mac mentioned," Joe said, pointing to the rock face to their left, up the hill a few yards. "Might as well check it out. Ready?"

Patek shook his head, then stood up, his hand resting on his holster. "No. But there's only a couple more hours of daylight left and I'm sure as hell not doing it in the dark, so, yeah, let's do this."

The outcropping was an actual cave, low roofed but dry and filled with what could only be described as a makeshift nest of branches, leaves, and filthy shreds of cloth.

"Jesus Christ." The stink was bad enough that he felt his eyes start to water, and he pulled his sleeve over his wrist, using the material as a filter to breathe through. It didn't help: there was a particular stench to rotted meat that you couldn't block out. "Is that another body?"

Joe used the toe of his boot to poke at the pile of debris within reach, not wanting to go too deep into the cave, for all that it seemed empty, and shrugged. His hand was on his pistol butt, too. "Could be. Maybe the rest of our missing persons. Part of the rest, anyway. Cannibal killer vagrants, loose in the Adirondacks. That'll make a good headline, don't you think?"

"Jesus Christ," Patek said again. "Call the goddamned Feds. This is their headache, not ours."

"Yeah."

They both backed out of the cave's mouth, retreating to the clearing, where nothing could suddenly scramble out of the shadows or drop on them from above. Keeping his right hand on his holster, Joe reached awkwardly with his left for his cell phone. Reception was crap up here, but they had one-touch direct to the station.

"Molly, it's Hansen. Tell our visitors to get the hell up here. We got something for them."

Their dispatcher responded immediately. "Animal, vegetable, or headache?"

Joe glanced back at the cave. "All of the above, sweetheart, all of the above. And you might want to send the coroner, too, although there's not much left for him to look at."

"Got it. You holding position or coming back in?"

"We're going to mark the spot and move on. I don't—" Joe saw Patek shift, his gun now in his hand, turning slowly, the way they didn't teach in the Academy. "Hold on."

He let go of the talk button and let his eyes skim the surroundings, trying to see what had set his partner on edge. Nothing moved, nothing smelled odd, but Patek had grown up here, was more of a country boy than he could ever hope to manage, so Joe was going to trust the other man's instincts.

And then something—an alley-born instinct—prickled,

and he dropped the phone, going into a crouch and pulling his own sidearm even as something charged at him, growling nothing at all like a bear or a vagrant.

There was a high-pitched scream, and the sound of rapid-fire gunshots echoed off the cliff, and then there was silence.

## Chapter 6

Martin was waiting just inside the barn when Jan got there, the massive doors pushed open just enough to let her slip inside, but not so much that anyone walking by might notice.

"That was fast," he said, giving her and her bags a once-over.

Jan shrugged. "It's not like I had much to pack." A week's worth of clothing, the secondhand tablet she'd picked up when they were on the run, after her apartment had been attacked—they had bought new tech for the Farm, specific to the needs of her team, but she wasn't going to take any of that. This tablet was battered, but it would do the job if she had to log in anywhere.

Abducted by supernaturals? Facing down a preternatural court to reclaim your boyfriend? Spending way too much time hanging out with a psychotic killer kelpie? Lost your job because your boss thought you'd lost your mind? Didn't matter—the email still came, and you either kept up, or you got trampled. Besides, she had her own job site to maintain, just in case someone actually stopped by to offer her work.

At least she had her meds and her inhaler and a backup prescription this time. Asthma sucked, especially when you were trying to escape from things that wanted to eat you.

Not that that was going to happen this time, she thought, rapping her knuckle once against the wooden door to avert any bad luck. This was just a reconnaissance mission, if unauthorized. The moment they found the queen, got into her good graces, and found out what her plan was, they'd alert AJ and he could set his own plan in motion for the actual capture. She would totally not-be-eaten.

"I don't suppose you—" he started to ask.

She offered him the second bag, a battered drab olive knapsack. "Underwear, socks, a pair of jeans, and two shirts, before someone else came in and I had to scoot." He had been sharing a bunkhouse with a dozen others, and she'd had absolutely no excuse to be going through his stuff. If he wanted toiletries, he'd have to stop at a CVS or something and buy them. Assuming supers needed any of that—though at the tree-shower, when they'd taken her to the Center, after her apartment had been attacked, there had been soap. No toothpaste or deodorant, though.

Live with someone for months, and you still didn't know them at all.

This was her first time actually inside the barn. She took a minute to look around. The old stalls had been broken down to make more room, obviously. There were four cars and one truck parked on the ground floor, the smell of metal and exhaust mingling weirdly with old straw and a lingering odor of horse. Jan's nose twitched, but it seemed that stable dust wasn't the sort to trigger her asthma. Or she hadn't been there long enough for it to, and hopefully they'd be gone before that changed.

Something moved overhead, where the loft had been adapted for more dorm space, but it was late afternoon, which meant that the diurnal residents were out doing their thing and the nocturnal ones were still sleeping, and the totally normal sounds of a car pulling out of the garage wouldn't rouse any suspicions.

And even if someone were to see them, Martin was always going in and out on AJ's orders, and Jan was…well, Jan guessed that she was problematic. She didn't think there was any word that she *had* to stay on the Farm or that anyone would think it odd if she went somewhere with Martin, since everyone there knew the story of how the two of them had gone through a portal—and back out—together. Everyone knew they were friends. Nobody would think twice about the two of them taking one of the cars for a drive somewhere, probably—maybe on AJ's orders. Right?

"Not that one." Martin gestured her away from the Toyota sedan and to the battered pickup truck. Jan frowned at it. That had been the truck that they'd kidnapped—okay, escorted—her out of the city in back when this all started. She knew firsthand that the seats were uncomfortable and the radio was crap.

"What if they need to, I don't know, haul something around?" she asked, making an argument for the vehicles with better suspension.

"There's another truck out back, if they need that. I don't like driving those other cars. They're…small."

The fact that she was discussing the relative merits and head space of cars with a creature who could change into a water-breathing horse at will was surreal enough to make Jan raise her hands in surrender. "All right, fine. Bump-o-truck it is."

She tossed her backpack into the front cab and slid onto the seat next to it. It was, in fact, just as uncomfortable as she remembered. Maybe even more so, because now she wasn't distracted by the weirdness her life had become or the fact that her boyfriend was missing. Her boyfriend was found, if still lost in his own way, and the weird…the weird had become normal.

"Get in and drive, swishtail," she said. "I need to get somewhere with actual 4G if this plan is going to work."

Even if they'd been willing to hang around any longer and risk AJ figuring out what they were up to, she couldn't send the email from the Farm's network—she knew that everything was monitored, because she'd been the one to set it up. If someone was paying attention and told AJ, there'd be a fight, at best, and at worst...well, better to get forgiveness later. Assuming there was a later at all.

Best-case bad scenario, if they couldn't actually find a witch who was willing to help them, was that they'd have little choice but to come slinking back with their tails between their legs, metaphorically at least for her.

"We'll find someone," she said. "We have to."

Martin gave her a look but pushed open the sliding doors, then got behind the wheel and started the engine. The truck pulled out of the garage without anyone coming down the ladder to stop them, and Jan hopped out to close the doors behind them, hopefully buying a little more time before anyone noticed the truck was gone.

Once she got back into the truck and Martin maneuvered it along the driveway to the main road, Jan pulled out her cell phone and started to tap at the keyboard, occasionally swearing as autocorrect and the bumpy ride turned her words into something else. She looked up when they approached the gate, but the guards barely even looked into the cab to see who it was before they waved the truck on.

Martin exhaled, his hands easing slightly on the wheel, and Jan just shook her head. What was there to question, after all? The guards were there to keep people out, not to lock them in. Someone would remember they had left and would tell AJ when he asked...but not until then.

So far, so good.

They'd gone about twenty minutes down the road, leaving the Farm—and farmlands—behind and were entering a more suburban area, with large houses set on gently sloping and well-tended lawns, before Jan finally got a signal back on her phone. It disturbed her a little that the moment the display appeared, she felt some tension slide away, as though merely being connected with the modern world, being back on the grid, would make things better. It wasn't as though they'd been cut off, after all, just had…limited bandwidth.

She had to admit, though, that seeing the emails go out one after another as her phone connected was a nice feeling.

Martin looked over briefly and saw her smiling.

"You got a signal?"

"Yeah."

"Okay. So what are you doing?"

"I told you. Contacting people who might know an actual practicing witch," she said.

"You know people like that?" Martin took his eyes off the road long enough to look at her with surprise.

"I maybe know people who know people. There are a lot of science-fiction folk in the tech community, and a lot of them are also pagans or, you know, otherly religious, alternate-lifestyle types. I figured some of them might know someone who was actually what we were looking for. Venn diagrams would suggest it works, anyway."

"What diagrams?"

Jan shook her head and sent another email off. "Never mind. Oh, look, there's a gas station. Hurrah. Pull over. I need a soda."

While Martin topped off the truck's tank, Jan went into the little convenience store and grabbed two bottles of Diet Pepsi, a package of licorice, and a bag of chips, because they seemed like things to have on a road trip.

The moment she got outside, she opened one of the bottles and took a long hit. There had been gallons of iced tea and fresh-made coffee at the Farm pretty much 24/7, but the only soda they seemed to stock was the ultra-high-sugar-and-caffeine crap that only hard-core programmers and speed junkies could run on. Jan had never considered herself an addict before, but the first rush of diet soda into her system was a revelation. Suddenly, she felt as if she could take on the world. Maybe even both worlds. She capped the soda reluctantly and went to use the bathroom around the corner, under the theory that you used one when you had it.

The bathroom was dingy but reasonably clean. She did her business quickly, washed her hands, then made the mistake of looking at herself in the mirror. The face that looked back at her was only partially familiar. The shadows under her eyes she recognized, but not the ones *in* her eyes or the faint but noticeable drop of her mouth. She tried to turn it up into a smile, and it came out as a grimace. And she needed a haircut, badly; the blond curls were almost down to her shoulders and would require more than gel and a brush to make them look presentable. Maybe she'd go back into the store and buy a baseball cap or something.

"Hey, Martin, do you need to—" Jan's words dried up as she came around the pumps toward the truck and saw the cover drawn tight over the bed of the truck...vibrate.

She blinked, and it stopped.

Maybe it was nothing. Probably it was nothing. The past few months of her life, though, "probably nothing" had usually turned out to be a steaming pile of something. She looked around for Martin, but he had gone inside to pay the cashier for the gas he'd put into the truck. She waited, and when he came out again, she waved her free hand to get his attention, then pointed at the truck.

He clearly had no idea what she was going on about.

Jan shook her head and started moving to intercept him

before he could get within earshot of whatever was in the truck. "There's something in the flatbed," she said quietly. "Under the tarp. I saw it move. Well, not move but—" She used her free hand again to waggle it sideways, trying to imitate the wiggle of the cover. Her voice was low, but she still felt as if it was carrying directly into whatever was under there, alerting it.

What if it was a gnome, one of the supernaturals everyone just called turncoats? She still had nightmares sometimes about the things that had come after her twice. Gnomes weren't shape-shifters the way Martin was, but their bones and skin were malleable, and her nightmares still featured their arms extending and grasping, reaching for her, tearing her apart the way they'd killed Toba, the owl-eyed supernatural who had volunteered to protect her.

Jan's chest hurt and her lungs felt squeezed, imagining one or maybe more underneath the cover, waiting, and if she went too close, they would ooze out, grabbing her, ripping her apart and eating her flesh. AJ had warned her back when this all started that gnomes liked to eat human flesh.

"Jan." Martin's hand was warm against her lower back, pressing just enough that her spine straightened automatically, and her chin rose in response. The small movement was enough; she shoved the panic away and forced herself to focus again on the truck, not her memories.

Her phone vibrated and buzzed softly in her pocket, indicating she had an email, but she didn't look down, not willing to take her attention off the truck. "Do you think...?"

"There's no way a gnome could have gotten onto the Farm, much less into the garage," he said, knowing what she was going to ask. "We have perimeter guards. You know that."

She did; in addition to the gate guards who weren't as useless as they seemed, there were supernaturals who moved around the boundaries of the property night and day, alert to anything out of the ordinary. The bansidhe that had saved her when Toba died was among them. The creature freaked her the hell out—she had learned that it freaked most of the others out, too—but the membranes under its arms were, apparently, the best intruder-sensors magic could make. And it *hated* gnomes.

"There's no way it could have crawled in while we were driving, once we were outside the Farm's borders?" The ride had been bumpy enough; something might have taken advantage...

"I would have noticed."

She took his word for that; she'd been too busy writing emails. "So, what is it?"

"Someone who decided to take a joyride off the Farm with us," he said. His forehead was creased and his mouth drawn down, the closest thing to a scowl she'd ever seen on him. Normally, he met even the worst setbacks or disasters with a calm, moderately amused facade, as though even facing death wasn't more than an inconvenience for the kelpie.

Before she could ask him what was wrong—beyond the obvious, naturally—he strode toward the back of the truck and unhooked the cover, throwing the tarp back with aggressive speed and then stepping away.

Jan jumped back, yelping in surprise when Tyler's dark head appeared over the edge, his hands reaching over to pull himself up.

"What the *hell?*"

"Don't send me back. Please, don't send me back."

His hands were gripping the side of the truck bed too tightly, until those slender fingers looked ready to shatter. He had never put on the weight he'd lost while the preter bitch was holding him, and his face was drawn tight, staring first

at Martin, then her as though he really did think they were
going to haul him back to the Farm.

The tightness in Jan's chest returned as she stared at him.
They should. They totally should send him back. He shouldn't
be out here, not the way he still forgot, still shied away from
anything strange or too loud. Tyler needed more time, he
needed to heal, and he sure as hell did not need to be chasing
right into the court of a preter queen, not after what those
monsters had done to him.

She was about to say that, too, when he cut her off.

"Please," he said. "I need... I heard what you were talking about. About finding a witch—" and his voice stumbled
a little on the word "—and finding the preter queen here...
I know them even better than you do. Whatever happens,
I'm supposed to be with you. I can feel it."

Jan was about to refuse, when Martin cut her off. "All
right."

Jan turned to Martin, slapping a hand against his chest and
pushing him back a step. "What do you mean, all right? This
is *not* all right!"

"Why not?" Martin removed her hand from his chest but
kept hold of it, his fingers curling around her own, cradling
the back of her hand against his palm. It was a habit of his,
from the first time they'd met, to hold her hand that way.
"Why shouldn't he?"

She stared at the kelpie and was suddenly, crashingly aware
that he really didn't understand all the ways that this was a
horrible, terrible, no good and very bad idea. *Supers,* she
thought to herself and then, more scathingly, *men.*

"Preters?" she said, not bothering to keep her voice down,
since there wasn't anyone else in the pump bay other than
them. "Bad mojo, brainwashing, capture, any of that sounding familiar?" And Tyler was still fragile, she didn't say out

loud, fragile enough that even she was too much to remember, too much to deal with.

"She's not here," he said quietly, still holding her hand, keeping her from turning away. "Stjerne's not here, Jan." And then, louder, he said, "Tyler came of his own free will, Jan. He obviously wants to do this. We're not going to send him back like a...like something that can't make up his own mind. And maybe he can help, maybe he's exactly the help we need, even if we find a witch willing to cast the spell. Like he said, he knows them better than we do."

That was exactly what Jan was afraid of.

"Thank you," Tyler said after he had climbed out of the truck and Jan had offered him her opened bottle of soda. He drank half of it in one gulp. Jan watched, not saying anything. Certainly not saying anything about how he used to despise diet sodas. It was wet, carbonated, and had caffeine; everything else was probably unimportant just then.

Jan took the bottle back, capped it, and put the bag of food and sodas into the car. Her jaw hurt slightly from all the things that she wasn't saying, so she exhaled, trying to let the tension go. It didn't work. "Do either of you need to use the bathroom?"

"No," Tyler said, and Martin shook his head. "Let's just get going, okay?"

"Yeah. Fine. I should make you ride in the back the rest of the way," Jan said to Tyler, even as she was opening the door to the cab and waiting for him to get in first. She would be damned if she'd be stuck in the middle just because she was the girl.

"We'll get a ticket if we do that and a cop sees us," Martin said, getting in on the driver's side. "And since I technically don't have a driver's license, let's not, okay?"

"Technically?" Jan closed the door and pulled her seat belt

on, having to adjust it slightly with Tyler next to her now. He turned to watch her, then looked for a seat belt, but there wasn't one for the middle passenger. She was actually surprised there was one on her seat; the truck was that old.

"At all." Martin shrugged as he started the ignition and pulled out of the gas station. "What? You need legal ID to get legal ID, and damned few of us are what you'd consider 'in the system.'"

Jan was caught between amusement and annoyance. The laughter won but only by a slim margin. "And you're driving instead of me because…why?"

"Because if you were driving I'd be stressing and being a pain in the neck. According to AJ."

"AJ is a control freak who couldn't be in any car he wasn't driving."

"Point not debated. But short of him being in the car, I drive."

"Chauvinist."

"Not even. I won't let him—" and the kelpie gestured with his left hand to the man between them "—drive, either. And it's not because you're human. Don't even go there."

Tyler shook his head. "I don't drive. Never learned how." Having said that, he lapsed back into silence, letting them banter past him. His gaze was focused somewhere beyond the road ahead, his hands folded in his lap as though he were afraid to touch anything. Jan noted, too, that unlike previous trips together in a car, when he would slouch and fill every available space, his legs were squared in front him, even on the crowded bench seat, leaving an inch or more between their thighs.

Whatever reason he had for coming with them, human contact didn't seem to be part of it. Jan couldn't see over him to the other side, but she was betting the same distance was between his other leg and Martin, too.

She let the matter of who got to drive drop and looked out the window. It all looked the same, just the paved road and trees and the occasional signs by the side of the road. Cars passed them going the other way occasionally, and there were cars far ahead and behind them, but it felt…lonely, somehow. "Where are we going, anyway? I mean, lacking an actual destination yet."

Martin shrugged faintly and drummed his fingers on the steering wheel. "I figured we might as well do a sweep for preters while we were out and about, waiting for you to get a lead. We shouldn't bother with anywhere a team has already swept and reported in, but that's mostly south and west, far as I know. So, north?"

It made as much sense as anything. They'd tried going in a logical manner, with AJ's predictive sweeps, and that hadn't turned up anything. So, why not whim? "I still don't see why you get to drive *and* pick the radio station," she was saying when her phone vibrated—she'd gotten a message, either an email or a text. Breaking off her complaint, she pulled the phone out of her pocket and checked the display. Three emails, actually—right, she'd forgotten to check at the gas station.

"Anything?" Martin asked.

"Shush," she said, reading. "Huh. That was fast."

"What?" Martin was drumming his fingers on the steering wheel more rapidly now, and she decided now was not the time to draw things out, no matter how his attitude about driving annoyed her.

"Two noes and one maybe. We've got a possibility in Albany. A friend knows a friend who says they have a friend who might be who we're looking for."

"Well, that's nicely vague," Martin said drily.

Tyler spoke over Martin's snark, his voice filled with an incredulity that was familiar enough that Jan felt her throat close up with emotion. "In Albany?"

Jan swallowed hard and nodded. "Yeah. That's where Katie— You remember Katie? With the poodle named, oh, god, what was it?"

"Archie," he said. "She named the dog Archie."

"Right." She had remembered that but wondered if he had. The dog had crawled into his lap and gone to sleep, and Ty had sat still all night, rather than wake it. "She says there's a witch there, one who might talk to us. A real, practicing witch."

Jan hadn't given specific details in her email, just asked if anyone knew of a real, serious practicing witch who was willing to advise them on a real, serious problem. Between that, and whatever her ex-boss was saying about her, Jan's reputation was either shot or made, depending on who was listening. She'd worry about that, along with everything else, later.

Assuming there was a later. If not, then, hey, drink up! as her old college roommate used to say.

"Albany. Huh." Martin shook his head and switched lanes, aiming the truck for the next exit, she presumed, to pick up a route that would take them into New York State. "Who knew that Albany was witchcraft central...?"


"What do you mean, they're gone?" Even as AJ said it, he realized how stupid that sounded. Meredith meant that Jan and Martin weren't on the Farm, which meant that they had left the Farm, which meant that they were about to get into trouble.

The bustle and hustle of the main room halted, not obviously, but enough that it was clear that everyone within ears-range—which went far for a building full of supers—was waiting to hear what had happened.

Meredith stared back at him, refusing to bare her throat in submission to his anger. She hadn't done anything wrong; she was just the messenger.

"All right," he said. "Fine. Go back to work. Everyone, go back to work."

After the first flush of irritation, he was more annoyed at himself, that he hadn't expected this. He had seen the expression on Jan's face, heard the frustration in her voice when she'd tried to talk him into her plan earlier. Some others of his kind might be able to claim they couldn't read humans or didn't understand their cues, but AJ had always prided himself on that very ability—it was part of how he earned a living, selling the parts from the cars his pack stole. If you couldn't read a criminal's face, you became a victim, not a trading partner.

Jan was uncertain, cautious, still a little lost among the supernaturals, but she wasn't a coward, and she wasn't a fool.

And Martin... AJ knew Martin by now. The kelpie was an odd and irritating mix of cold-blooded pragmatist and gooey sentimentalist. Normally, that wasn't a problem; when you invariably kill the ones you get gooey over, the problem self-solves. But the bond between Jan and Martin was real enough that he would go along with whatever she decided.

So, they had a human who needed to feel useful, a kelpie who wanted to help the human feel useful, and a truck, all missing. And since he'd nixed their ideas on how they wanted to help, he had to assume that they had gone ahead with it anyway.

"Idiots," he muttered. But they were idiots beyond his protection now.

Martin would keep her safe. AJ trusted that, after everything the two of them had been through. He'd keep his instincts under control, for her. And that was good. Beyond the fact that the human was useful—despite her own feelings on that topic—AJ liked her. He hoped they managed not to get killed.

"Boss?"

A *yōkai* stuck his head in through the window, his elongated neck reaching in easily. "Um, boss?"

"What now?"

"The other human's gone, too."

Huh. That he hadn't expected. AJ rubbed at his muzzle, trying to keep his teeth from showing in a snarl that would only unnerve the others in the room, and hrmmed at the back of his throat in a noise that was not a growl, damn it.

"All right. That's…not a bad thing." He hoped. "Get Zan in here. I want to ask a few questions of the damned 'corn, but we can use this."

Somehow.

"And send a message to the Huntsman," he added, throwing it out for someone to pick up and run with. "If our humans are getting involved, I think this just became his fight, too."

The Huntsman was old, but he was canny, and he still cared about his species, as much as he might deny it. AJ's missing threesome was going to need help eventually, and he couldn't spare anyone else.

"And what the hell is going on with the California team?" he barked at the rest of the room, aware that they were all still paying more attention to him than their own assignments. "It's like every one of you loses the common sense you were hatched with—not that there was much to begin with—the moment you leave this house. Someone get me a report on California, before I have to eat someone!"

Around him, the hustle resumed.

* * *

The morning light filled the bay window of the council room, catching on the polished brass figures and making the polished wooden floor gleam with red highlights. The small table had been placed directly in the sun's path, a simple blue vase with a single daisy stuck in it resting on the surface. Nalith studied the flower, then picked up her pencil and added a line to her work, frowning as she did so.

A human male stood to the side of the easel, just far enough to be outside her space but close enough that she could summon him with a gesture. He watched her, but his blue eyes were clouded, his expression vacant.

"You drew this so easily," she said. "You made it more than it was."

She had found him in town, working on this easel by the creek, sketching a simple clump of flowers that had somehow survived the first early frost. When he had looked up, smiling at the woman who had paused to watch him work, she had decided to keep him. Like the first human, he brought art to her. Unlike that first, he *created* it. He was the fecund soil, the remembered song, the missing spark. He *would* show her how it was done.

"Let the pencil rest lightly in your hand," he said now. She looked at the pencil and opened her fingers slightly, so that she barely held it. "Like this?"

"Yes."

He was a handsome man, well formed and graceful, if carrying more weight in his middle than she found attractive, but she cared not for his physical presence, only what was inside his head. Nalith lifted the pencil to paper once again and added another line, then another, attempting to re-create the shadow she could see under the petals.

There was a movement in the hallway outside, the faintest suggestion of someone awaiting an audience. Nalith, not looking up from what she was doing, made the faintest nod, and the creature crept into her presence.

"The houses you approved of are cleared, my lady."

At that, Nalith did look up from the sketch pad, both slightly irritated by and, she admitted only to herself, pleased for the interruption. No matter how many times she attempted the simple sketch, no matter what advice her new pet gave, the results did not satisfy her. Having something else to focus on, especially something already completed, was a good thing.

"Houses?" She could not recall what the creature spoke of.

"The locations you had chosen to house the expansion of your court, my lady. Two houses, ready for your filling."

She knew quite well that she had chosen no such thing; the brownie had suggested it and, after her nod of approval, had organized the acquisition for reasons of its own. But it was a good idea, and the creature had proven willing to credit her all the success and shoulder all the responsibility—and, if needed, the blame. Nalith could not fault it on its performance.

In fact, it deserved a reward, of sorts.

"Two houses," she said, as though only now considering the ramifications of such things. "They are not within this enclave, but some distance?"

"Yes, my lady. In surrounding townships, to better extend your reach and yet cement your hold on this territory."

"Indeed. Well done. The court will well-fill such distances, but I find that when out of sight, some courtiers tend to… unregulate their behaviors." Not here, but back there, if she did not cast an eye on the court, they would ferment gossip and disquiet. She expected no such ill behavior here, but best to be prepared rather than face an unpleasant surprise later. Back there, a single word would strike down any who annoyed her. Here…she had fewer weapons to her command, but that did not mean she could not shape new ones.

Yes. She had not planned this, but it suited her needs to do it now. She would use these houses. And that led to an excellent, and useful, reward for her little supernatural.

"Tell me, brownie. Would you oversee these Extended Courts in my name and under my word? Ensure that all within adhere to my pleasure and my whim?"

The brownie should have looked staggered at the level of trust she granted him, but instead a crafty expression crept into its eyes, calculating the offer against its own plans. Nalith had once thought these supernaturals were placid, ambitionless creatures, but every day in this realm taught her otherwise. The creature thought to use her? She was amused and saw no reason to not let it continue, for a while at least. Ambition could be molded into *useful* things, after all.

"My lady, it would be my honor and my privilege to serve you in such a fashion," the creature said now, finally coming to a decision.

"Then all we need are courtiers to fill these houses, West and East." Nalith smiled, catching sight of herself reflected in the window, her lips pale and her cheeks blushed high under dark blue eyes. Beauty, as humans saw it. Danger and power to the supernaturals. A weapon to bring her what she most desired. "Courtiers suited to my whim. And that shall be *my* pleasure…."

Placing the pencil on the ledge of the easel, she strode past the artist, still waiting on her command, and went through the front of the house, stepping through the door and onto the porch that wrapped around the structure. The brownies had painted the house white on her orders, a glamour of her own making stirred into the paint, and it glistened in the sun with a faintly metallic aspect, enough to draw glances but not so much that any would know *why* they could not look away.

Nalith rested her hands on the railing and considered the lands around her domain. She had chosen well, for all that the area surrounding was not so well served with amenities as she might have wished. The road in front of the house was wide and well repaired, the trees rising in front of her tall for this area, if nothing at all like the great trees of the other realm, whose leaves chimed in the breeze and whispered in the night air.

Still, the leaves here, while silent, had turned from green to gold and scarlet since she had taken residence, and that, too, pleased her. Soon enough the cold season would take hold when, her court had told her, the leaves disappeared and white rain limned their branches. She had never seen such a thing herself, but this, too, pleased her: a new experience to anticipate.

Not barren, this place. She could feel it within the elements, carried on the breeze, stirred in the water, growing in the soil. Warmth—not the painful glare of the sun but the sudden crack of lightning, the molten flow of lava—filling her with promise.

The only things that did not please her were the other structures on this street. Her lip lifted in an elegant sneer. Beings not of her choosing lived in those structures, filling them with their noisy, useless selves. She would have only the finest near her, those who filled their days with performance and creation, not slovenly behavior and consumption.

But if they were to avoid a repeat of the last attempt to build a court, where she had moved too swiftly and drawn attention before she'd been ready, then slow steps were the best. In this, the old ways were still the best, to lure rather than take. Slower but safer. Start outward and bring her grasp in, clearing the way steadily but without notice. Capture them all without a shout. Humans and supernaturals alike.

Then, when she was ready, when the fire within her was ready, they would all know who ruled in their midst.

# Chapter 7

Jan hated road trips. Her ass was numb, and her shoulders ached after two hours in the same position, the door handle digging into her on one side and the space between her leg and Tyler's almost as painful.

"Pass me the soda?" Martin said, holding out his right hand.

"All gone," she said and held the empty bottle upside down to prove her point.

The sodas were long finished, the licorice and chips nothing but memories, and all three of them were sick and tired of being in the car, and probably sick and tired of each other, too. On the plus side, after an argument over what radio station to put on that had ended in the radio being turned off entirely, Tyler had started taking more part in the conversation. He still didn't sound like "her" Tyler, but it was a start.

She still thought him going anywhere near a preter was a crap idea, though.

"We could pull off and look for a convenience store," she suggested, hoping for a break to stretch her legs.

"No." Tyler shook his head. "He's already jittering too much. No more caffeine for him."

"Who're you, my mother?"

"Don't," Jan said, warning them both. "I swear, I'm half-tempted to bitch slap you both."

"Don't slap the driver," Martin warned, and a sound came

from Tyler that made them both look at him, Jan worried, Martin confused.

"I'm sorry." He was biting his lips hard, staring straight ahead. "I just... We're in a pickup truck driven by a kelpie, heading to find a witch, driving up the Interstate to stop an invasion from another realm by *elves,* people, and..."

He started to laugh. It was a hiccuping noise, more than a little hysterical, but it was real laughter, and the tension that had built up around the three of them during the drive faded a little.

About forty-five minutes later, in the middle of a contentious discussion about music from the 1950s that was mostly Ty and Martin arguing over Elvis, she spotted the sign for their exit and breathed a sigh of relief. One more rendition of any Elvis song, and she was going to push them both out of the truck.

"So, this is Albany." Martin came to a pause at the end of the exit ramp and checked his window, then pulled into city traffic. "Never been here before."

Tyler looked out the windshield at the buildings around them and made a face. "It's..."

"It's a city. Stop being such a small-town snob," Jan said. "Turn left here. No, the next street, not this one."

It was nearly dark by now. The truck trundled through the city, following the directions on Jan's phone to a neighborhood of old houses and almost-as-old trees. Kids were playing on the porch of one house, and teenagers leaned against a parked car, drinking something out of a brown paper bag, their shoulders hunched against the colder night air. If she'd ever had to say where a witch would live, she wouldn't have picked this street. Then again, why not?

"See?" Jan said to Tyler as Martin maneuvered the truck into a parking spot by the curb. She lifted her chin in the direction of the teenagers, who were studiously ignoring them while taking sideways looks. "Get away from the highway, and it's just like back home."

"Not really," Tyler said, getting out of the truck after her and stretching his arms overhead until she could hear his back crack into line. "But yeah, okay, it's not all depressing."

Jan smiled and looked over at Martin. He looked as if he would rather be anywhere else.

"What's wrong?" she asked him.

"I don't know. I just… I don't feel good here. Being here. It's probably nothing. Which house?"

"That one." Jan pointed at the gray two-story building with darker trim on the porch. The house was somewhere between "old" and "really old," but even in the dusk she could tell that the paint was reasonably fresh, the small patch of grass was neatly trimmed, and there were planters on the porch filled with herbs and flowers, giving it a cared-for appearance. And the number painted on the left post matched the one in her email.

This was where the witch lived.

"Time to get this over with, then, I guess," the kelpie said.

Jan led the way up the stairs, Tyler behind her, Martin a few steps behind him. Before ringing the doorbell, she looked back. Despite his words, Martin was visibly tense, and that was making Jan tense up, as well. Only Tyler seemed unconcerned.

The doorbell was a sweet-voiced chime, repeating three times. The heavy wooden door opened, and a woman looked out at them with polite interest. "How may I help you?"

Jan wasn't sure what she had been expecting—a wild-haired hippy-dippy type maybe, covered in tie-dye and magical charms, or a New Age type, or even a goth chick in black and satanic symbols. It certainly wasn't a thirtysomething woman with a neat, professional-looking haircut, wearing jeans and a USAF logo T-shirt.

"Um, Elizabeth Pasteur?"

"That's me." Her gaze met Jan's easily, then she flickered to Tyler, and something in her face changed. "Oh. Oh, dear." She pushed open the screen door and stepped back. "Come in, please."

Jan crossed the threshold, Tyler behind her. Martin hung back, and Elizabeth waited. As he stepped onto the porch, the witch blocked him. Not aggressively, not barring him, but forcing him to pause. Not quite a standoff, but the tension crackled in the cool air. Tension and something else that made Martin back up a step, the heavy clunk of four hooves audible on the porch.

Some kind of barrier, Jan realized. Magic? Enough to make him uncomfortable, even outside her property, on the street. It was obvious the woman knew he wasn't human. Jan cursed, annoyed that she had become so used to supers she hadn't even thought that might be a problem. Witches didn't like supernaturals, Martin had said. They had history.

"It's okay," she said. "He's a friend."

She either didn't hear Jan or didn't care, still blocking Martin from entering. "What is your intent here?"

Martin looked at her, then let his gaze move to where Tyler and Jan were already inside the house. "I am here to seek aid and information, not to cause harm or mischief to any within this house."

The words, oddly formal, seemed to satisfy her, and she stepped back, letting him pass.

The kelpie met Jan's gaze with a bland expression, but she could read him now: he didn't like witches, either, didn't trust them. But they needed this woman's help, so he would deal.

Inside, the house had a definite New Age vibe, Jan decided. Not that there were crystals and smudge sticks perched everywhere, the way she'd seen in some of the shops and coffeehouses she'd wandered into over the years, but there was a large crystal globe set in the middle of the coffee table, and the herb planters outside were echoed by pots set in all the windowsills and nearby floor. She might have dismissed it all as stage setting, except for what had happened out on the porch.

Jan still wasn't sure she believed in witches, but she'd learned to recognize power.

"Please, have a seat." Their hostess gestured at the sofa and chairs grouped around the coffee table. "How may I help you?"

The wording, repeated, struck Jan: not "what do you want" or "can I help you" but "how may I." They taught that to phone operators, she knew from a college job, but this sounded... warmer. As if she really meant it.

"What makes you think we need help?" They did, of course, but Jan didn't like being put on the defensive when she had planned to take the offensive.

"An elf-shot human and a water-sprite come to my door, I assume they're not trying to sell me Mary Kay products." She tilted her head and looked at Martin. "Are you?"

At a loss, Martin looked at Jan, whose lips twitched despite herself. Not a preter, she reminded herself. Human. "No," she told the woman. "We're not. Your name was given to us as..." She hesitated, not quite sure how to phrase it.

"You need a witch," Elizabeth said easily. "And here I am. How may I help you?"

They'd talked about this during the trip up here. Or rather, she and Martin had; Tyler had remained quiet on this topic, never volunteering an opinion.

Now Ty sat next to her, his knee not quite touching hers

but closer than it had been in the truck. She wanted to put her hand on his leg, run her hand across his hair the way she used to when they were curled up on the sofa, watching the rain hit the windows.

She was afraid if she did those things, they wouldn't feel the same.

"We have reason to believe that the elf-queen is here," she said instead. "In the sunlit lands." The phrase sounded stupid to Jan, but Martin had insisted. Remembering the weird twilight skies of the preter realm, it did make sense and was apparently the traditional description.

After the way Elizabeth had reacted to Martin on the porch, Jan had been afraid the woman would react badly to their needs or maybe throw them out. Instead, Elizabeth blinked and drew back a little, leaning against the back of the chair she had chosen. "Indeed."

"You're not surprised," Martin said, his earlier tension gone but replaced with something new, more anticipation than worry.

"No. I wish I were, but…no." The witch shook her head and fiddled with a beaded bracelet on her left wrist, rolling the beads under her fingers like a rosary. "There have been things recently, vibrations in the world, out of order. Vibrations I could not recognize, did not understand. And in the past few months, they have become…more disturbing. If what you say is true, that would explain a great deal."

"Could you, can you identify where those vibrations are coming from?" Jan didn't want to let herself think it could be that simple, that easy. Then again, why not? Most things were simple, once you understood what to look for.

But not people, she reminded herself. People were complicated. *Don't trust her too easily; you don't know anything about her, and even if she knew Martin wasn't human, that doesn't mean it's a* good *thing.*

Not everything in this world thought elves were a bad idea.

"I could identify them, I suppose. Why should I?" Elizabeth raised a hand to stop any objections that might come. "I'm not saying I won't, but the spell is not without risk to me. So why should I?"

"Because otherwise, her court will come to find her," Martin said. "Soon. Now. Her original court, all the lords and ladies of the sunless lands. They have access now, access *they* control. And they will not leave, after. They are changing, abandoning tradition. They plan to claim this land and all who live within it." Martin's voice dropped, an intimate, convincing tone. "You dislike me. But we share this world. We both belong. You know they have no true love for humans— and a human with a touch of magic they will love even less."

Jan still didn't understand how a human could work magic, and Martin hadn't been able to explain it to her; but clearly, from the way Elizabeth's face tightened, the preters knew about it, too, and didn't like it.

*Supernaturals, preternaturals, and witches, oh, my.* Every time Jan thought she'd figured out her new reality, another twist showed up.

"And if you find her first?" Elizabeth asked.

"We can stop whatever games they want to play. We can block their access." Jan said it as if she believed it, as if it was a done thing, and all they had to do was go through the paces. The fact that it was all bullshit and hope-so and best-case scenario didn't make it sound any less impressive.

Elizabeth didn't look impressed. But she did look a little calmer and stopped playing with her bracelet. "All right." She seemed to be talking to herself, though, not them. "All right."

Jan didn't know what to expect. For all that she'd spent

the past few weeks living with werewolves and trolls and winged things and god knew what else, the idea of witchcraft had kind of freaked her out, when she thought about it. Which she'd been trying not to do. Maybe because this was a human thing, apparently, and until now she'd been able to keep "human" to mean "normal."

*Normal* might be a meaningless term now. The New Normal was Weird. Jan was aware that she was skirting dangerously close to hysteria and dug her nails into the palms of her hands, concentrating on the pain until she felt the hysteria subside.

The other woman got up off the sofa and went to the console table against the wall, picking up a wooden box about the size of her hand. The wood gleamed as if it was old and well cared for, and as the witch brought it back with her, Jan could see that something had been carved into the sides and lid. From where she sat, the design looked like endlessly twining vines, or snakes, but she wasn't going to get up to look more closely.

She'd been spending enough time with the New Normal to remember Pandora's box.

"Unfold that map on the table, please," Elizabeth said, not to anyone in particular. Tyler reached over to pick up the map—just a basic AAA road map of New York State—and opened it, laying it carefully on the coffee table in front of the witch.

Elizabeth placed the box on her lap and lifted the lid. Jan had enough of an angle from her seat to see that the inside was lined in dark green, and it contained more crystals, although much smaller than the monster on the table. The witch lifted out several of the stones, dangling from chains and cords, and considered them, then let all but one drop back into the box.

From the soft thump they made, Jan figured the lining was probably velvet, like that in a jewelry box.

The crystal she'd kept out was clear, about the size of a thumb, and strung on a thin silver chain that let it swing easily. The overhead light caught at it, casting tiny rainbows across the map.

"There is magic everywhere," the woman said, and it wasn't quite a conversation and not quite a lecture voice but fell somewhere in between. "All a witch does is listen for it, listen to it, and then...ask it to move."

"That's all?" Tyler's voice was amused, dry. Jan looked over at him and saw that familiar, long-missing expression on his face—partially amused, partially disbelieving, and totally engaged. Her eyes prickled with tears, because she had missed it and because someone else had caused it to appear. She squinched her lids shut until the prickling stopped and then opened them again.

"The difficult part is shutting up enough to listen," Elizabeth replied. "Most—human and non—have trouble with that part."

Since none of them could argue with that, they didn't.

The crystal dangled over the map now, the chain held against her palm. The witch's eyes closed, and her face went peaceful, the lines around her mouth and eyes easing. "Hush and listen to how the universe moves...."

Jan held her breath, not sure what was going to happen but braced for pretty much anything. Across the coffee table, Martin was sitting on the love seat, his gaze intent on the dangling crystal. In that instant she could *see* the hazy outline of his other form, his long face shifting to a brown muzzle, ears tilting alertly, his shaggy black hair almost exactly the same as it fell into his eyes....

Magic everywhere. And she had spent most of her life utterly unaware.

Despite everything, despite the danger they were in, the sense of urgency still beating under her chest, Jan wouldn't have traded this for all the safety in the world. Not even for Tyler to be well and healthy again, and the guilt for that was like heartburn in her chest.

The crystal jerked, even though the witch's hand remained steady. Next to her, Tyler drew a harsh breath in but didn't say anything.

The crystal jerked again, with a definite lean to the left. It spun counterclockwise and stopped.

The witch lowered her hand slowly, until the lower edge of the crystal touched the map.

Martin leaned forward and read the markings upside down. "Little Creek."

"That's where the new magic stirs," the witch said. She sounded exhausted. "Of course."

"Of course?" Jan looked away from the map and into the other woman's face. "Why 'of course'?"

The witch moved the crystal away, placing it carefully on the table next to the map, and moved her hand back to the map. "Here." She pressed a spot to the left of Little Creek with her thumb. "And here." She marked another spot with her pinkie, spanning the space between with her hand. "There have been murders in the past couple of months. Particularly bloody ones. Entire families. They were calling them wild-animal attacks at first, and then they went out of the news entirely. And then, this week…" Her expression closed off briefly, her thoughts going somewhere else. "They haven't released the news, not officially, but two police officers investigating the murders disappeared. In the mountains."

Elizabeth sighed and moved her hand back to her lap,

touching the bracelet again. "The night air has been restless for weeks, whispering of something ill-come and unwelcome in the hills. I had hoped that someone would come. Someone who could deal with this."

"You didn't want to look until it was someone else's problem."

Jan bristled at Martin's tone, oddly offended on the woman's behalf, but the witch simply gave him a tired smile. "Borrowing trouble rarely ends well."

The witch didn't look magical or impressive. Then again, neither did Martin, truly. They looked like two ordinary, not particularly special people.

Somehow, weirdly, that made Jan feel better. She didn't look particularly special, either.

"Are we certain that the magic is connected to the murders?" Tyler had pulled back again, his voice barely loud enough to be heard. "Maybe it's just coincidence."

"Coincidences do happen," Martin said, but he didn't sound confident enough for anyone's reassurance.

The witch put her box of crystals away and rummaged in a drawer, pulling out several packets. "Wait here," she said and went through an open doorway at the back.

There was an uneasy silence among the three of them.

"You think the queen was involved in those killings?" Jan asked.

Martin touched the surface of the map, moving it slightly across the table. "I think that she thinks that the queen was. And right now, she's the only eyes on the ground we've got."

"On the ground and a hundred miles away," Jan pointed out.

"She did more from a hundred miles away than anyone AJ sent out."

"Yeah." And this was more than they'd had before.

The witch came back with three little sachets in her hand, about the size and shape of tea bags.

"Here." She handed one to each of them. The unbleached linen was scratchy and filled with something that crackled. Jan lifted it to her nose and sniffed. Lime and something that smelled a little like pizza, or maybe pine? She looked at the witch, who was staring at her with an unnerving steadiness.

"Lime, sage, and pine. And a pinch of fennel. Keep it on you, in your sock or tucked into your bra, somewhere it can't be easily taken from you." She lifted one shoulder slightly, a philosophic shrug. "I wish I could do more, but…"

"It's a protection spell?" Martin had already put his sachet away. Jan hesitated and then tucked hers into her pocket, the one opposite from her inhaler.

"Protection and healing, combined to deter injury. If you are facing violence, it might turn a blade or ill wish away from you. Plus—" and here she smiled a little "—it's a soothing smell, and I've found that it helps with clear thinking."

When it became apparent that Elizabeth had given them all the aid she could—or would—there wasn't much left to say. The three visitors got to their feet, tucking the gifts away and offering their hands in thanks. Elizabeth took each gravely, ushering them to the door.

As they were leaving, the witch placed her hand on Jan's elbow, keeping her there a moment longer.

"You're not elf-shot," she said. "But they've marked you, too. You've made a bargain with them."

"Yes." Jan looked over her shoulder to where the men waited, already on the walkway. "To bring him home, to give us time to fight them."

"That's dangerous. Deals with the Others…that's a deal with the devil in another guise. There's always a higher cost than we think." Her other hand reached into her pocket and brought out a small brown shape, a little smaller than the sachet. She pressed it into Jan's hand, and Jan took it automatically, her fingers curving around it. The shape was cool, like stone, and when she looked closer at it, she realized it was carved in the shape of a horse, with an arched back and small blue dots set into its haunches.

"It's a fetish," the witch said. "It brings healing and the power of the herd. I put him in my pocket this morning, not knowing why. Now I do."

Jan's thumb rubbed over the figure—the fetish—almost absently and felt the stone warm under her touch. On closer inspection, the brown was flecked with red and gold, and she thought of Martin's other form, the way the water had clung to his hide when they'd escaped from the troll-bridge and how his eyes flickered sometimes with gold.

Jan opened her mouth to ask a question—what, she didn't know—and Elizabeth put her fingers against Jan's mouth, silencing her.

"Trust and go," the witch said.

She rejoined the others in the truck, the small figure still clenched in her hands.

"We're not going to get anywhere tonight," Martin said. "It's too late, and I for one have no interest in driving around after dark without a clue where we're going. How much cash do you have on you?"

"You're kidding, right?" Jan shook her head. "You don't have another friend you can call on to loan us crash space?" That was what they had done before, when her apartment had become unsafe. It hadn't exactly been Hotel Paradise, but there'd been a roof and running water and a bed that had been reasonably comfortable.

"I didn't think I was going to need bolt-holes all over the East Coast," he said, a touch of irritation in his voice. Supernaturals didn't seem to need as much sleep as humans, but it had been a hell of a long day; he was right, they needed a break.

"There're blankets in the back," Tyler said. "It's not ideal, but we can sack out in a rest area if we take turns."

Jan looked at Martin, who gave a curt nod. "Good enough. Let's get the hell away from this house. It's still giving me itches."

When their car had pulled away, Elizabeth closed the door carefully, then locked it and ran her hand down the seam between door and frame, her mouth shaping a silent prayer. She then went back into the main room and settled herself on the sofa, her legs crossed underneath her. Breathing in, then out, she reached out to feel the wards that protected the rest of the house, making sure that each one remained intact.

Why hadn't she done anything, they'd asked. Because she was scared. No: she was terrified. The first time she had sensed magic shifting in her area, had reached out to identify it, things had appeared soon after. Things that smelled of anger, entrails, and greed. Things that lurked in the shadows, watching.

She was not the only one who knew how to listen. And there were things out there that hated any other voice but their own. Bad things. Violent things.

She was able to keep them out, but not for long, not if they brought more. She could leave, flee during the brightest hour of the day, find another place to stay, keep herself close so that they could not find her again. But there were people who needed her, people who needed to find her. She would remain.

Elizabeth had no illusions about herself. She was not brave; she could not fight this battle. But she would not flee it, either.

And when those in need called to her, be they human or other, she would not turn them away.

Her hands reached out to the crystal in the center of the table and touched it gently, the tips of her fingers resting on its surface. "Feel the universe move. Move with it." It was a mantra, not an invocation, meant only to calm and center her. Then she exhaled and took the next step. "Show me those I can help."

Inside the crystal, a faint golden flicker gleamed to life.

His *stolnik* came to him at dawn, the younger being already draped in formal gear, holding the day's robes in his hands, ready to dress the consort.

"They are ready."

It wasn't a question requiring response. The consort did not care if they were, in fact, ready: they would *be* ready. He had given his word to the mortal that she would have her time, so long and no more, to ready herself for what would come. Time ran differently here and there, but he could feel the moment coming, the pulse of magic connecting their two worlds. He did not understand why his queen had found it so alluring, but he would follow. Follow and lay waste to all she now held dear, claim the rest, and leave her no choice but to return.

The *stolnik* draped the robes over his shoulders, adjusting them just so. He allowed it, caught up in his thoughts. The throne room was empty of the usual throngs, the sun yet rising over the plains outside, the Mountain still in shadow and Under the Hill still sleeping, save the consort and his companion and the nine standing in front of him. Nine plus nine humans with them, hollowed-out and waiting.

There should have been ten. The irritation of that scraped at his bones, not so much for the loss of one portal—nine would be enough, no matter how the magic now made them itch for ten, the sense of a pattern incomplete—and not for the delay that agreement had forced on them, but for the ease in which the human had opened a portal of its own, to escape.

Unheard of for a human to do such a thing. Another pattern broken, another thing askew. The one who had come here and left again, stealing back their tenth portal-holder, proved that they could leave as they desired...which raised the possibility that humans could come as they desired, as well.

That could not be allowed. This was *their* magic, fairly stolen. *They* had shaped it, and they would control it. And if that meant every human born must be chained or die, then it would be so.

The consort would take great pleasure in destroying what had so fascinated his queen and lured her from the Hill.

"Unleash them," he said and turned away, secure that the others would do as commanded. There would be no subtlety now, no gentle seduction. The supernatural that had accompanied the human would doubtless spread word among its kind, play up its success, its escape. They would resist, think that they could hold off their inevitable decline.

It did not matter. For whatever unknown reason, the balance had shifted, the magic had changed. His queen might have been the first to scent it, but *he* had perfected it. They no longer needed to wait, to lurk, to take in small bites what they should devour. The portals would be opened and held, and then the court's harriers would sweep in, reclaim Nalith, and eradicate the supernatural vermin who had defied them, once and for all.

And then the court would claim the human world entirely, the way they should have, centuries ago.

# Chapter 8

Glory woke up with a strange man in her bedroom. Not that this hadn't happened before, more than twice, but usually the men were young, nice to look at, and curled next to her in bed. Or, sometimes, getting dressed, dropping a kiss on her lips as they hurried off to work or wherever they were going. They weren't usually old guys standing, fully dressed, staring at her.

Staring at her, holding a mug of coffee in their hands.

She licked her lips and said the only thing that came to mind. "Normally, thieves take the espresso machine, not deliver the product."

He smiled a little and held the cup out to her.

She sat up, careless of the fact that she was naked, and took it. Her dreams had been jumbled, loud and confusing, and coffee was just the thing to clear her head. And yeah, taking coffee from strange men who appeared in her bedroom was maybe not the wisest of life choices, but she wasn't exactly the poster child for giving a damn.

"You need to go."

"What?" Her eyes were focusing better now. He was tall, old but still in solid shape, and wearing a hip-length brown leather coat that she seriously and immediately lusted after.

He also had what looked like an ax buckled at his belt, and knee-high boots that had to be custom-made. If he was playacting, he had a brilliant costuming department. He was also older than she'd thought at first. Ancient, she thought, sipping her coffee. His eyes were ancient.

"The witches are calling. The time for us to stand aside is over. You need to go."

There was a stranger standing in her bedroom, handing her coffee, talking about witches, and telling her to go…where? She was still dreaming, wasn't she? That would explain it. She'd fallen asleep at her desk, facedown and drooling over the latest report from Jan and her merry bunch of maniacs, and—

This wasn't a dream. She knew the feel of her sheets, the sound of the radiator clunking behind her, the weird quiet of her building when she woke up too damn early in the morning. Her dream had been noisy, confusing, filled with voices yelling and the sound of ice moving across the world, slow and unstoppable, leaving a flat, glassy plain behind. And the sound of a clock, a clock like she didn't have anywhere in her flat, an old-fashioned ticking, marking off the minutes.

Metaphors, she knew it was all metaphors, the usual dream BS her brain kicked out when she was stressed, tied into Jan's deadline, the deadline they were all working under, but at the same time it wasn't. And this, the guy standing in front of her, wasn't a dream.

"They're coming." Her hands felt cold, despite the coffee, despite the heat kicking in through the radiators. Tick-tock.

"They're coming," the Huntsman agreed. "We must go."

Only lost tourists came down the road that led to the Farm—that was precisely why it had been bought years before. The property was isolated, in a part of the state where people respected that in their neighbors and never asked about the odd assortment of individuals who came and went.

So when a sedan pulled up to the gates of the Farm—the property wasn't actually fenced, so the gate was more of a

checkpoint on the single road that led up to the main buildings than an actual barrier—the guards were prepared to send
whoever it was back with directions on how to get to the main
road, or Boston, or wherever they had been planning to go.

When a human woman in a dark red business suit got out
hauling a suitcase and paid off the driver before the guards
could say word one, however, they thought they might have
to revise their strategy.

She extended the handle on her luggage and, pulling it
behind her, walked up to the guards as though she were an
expected and honored visitor.

"I'm here to see Jan." Her accent definitely wasn't local,
her enunciation crisp and musical all at once, but neither supernatural could quite place it.

"Excuse me?" Grady was a faun and not particularly good
at an innocent expression, but he did his best.

"Jan. Your pet human." The woman narrowed her eyes at
him and then, in a voice that carried a definite edge of do-
not-fuck-with-me, said, "AJ will want to see me. Now."

Grady blinked, nodded, and opened the gate for her as
though she'd been expected for hours. She nodded regally
at both of them and set off up the road, pulling her suitcase
behind her.

Once she had gone through, he turned to his cohort with
a wild-eyed expression, his skin chalky under his fur. "What?
Were you going to stop her?"

"Nope," his cohort said. "Let that be *his* problem." Max was
*lupin*; he had no problem whatsoever letting his pack leader
deal with alpha females.

The track up from the gate seemed steeper than it actually
was. Glory was tired, seriously jet-lagged, and in dire need
of a decent meal and a steaming strong cup of coffee. And a

shower, a shower would be lovely, too. In fact, if someone could point her to a coffee shower, she might be able to die happy.

When Jan had called this The Farm, she'd thought the other woman had been joking, maybe making a spooks reference. But no, it was really a farm, with too much open green space for anyone's comfort. She thought about what it would be like out here once the sun went down, and shuddered, walking a little faster up the path toward the grouping of buildings. She knew that everyone—everything—here was working for the same cause, and she'd been talking to enough of them to, mostly, get over the instinctive shudder of atavistic unease when something obviously non-human appeared, but there was a world of difference between talking to someone through a vidscreen and knowing they were all around you.

Her reaction—creatures were all right so long as they were on the other side of the ocean? Did she really think there were none in London, probably riding the tube with her?—would have amused Glory any other time. Not now, not with the tension the man in her bedroom had instilled in her having grown during the flight, the more so because she couldn't reach Jan on the phone. And then for the boys at the gate to not acknowledge that Jan was here...

Something was wrong.

There were half a dozen buildings at the top of the hill, and Glory was in no mood to track through each of them to find her quarry. She paused where the road turned into a series of paths, and studied the activity around each building. There weren't many people out and about midafternoon, and the ones who were all looked intent on their destinations.

A slender, lizardish-looking creature passed her, not quite close enough to grab. It was vaguely familiar, although right now, that didn't mean a whole hell of a lot of anything. She dropped her luggage and put a hand up in its face, stopping it in its tracks. "Seth. Where's AJ?"

The super paused to look at the human who had accosted him, blinked hard enough that his underlid almost stuck, and then said, "Glory?"

She'd been right, this was one of the supers she'd met during their Skype meetings. Or its twin sib, anyway. "In the Britannic and extraordinarily jet-lagged flesh. Where's AJ?"

The supernatural shifted the file he had been carrying to the other hand, grabbed hers—the one not pulling her suitcase—and practically dragged her up to the main building to where AJ was having a cup of coffee in the kitchen.

Or rather, he was trying to have a cup of coffee and kept getting interrupted by people dashing in and out to either ask him something, tell him something, or hand him something. His heavy brow was drawn together, and his teeth were ever so slightly showing, but nobody seemed to notice or worry that the *lupin* looked one comment away from biting someone.

Instead, he answered questions, listened to information, and accepted whatever was given to him, while his coffee sat untouched.

"Boss!" Glory's guide pushed past everyone else, hauling her with him. She had abandoned the suitcase at the front door as a matter of practicality.

The werewolf—and really, she couldn't think of him any other way, no matter what Jan said—looked up and saw her, and Glory suddenly had an idea of what a bunny felt when the hawk swooped overhead, because all she wanted to do was go very, very still and pray his attention moved on to someone else.

"So, you're AJ," she said instead. "You look wolfier in person."

There was a snicker from somewhere in the crowd, and AJ's

gaze got even more intense. Then his jaw dropped in what she hoped to hell was a grin, and he said, "And you smell like fear and sound like sass. Did Jan tell you—"

Glory shook her head. "Some bloke showed up. In my bedroom, I might add. Told me Jan was off doing something else and you people needed me. Human, old, sword and leather? Sound familiar?"

"The Huntsman," AJ said. "Huh. I didn't have to poke him after all. Good, old man. Well played. Galilia!" He yelled that last, and everyone jumped.

"What?" A woman's voice came back, irritated.

AJ jerked a thumb in the direction of the voice and said, "Follow her. Get your ass to work."

Glory could work with that.

"Hey!" AJ yelled after her, before she'd taken more than three steps.

She paused, half turning. "What?"

"The old man didn't come with you? Where did he go?"

She shook her head and shrugged. "Do I look like the social director for— No, he didn't. Said he had something else to do, and that's all I know. I can get to work now, boss?"

AJ waved a hand, releasing her, and she left, shaking her head. "Janny girl, if anything, you *underplayed* how crazy this place is...."

The blankets in the back had turned out to be sleeping bags. They had pulled into the first rest area they could find, parking at the far end of the lot, and alternated turns, one of them awake while the other two slept, until the sun rose. Grubby and cramped but rested, they'd cleaned up as best they could in the bare-bones washroom and then found a diner for coffee and breakfast.

Once or twice, one of them would start to say something,

open some topic of conversation, but it petered out. Jan felt a gnawing in her stomach that had nothing to do with the toxic sludge the diner called coffee, matching the frantic tick-tick-tick that had kept her company for so many weeks, and she let the heels of her hands press against her closed lids, trying to still her thoughts.

"Come on," Martin said, his hand resting over hers and then ghosting over her hair. "Time to hit the road again."

They followed the GPS toward Little Creek until it first started sending them in circles, and their signal spluttered and then disappeared. After that, Jan navigated by gut feel north on the highway until it led them to the turnoff for their destination.

They almost missed that single overhead sign for their destination, the sun's glare making it difficult to read, and only Jan's sudden yelp and Martin's reflexes kept them from driving right past the marker.

"I'm surprised this was even on a map," Jan said, looking out the window as they came off the highway.

Little Creek wasn't a city. It was barely a town; there was one small sign advertising its existence, then a narrow wooden bridge across what had to be the Little Creek of its name, and maybe fifty houses scattered around a single main street that held all the basics of country life.

"Mama's Cakes? That's cute." Jan was scanning the main street as they drove by. "A bakery, one pizza place, and a bait-and-tackle store...at least they have a library. That is also the post office."

"At least the truck looks totally natural here," Martin said.

"Oh, yeah. Trucks and overalls and no phone signal worth a damn." She scowled at her phone and then put it away in her bag. Something pricked on her arms again, a sense of unease that she wanted to write off to being out of roaming range but knew wasn't. *Here there be preters.*

"The witch was right," Martin said, ignoring both of them. She knew that his ears couldn't actually flick with interest, not in this form, but his body language was giving the impression of exactly that. "There's something here. Something preternatural. I can feel it."

"Keep driving," Jan said. "Humans are safe, but if you can feel her, she can feel you, right?"

The kelpie nodded, his hands too tight on the wheel to be as casual as he was trying to sound, but he kept the truck to a slow, steady pace, not attracting any attention. They'd run into that problem before, which was part of why AJ had dragged Jan into the fight to begin with. She could get up close and personal when they couldn't.

But the witch had been able to tell that Tyler was, what did she call it—elf-shot? Jan hadn't thought of it before, but could the preters tell? Would his scent, or whatever it was, call out to the queen, even though she hadn't ever met him?

And if so, was that a good thing or a bad one?

"Figure out the trap, then set the bait," she said to herself, then shook her head when Martin turned to look at her. "Nothing. Can you tell where she is?" Her prickling told her there was danger, but not where.

"Not exactly, no. Near. In town. And she's been here for a while. The others, they left just a trace, and it disappeared after a bit. This is more like a pool of smell. Like…like the court, back through the portal."

"So we're in the right place," Tyler said.

"Yes."

Jan bit her lip, wanting to offer reassurances but unsure how they would be received. This wasn't the bitch who had tortured Tyler, brainwashed him, and nearly killed Jan, but

Jan wasn't sure that was going to matter once they were face-to-face. Would he be able to handle it? Would *she?*

"Keep going," she said.

At the far end of the street, there was a huge mansion on the hill to the left and what looked like an RV haven to the right. Then they were out of the town itself, such as it was, and into what looked like a national park of some sort. Or somewhere large trees had been growing for a long time, and there wasn't much—any—traffic sharing the road with them.

Martin pulled onto the shoulder the moment he felt safer and then turned to look at them. "So. We know she's here. What now?"

Jan had to cough once before her voice would come up strongly enough to be heard. "Even if she scented you, just one unfamiliar supernatural wouldn't set her off. There are probably a handful in these hills anyway, if they haven't all run. So, we have a little time to think."

"We should let AJ know…" Martin started, then let the suggestion trail off.

"She'd scent them coming and be gone again, just like last time, wouldn't she?"

"Probably."

They both turned to look at Tyler, surprised that he'd finally spoken. He stared out the windshield, and his jaw shifted a little, but he didn't say anything more at first. Then he sighed. "If she's anything like…the others, then she'll be too arrogant to leave without a clear threat. Just us, though, we wouldn't be a threat. And even if she smells Martin, having been driven away once, she'll be even more determined to stay this time. Her pride will be hurt."

"Will that make her more cautious or more careless?"

Tyler shook his head. "I don't know. If it were…were Her—" and Jan could still hear the capital letters in that

"—then I would say more aggressive, angrier. But the queen…" His shoulders raised in a shrug. "There was no queen in the court when I was there. I don't know how that changes things."

"She was their center, their stability," Martin said, "the single point of order in their chaos. That's why they're so screwed up and angry now."

"Will she be stable without them? That's why she needs a court here. She needs the audience, needs to be needed. Drama queen, literally." Jan thought about that, chewing her lip, while the other two waited.

"We'll play it both ways," Jan decided, wondering when the hell she'd been put in charge. When she'd decided to leave the Farm and they'd both followed her, she guessed. "Stability, familiarity, and challenge, those're our ins."

Martin shook his head, then reached up to run his fingers through his hair, a sure sign that he wasn't happy. "You want us to go in there, all three of us? Him?"

"Right here," Tyler said mildly.

"Hell, no, I don't want to. Do you think I'm insane?" She glared at both of them. "Don't answer that. But what did you think was going to happen when you said to let him come, that we'd leave him on the curb outside? She's going to be on the alert for attack. The three of us have a chance to… sneak in."

"Sneak into the court?" This time it was Tyler who looked at her as though she had lost her mind.

"We did it once before," Martin said, purely contrary, as though he hadn't just been arguing against it.

"Technically, we didn't so much sneak in as march in blindly." They had followed Tyler's trail to Under the Hill and bullshitted their way in and then bluffed their way out. The memory and the awareness of how easily everything could have gone wrong were part of Jan's ongoing nightmares.

She shook off those memories and focused on the here and now. And the deadline, still ticking away. Three days now, or was it two? She was starting to lose track, the tick-tick-tick too tightly packed in her brain now for clarity. "We're here. We managed to do what the others couldn't, by virtue of being human. And flying under the preter radar. AJ couldn't have gotten a witch to help, even if he'd asked around—she barely let you in the door, Martin, and only because you were with us, and she was already worried."

She waited, and the kelpie nodded once reluctantly. "Witches don't have much love for any of us. We might have been able to convince her, but it would have taken time. And AJ—well, *lupin* aren't exactly trusted by humans, above and beyond."

"I can't imagine why," Jan said drily. She had learned to like AJ, but at their first meeting, if she hadn't been so scared, she probably would have pushed him under the bus they'd yanked her from, just for being such an intimidating, growling ass. And that was before she'd learned what he was. *Lupin* weren't werewolves, not the way humans understood it, but they *were* predators. Predators who were an unapologetic match for humans.

"So, we're here, we know where she is, and she's not expecting us. I say we at least try."

"Try what?" Tyler said, and she knew—the way she'd known before, when he was still healthy, normal, push-her-buttons Tyler—that he was trying to get her to say it out loud, to make it real. Back then, she might have blushed, backed down, thought her idea too silly to actually say out loud, be taken seriously.

She had learned to say impossible things a dozen times before breakfast since then.

"Try to work our way into the court. No, listen to me." Jan

went on before he could protest—or worse, if he didn't. "She's building a new court here, so that means she needs people around her to fill that court. And we know she didn't take any of her own kind with her. If she's curious about humans, the way we thought she might be for her to come here, want to stay here, then we go in and play that up. If she's looking for supers to be her new courtiers…" Jan swallowed once, then forced the words out, looking at Martin. "You can play up the crazy-ass dangerous side you showed the other preters. Maybe. Or if she wants—"

"If she wants a demure, useful tool, I can do that, as well." Martin didn't sound happy, but he wasn't arguing against it, either. "You're right. I don't like it, but you're right." His jaw moved, as if he was chewing, and his steady brown gaze held hers as he thought. She watched, fascinated as always by the golden glints deep within his pupils. She wasn't sure if it was an all-supernatural thing or only specific types, but she found herself looking at eyes more carefully now, looking for it.

"It's definitely her," Martin went on. "The air in this town vibrates from her presence, like the after-crack of gunpowder. How the hell did any search team miss this? I know AJ sent teams up here—hell, we're not *that* far from the Farm itself!"

"It's obvious to you, to us. But we've been there," Tyler said. His voice was so low, they could barely hear him. "We've been surrounded by them, scraped raw by them. How could *we* miss it?"

Jan reached out and took Tyler's hand in hers without thinking, the same way Martin did to her. Unlike previous attempts since they'd returned, this time his fingers closed around hers without hesitation or flinching.

If nothing else, that much good had come out of this.

"So," she said. "We're going to do this. How, exactly, are we going to do this?"

★ ★ ★

Little Creek was small enough that there was no buffer between the rest of the world and the stench of preter. The moment Martin walked over the bridge and into town proper, the sun fading at his back and shadows ahead, it hit him all over again, even more strongly than when they had driven through. The worst part of it was that the awareness wasn't unpleasant; all this would have been easier if it had been unpleasant, if the preter were repugnant. They weren't. They were elves, legendary even among the supernaturals of this world for their exotic, fearsome glamour and grace. Feared, despised…but also legend.

He had waited twenty-four hours while Jan and Tyler went on ahead, taking the truck out to an old logging road and hiding it there, then walking back. He had taken his time, giving the humans their chance first. It was a risk trying to slide three people into the court in the same week, but with luck, no one would think to associate two humans with a kelpie.

He had also, on Jan's instructions, once he'd gotten a signal on her phone again, sent a message to Galilia and to Glory each, telling them where they were and what they were doing. If nothing else, at least AJ would know what had happened to them.

Assuming they weren't too busy holding off the end of the world. When was the deadline up? Jan had been the one to make the bargain, the one keeping watch; Martin had no real sense of time normally, and recent events had disoriented him more than he wanted to admit. Soon, though. Very soon.

Elves were legend, but he had seen them up close, seen them in their own court, been surrounded by the force of their very nature, and he would never admit to Jan how close he had come to not fighting them, to giving in and staying there.

He hadn't. Of course he hadn't. Jan's safety had depended

on him. AJ was counting on him. The awareness of those things had been reins on his neck, focusing him. He was needed; he would stay on the straight and narrow for as long as he was needed.

He did wonder, though, if the other creatures of that world were just as appealing—or if the court had destroyed them all, turned them into nothing more than mindless servants to their glamour. They had seen others in the preter realm, unknown species, but they had been dumb animals or corpses left in the wake of Tyler's captor as she returned to the court. There was no way to tell what those might have been, breathing and vibrant.

The thought of that happening here, of this world becoming nothing more than a shadowed showplace, a backdrop for preternatural vanity…

He wasn't worried for himself. Martin wasn't much on self-awareness or long-term thinking; he took the moment and then he took the next moment, and whatever happened then, happened. He thought that many of the supers would fade back into their hills and rivers, become shadows themselves or adapt to serve the court. But *lupin* like AJ and Meredith would fight and die. And humans…

He had seen what happened to humans when preternaturals touched them.

Martin was under no illusions about himself, about what he was, what he did. As he'd told Jan once, it was a thing. But he did not toy with his victims, did not take pleasure in their suffering.

He looked at Janny and saw a human, a *person*. A friend. Stubborn, fierce, and loyal enough to trust him even when everything she knew said not to.

A preter would look at Jan and see only a servant, a mirror to reflect their own vanity. Or worse, use and then abandon her to become one of the Greensleeves, lingering outside the court forever hoping for some scrap of attention, some touch of favor.

Caught up in his thoughts, Martin suddenly realized that he had walked into what passed for a downtown, the tightest cluster of storefronts along the main road. His nerves went tight, the urge to change shape humming at him: an instinctive reaction, not useful. This was a human place. Most of the stores were closed, a few restaurants glimmering with light from within, people moving inside, crossing the street, or walking along sidewalks. A few, not many. This was a town where dinnertime was a serious thing, home from work, with family, tucked away for the night.

Away from things that might be hunting in the dusk.

He turned right, away from the center, up a wide, tree-lined street, until he came to the place that practically vibrated with wrongness, with unbelonging.

They were watching him.

His feet had carried him to the turn in the road and then stopped. Waiting.

It didn't take long. There were two figures walking toward him, for all intents and purposes taking in the evening air, but he knew them for what they were: guards.

"You."

"Me," he agreed, amiable, even as the reed-thin figure stepped up and tried to get in his face. He had no idea what it was: most likely AJ or Elsa would know, but he'd never bothered, before all this, to learn the different species. He could break it in two if he tried probably. He resisted the urge to shift, to give the creature a hoof in the face, another to the gut. That wasn't what he was here to do. Not yet, anyway.

"What're you doing here, brook horse? The creek's already owned."

He'd known that, too; walking over the rickety wooden bridge, he'd seen the reflections underneath where no light should be glinting. The naiad there had winked at him and let him pass. They understood each other well enough; she wasn't going to get involved.

"I'm looking for Herself," he told the other guard, ignoring reed-thin entirely.

"Whoself?" The other one looked human enough to pass on the street without blinking, but he could see the rustle of downy feathers on its neck, see the way its arms didn't joint quite right, the way it hid its hands from sight.

"Oh, give me a break," he said, not having to fake his exasperation or annoyance. "Tell me she's not accepting anyone to her court, fine, I get that. But let's not pretend we can't scent her all over this town. Now, I've walked two days to get here, I'm tired and dry, and either you let me go on up and present myself or..."

He let just a hint creep out, but it was enough for thin and weedy to shift—not stepping backward exactly, but wanting to. Martin allowed the hint of a smirk to creep out. Kelpies were loners, didn't have to worry about alpha intimidation tactics, but he'd been watching AJ for long enough to pick up a few tricks.

He could feel other supernaturals gathering around him, silent and unseen but definitely there. None of them made a move, though. Nobody wanted to fuck with the craziest SOB in the crowd, not unless they wanted to make a name for themselves, and anyone who wanted to make a name for themselves wouldn't be content standing guard duty so far from the actual action, away from the queen's direct sight.

"Let me present myself," he said again, keeping his body still, his expression flat. "Let Herself decide."

He didn't see any communication between the guards, but

he felt the ones behind him move away, and tall and skinny stepped aside, rejoining his downy companion on the side of the road.

Refusing to turn his head enough to check what was happening on either side of him, Martin went on at his normal pace, a steady, loose-limbed walk that had him up the street and on the sidewalk within minutes.

The house itself looked...ordinary. It was set on a corner lot, sloping grass running down to the cracked sidewalk, a great tree planted in front, towering over the roof, showing full autumn colors that glimmered red and gold even in the dark. The building itself was three stories high, with a porch that wrapped around the front, and a bay window filled with colored glass that shone from within, a warm, welcoming glow. Two figures—one definitely human, an older male, the other too short and squat and scaled to be anything other than a super—lounged on the porch, their feet up and their attention square on him.

Guards, of a higher level than the ones on the street. And a human among them; Jan had been right.

The house might look ordinary, but like the Farm, it housed things far from ordinary.

"I've come to seek service with Herself," he called, not to the figures on the porch but those undoubtedly waiting beyond, behind that wooden door. "Will she consider me?"

There was a long pause, the air heavy with the weight, and then it eased, and the door opened, letting more of that warm glow escape.

"You're in luck," the smaller figure said, its voice a gravelly croak. "Evening's when she's in best humor. Go in, and do your best." Its mouth split, froglike, and showed a shark's row of teeth. "If your best don't please, we'll see you out here again soon enough."

Martin nodded and climbed the steps and went past them, giving them neither the satisfaction of fear nor the instigation of a sneer. First, he had to get into the court. Then...

Then they'd clean it up and take the trash to the curb.

## Chapter 9

Twenty-four hours was both no time at all and an incredibly long time. Long enough to get from London to what Galilia referred to half-affectionately as "deepest, whitest Connecticut." Time enough to work and sleep and wake again surrounded by an entirely different world.

Glory drank her coffee and ate the food she was given that first morning—scrambled eggs, bacon, toast, and surprisingly good jam—packed herself up, and went to work. And tried not to think about *what* she was working on.

Patently impossible, of course.

Without Jan—and nobody seemed to know where she had gone exactly, or if they did they weren't telling, and only the fact that both Tyler and that horse-faced boy, Martin, had gone with her was keeping Glory from freaking out about that—Glory had to figure things out on her own. Galilia and the others on the team did their best, but they didn't *understand*.

Magic, fine. If there was science, why not magic? But it wasn't like jam and toast; they were supposed to stay separate, weren't they?

But it wasn't. Separate, she meant. It was all mixed up and jumbled, and hearing about it had been one thing, one kind of manageable crazy. Living in it…Glory understood now, maybe, what had kept Jan here, rather than running when she'd had the chance. Not the glamour, in any sense of the word, or even the fascination of, oh, dear god, fairies—or *jiniri*, or werewolves, or trolls, dear god, utterly polite trolls asking if she wanted tea, no. It was the quicksilver flashes of a different way of thinking, a different way of *being*, that every now and again would rip through Glory's awareness, triggered by something one of the others would say, making her look at something she thought she had seen a hundred times before and see it in an utterly new way.

You always got that with new coworkers; that was part of why she liked changing jobs as often as she did. But this was a whole new level of seeing. No, not a level. A whole new set of *eyes*.

Glory never wanted to go back to her old life, and *that* scared the hell out of her.

It wasn't until the day after, time spent either in the workroom going over every bit of data they had on the most recent preternatural incursions, talking over every bit of data they had, or, for a few hours, sleeping in a narrow bed in the attic room that had been Jan's and dreaming about the data they had, that everything came together in Glory's head. She stopped halfway through her sandwich and changed the topic of conversation entirely.

"So, magic is actually a thing."

Galilia put down her own lunch and looked at the human, waiting for more context. "Yes."

"But it's a thing you can't manipulate directly. No supernatural can?"

"It depends on how you define *manipulate*. Or *directly*."

"Or is?"

"What?" The *jiniri* looked at her in confusion, while Alon, a squat, lizardish super, coughed into his hand, grinning.

"Never mind. Go on. Magic is an actual thing, but…"

"Less a thing than a force. No, not a force. You can manipulate a force, influence it. This is…"

"Like maths," Glory said. "We assign a value to things, and we manipulate them, but we're not really changing *it,* just how we perceive it. Like time."

"Time?"

"Time isn't real."

"What do you mean, time isn't real?"

Glory shifted in her chair, aware that messing with the perceptions of human coworkers might be a safer game than doing the same with supernaturals. Jan had warned her that the preters, at least, didn't like having to see things a new way.

*It's not so much that they're hidebound,* she had said early one morning over the crackling vid-connection. *It's…they don't think the same way we do, I think. They can see the forest and the trees, but they can't make a new path through them when one already exists. That's why them suddenly changing how they did things, how they* could *do things, is such a big scary deal.*

"Okay, time is real," Glory said now. "But it's real because we're putting labels on something so that our brains can comprehend it. There's a theory, and never mind the theory because that's way off track, but my point was—" and she'd had a point, she knew that "—magic is like time. It *is,* but we can only label it, not manipulate it. Not really. But there are things that can, maybe, mess with time. Real time and our perception of it."

Glory's brain hurt. She was good at practical things, solid things like maths and coding, not theoretical physics.

"Except some humans can," the *jiniri* said.

"What?" Glory's head came up, and she stared at the other woman.

"Some humans can manipulate it. Witches."

"That's what the Huntsman said," Glory recalled suddenly.

"It was all pre-coffee hazy and then jet lag, but he said that witches were calling or something. That's why he got me, why he went off doing god knows what. There *are* witches?"

"Maybe?" Alon looked uncertain, which already Glory knew was unusual. "I've never actually met one. Stories say they don't like us."

"Huh. Witches. Actual witches? Well, why the hell not. Bet I've met one. More than one." Glory frowned, another thought occurring to her. "And I bet Jan has, too. Or knows someone who has. That's where she's gone, both of them. Lay odds on it."

The *jiniri* considered that and then dismissed it as not being relevant to the current discussion. Glory could tell AJ later, if she thought there was need. "So, what does that have to do with us figuring out how the preters are using technology?"

"Because suddenly I'm not sure they are," Glory said. "Using it, I mean. Not the way I use it, and not the way you use glamour, as an active thing. I think magic is like time." She looked at her companion and shook her head, exasperated. "A construct, a…a force that is variable, undefinable until we force a structure on it. We've been trying to figure out how they're using it, when we should be asking how they *see* it."

"Because what we see changes how we act. And the structure they put on magic changed them in turn." Galilia got it.

Alon was a little slower to catch up. "But why…why restructure it, after so many centuries?" he asked, not quite accepting her theory yet.

"Two thousand and eight. That's when it started, back then?"

All three of them turned to look at the whiteboard propped against the wall, covered in colored marks of a time line.

"Yes," Alon said. "Or at least, there weren't any reports of anything unusual happening before then."

"So what changed, then? What could have changed the way they saw magic?"

Alon's eyes went wide, and the scales along his arms went from a cool green to a dark, intense crimson. "Oh. Oh, fuck."

"What?" Galilia looked at him, expectant.

"I just... Oh, fuck."

"Al, if you don't get something coherent out of your mouth in the next ten seconds..." The *jiniri* stood up and looked surprisingly imposing for something so slight.

The lizardlike super waved its clawed hands in tight circles, as if he was getting ready to lecture them. "We've been looking at the preters and not the humans, because hey, magic, right? And witches aside, humans don't use magic. But what you said about time?"

"Al..."

"The LHC."

"The what?" Galilia turned to look at Glory, hoping the human would be able to translate.

"The Large Hadron Collider," Alon clarified. Gali still looked confused, but Glory nodded for him to continue. "Back in 2008, that's when the LHC went online," Alon said. "They were trying to— I don't even know what they were trying to do, but it involved particles and the basic laws of physics and—"

"And string theory," Glory said. "I remember reading about it. They're... Yeah. If magic's world stuff, all around us, then it's going to interact, and if scientists are shoving particles at really high speeds...Jesus, you think that someone got their physics in the preters' magic? I don't suppose we've got a pet physicist around?"

Both supernaturals shook their heads.

"Didn't think so. Doesn't matter. Not like we can go ask them to turn it off, and the damage's already done, obviously, if the preters have changed how they work their mojo. Once shit like this goes down, you gotta deal, not denial. Jesus," she said again. "Fucking string theory, seriously?"

Alon was practically bouncing up and down in suppressed excitement. Glory almost laughed; she might not know its species, but she knew geek when she saw it.

Galilia brought them back around to the original question. "So, how do we stop them? How do we—in, like, twenty-four hours?—prevent the preters from opening more portals?"

Glory sighed and rested her chin on her folded hands. "That's the problem. We can't."

*Time. Time is up.* Jan woke with that thought thrumming in her head, fight-or-flight instinct firmly tuned to *flight* before she remembered where she was and what she needed to be doing.

The urge to flee still lingered, and she had to force herself to stay still, to keep her head on the pillow and her breathing calm until she could trust herself to stand up and not do anything stupid.

More stupid than they'd already done, anyway.

Either stupid or brilliant. Yesterday, they'd managed the first goal—infiltration— and only the first, and Jan still wasn't sure quite how they'd managed that, even.

*My lady. Humans, to see you.*

The supernatural who'd greeted them at the door had barely come up to Jan's knee, but his eyes had been cold, and his voice had held a sneer, as though humans couldn't possibly be of any use whatsoever. Tyler had shivered slightly as they'd walked inside, her arm tucked into his to keep him from bolting, but when they'd been ushered into the queen's... throne room, for lack of a better term, he'd straightened up and dropped her arm as if he'd never met her before.

*Humans? I will see them.*

Jan had seen preters before. She was prepared for the lean, elegant beauty, cool exoticism, a dangerous veneer hiding more danger underneath.

She had not been prepared for a woman—a preter, clearly, with the same narrow, elegant, almost too-sharp face, dark hair pulled back in a ponytail—with sleeves rolled to her elbows, fingers covered with chalk dust, blues and greens to match the canvas in front of her. A woman who'd been more interested in what was on the canvas than the humans being brought in for her attention.

"That's not it," the preter had muttered, her lips pulled back in an expression of distaste. "That's not it at all."

It was a particularly bland and amateurish canvas, Jan had decided, catching a quick look at it as they were brought around to face the queen. Like someone who'd caught half a glance of Monet's work and decided they could imitate it… and couldn't. At all.

"You need to draw the lines up more," she'd said without thinking, stepping past Tyler, past their startled guards, past the man—another human—standing at the preter's side like a butler, waiting for her next comment. "The browns need to balance all the green and blue. Otherwise it just turns muddy."

The queen had turned those eerie pale blue eyes on her, the narrow mouth with too-sharp teeth lifting in what seemed an almost welcoming smile.

"You know art?"

There'd been an almost predatory hunger in those words, not a casual inquiry at all. Jan had swallowed but—remembering the lessons of her encounter in the preter court before—had held that unnerving gaze without blinking. "Some." Her work was technical, but she had drawn a lot on graphic-arts theory. "And I know design and color."

Somehow, impossibly, that had been the right answer. The preter had dismissed the human next to her, sending him off to sit on a cushion at the far end of the room like a pet, and spent the next few hours making Jan recite everything she knew, every detail she could remember from her college courses.

*Keep yourself useful,* Martin had told them before they'd split up. *Become as essential as you can. That will protect you.*

Now she slipped out of bed, the sheets slithering around her as she moved. Still trying to adjust to the new surroundings, she had to pause a moment and remember where everything was before she reached to the nightstand for her morning routine of pills. Birth control was less of an issue these days, sadly, but her asthma medication—Jan had gone without a few times since her life had been turned around and shaken in a can of crazy, and she wasn't going to do that again. You never knew when you'd have to run, or fight, or panic. Breathing wasn't optional.

The floor was polished wood, cool and smooth under her bare feet. She pulled the robe—thick cotton, basic but comfortable, like all the clothing she had been given—off the back of her chair and wrapped the belt securely before going to the door and looking out into the hallway.

The house was three levels; they had been settled on the second floor. Upstairs, in the attic, or what might have been the servants' quarters, was where the brownies stayed. A pack, they were called, and that had made her wonder which had come first, the term for them or the Girl Scouts' usage. The other supers lived outside, she guessed; she had seen them coming and going, and there was a small campsite set up at the far end of the lot, by the trees. Maybe they had tree houses in the copse or something.

This hallway had four doors, two bedrooms to the front

of the house, two to the back. They had the left-hand back room. The other rooms had been given to the three humans the queen had taken already: an older man who seemed to handle the jungle of media stuff crammed into the main room; Patrick, a tall, long-haired man who didn't talk much; and the painter, Kerry, who was trying to teach Nalith how to draw.

Trying and failing. Nalith understood the mechanics clearly enough, but nothing seemed to stick, no matter how many times Jan and Kerry explained that it wasn't about replicating the flower exactly but re-creating it in a different medium.

Nalith. The queen was not what she had expected at all. She was…

Jan leaned against the door frame and reached up to touch the silver chain around her neck, her fingers running along it nervously. It itched where it touched her skin, but Nalith had warned her not to remove it, that it would allow her access to the court and protect her within its boundaries.

Tyler had almost bolted when Nalith had dropped a similar chain over his head, and the queen had paused, placing her delicate, elongated hand flat on his chest.

*You have been touched by our metal before,* she'd said, not quite a purr. *You have been the thrall of that world…you were a portalmaker.* Those blue eyes had looked him up and down, and Jan had tensed, not sure what they could do, two humans surrounded. And then Nalith had looked at her and then back to Tyler and laughed.

It hadn't been a cold laugh.

*You took him,* she'd said to Jan. *Took him from them and came to me. Wise human. Wise.*

And that had been that. No questions, no mind games, no anything. They'd been accepted in the queen's court, given food and clothing and a role to play. They were waiting only for Martin to arrive and work his way in, as well.

And then…

There was a sound, and Jan turned to look over her shoulder. Tyler was curled on his side, on the far edge of the mattress. They shared a bed now, but not comfortably. Not the way they used to, curled around each other, sharing a pillow, her head against his shoulder.

Still. He remembered her, who she was, if not what they had been to each other. He didn't shy away from her company or her touch. He was here with her, on this adventure, alert and aware and fighting to take back what had been stolen from him. It was enough.

She would protect him from everything else. Even the queen, if it came to that.

Nalith. Jan frowned, something prickling at her, making her rub her arms as though she were cold. The preter was alien, strange, disturbing—but she was something else, too. Not like the others Jan had encountered, here and Under the Hill. Something burned behind those eyes, in her voice, and that heat made Jan more nervous than before. Cold appraisal, disdain; those were things she had braced herself against. Not this.

The plan was already off-kilter. She wished Martin were here so she could talk to him, figure out what to do.…

"Human."

The voice floated along the hall, although it was so soft it should not have been heard a foot from the speaker, much less a full flight above. Nalith could have been calling any one of the four of them, but Jan knew it was meant for her. Knew that Nalith was aware she was awake and desired her presence.

"I come, my lady," she said into the air. If her throat was tight and her words thin, the preter queen did not seem to notice—or deemed it unworthy of remark.

Jan took a few minutes to dress, pulling out her jeans and

a loose-necked sweater of the same cotton as her robe, and brushed out her hair. A shower would have been nice, but there was no time; already she knew that you did not delay when the queen summoned you. She touched the inhaler in one pocket, the sachet and the small horse the witch had given her in the other, gathering courage, and then went down the stairs, through the kitchen, and into the front of the house, where the court gathered.

Jan paused in the doorway, her feet still bare against the wooden floor, and studied the creature who had instructed them to call her not "queen," but "my lady." No, the preter was nothing like what they had been expecting.

They had expected, readied themselves for, a preter queen: cold and harsh, selfish and calculating. Nalith was selfish, true. Every thing and every living being in this house moved around her, acted and reacted according to her whim. Within hours of their arrival, that had been made clear to them both. The queen was calculating and harsh and utterly, undeniably alien. Simply standing in the same room, Jan could feel the prickling unease that came from nothing else.

Jan had expected that, prepared herself for that. She had not prepared herself for *Nalith*.

They had theorized that she would be drawn to humans, that her purpose in coming to this world centered on that need. And although the majority of the court were supers, her reaction to them seemed to support that theory. But the humans she was gathering to her were not warriors, not wealthy or particularly good-looking, the way all the humans Under the Hill—or even the Greensleeves, the abandoned ones—had been. They were artists mostly. Creators. Patrick, who turned bits of wood into abstract shapes and spirals that caught the eye and invited contemplation. Kerry, who, when he wasn't waiting attendance on the preter, could dab the back of a spoon into paint and create the shadow of a cat, lounging along a ledge. And now Tyler, who had been tasked to sit at Nalith's feet and sing to her. His voice wasn't professional quality, but it was pleasing, and he'd always been able to carry a tune well.

And his brain remembered a hundred or more songs that Nalith had never heard, from traditional folk songs to pop ditties.

And there was the older man, who had not yet been introduced or spoken to them, who seemed to know about opera and ballet and made sure all of Nalith's programs were recorded properly on the media system he had set up.

It didn't take a genius to realize that the preter queen was fascinated by beauty, by art, by the act of creating art, both decorative and performance. That was her criteria for humans, for membership in her court.

Jan couldn't draw, couldn't paint, couldn't do anything artistic, but she hadn't lied about her design skills. She understood how things fit together, could see the patterns. She had a suspicion that Nalith wanted Jan with her during her drawing lessons, to give her feedback on a shape, a color, a choice, a placement. Like a pet decorator, some kind of Tim Gunn to elves?

There was no way they could have predicted this. No way to have expected it. And even as it gave them entrée to the court, Jan wondered what it all meant. How did you take over the world with *artists?* What was Nalith's plan?

It didn't matter, Jan reminded herself. Whatever the preter queen had wanted when she'd come here, it didn't matter. She'd woken up this morning because the tick-tick-tick inside her bones had stilled. The ten weeks and ten days and ten hours they'd been given were up. The preters would no longer be barred by their word from opening portals and coming into this world. AJ and the others would have their hands full if the consort kept his threat, and she had no reason to believe otherwise. They—she, and Martin, and Ty—were the only ones on scene. They had to find a way to use the queen, to turn her into a tool to force the court back, once and for all.

She must have made some noise, disturbed some waft of air, because the preter queen looked up then and saw her there.

"Ah. Human Jan." Nalith motioned, one elegant hand curling less in invitation than command. "Come to me."

Jan went.

Today they weren't, apparently, going to discuss colors. Nalith was sitting on an antique love seat upholstered in gold velvet, the woodwork gleaming of polish. She wore dark blue, a long skirt and sweater, with her long legs stretched out in front of her and an expression that, on a human, Jan would have described as pensive. Her elegant hands were now resting in her lap, still. Jan had already learned that boded ill.

"My lady?"

"Why does the light change?"

"My lady?" she asked again, less cautiously.

Nalith repeated her question. "The light. Each day, it changes. You have been to both realms. Why does it do that here?"

Jan thought back to the preter world, the continuous overcast that seemed to last forever, broken only by odd intervals of night. She followed the queen's gaze to the side window, where a patch of early-morning sunlight crept along the floor.

"I…" Jan closed her mouth and tilted her head, considering how to answer. "There is a scientific explanation that I would have to look up," she said finally. "Perhaps we should recruit a meteorologist, who could answer your questions more effectively?"

"Perhaps," Nalith said in the tone that meant *not really.*

She wanted an answer now, not to wait. "It vexes me, this changing."

She was taking it personally. Why? Jan cast her gaze around the room and saw the easel, shoved off to one side, the pastels sketch she had been trying to do the night before now abandoned.

Ah. The queen had been trying to draw in the morning light, and it had been different from the afternoon light. Jan tried to think of something useful to say, something that might interest the preter enough to distract her from her potentially deadly vexation.

"The morning light is cooler because it has not had so long to warm in the sky," Jan ad-libbed. "In the afternoon, the light is warmer, it has a deeper glow to it. And at night, the moon and stars give us the coolest light of all, because they have no fire."

For utter bullshit, it sounded pretty good. Jan held her breath, waiting to see if Nalith would buy it.

The rattlesnake-quick slap across the face answered that. Jan didn't bother picking herself up off the floor, staying on her knees, her head down, staring at her hands held loosely in front of her, trying to project *not a threat not a threat not a threat* as clearly as she knew how.

"Do not think me a fool because I am indulgent with you," the queen said, and the cool disinterest was more terrifying than anger might have been. "I am your lady, and you will be respectful."

"My lady, yes, my lady. It is true, however, that the morning sun will bring forth cool tones, and the evening warmer ones. This is what you discovered, yes? That the colors look different in the morning than afternoon?"

"Yes." Nalith raised her chin and looked at the half-finished picture propped against the opposite wall. She was considering Jan's words, distracted from further violence. "And so, I should work on the piece only in the same light, to make sure the view is consistent. That is the trick to it?"

Jan stayed down on the floor, keeping her breathing steady, even though she was shaking with anger and fear. "I believe so, my lady. And…" She tried to remember the tricks she had learned when she was first putting together websites for clients, years ago. "There is a thing, a Pantone color chart. It might be helpful. I do not think there are stores here that would carry one, but I may order one for you, online?"

Jan didn't know if there was a computer in the house or not, but surely with all this media setup there had to be, or someone knew where there was an internet café somewhere, or maybe in the little library/post office in town. First, though, she needed permission to leave. Her phone had lost data and voice signal the moment they'd gotten into town, although she didn't know if that was merely the crap signal out here or if the preter had magic'd the area somehow. Yeah, AJ and Martin both claimed that supers and preters couldn't actually *use* magic, but they hadn't told her about witches before, either, and witches apparently *could* use magic, so she wasn't discounting anything.

But if she could get access to the internet, without someone or something looking over her shoulder, then she could send a message to the team back at the Farm, let AJ know where they were, what was going on, telling them to bring the cavalry. She had asked Martin to find enough signal to send emails from her phone before he joined them, but—

"Perhaps," Nalith said, interrupting Jan's thoughts. "Perhaps another time. My mood is not suited for such pursuits now. I wish to be entertained."

Jan had assumed that the queen would have her turn on the wide-screen television on the wall—the preter had developed eclectic tastes, from *Sesame Street* to opera to crime dramas, and the only thing she seemed uninterested in were reality shows and QVC-like channels, although she occasionally paused her restless channel-surfing to watch some reality TV. Instead, the preter stood and gestured with her hand. "Come."

The queen's mood swings were already becoming familiar. Jan did not trust them enough to raise her head but got to her feet and tamely followed the preter through the house, skirting the kitchen, and out into the back yard.

It wasn't so much a yard as a field, extending an acre or more to where trees lined the property, hiding the neighbors from sight. Not that any neighbor had shown any interest at all in what went on there, from what Jan had been able to determine. So much for small-town curiosity. Or maybe they had been curious and learned better of it.

While there was a porch that wrapped around the front of the house, in the back some previous homeowner had built a two-tiered deck that was completely out of character for the style of the house but made a great lounging area, with steps that led to a narrow, flagstone patio.

Several of the brownies who seemed to run the house proper were lounging around, but they jumped to their feet when Nalith came outside. Jan stayed back a step; brownies might be helpful homebodies according to legend, but she didn't like these ones at all. They looked at her as if they'd just as soon lock her in the basement and throw away the key. It was small consolation to discover that they looked at all the humans like that. Weren't brownies supposed to be friendly?

"My lady," the one who seemed to be their leader said, making a bow that almost scraped his nose on the porch floor.

"The kelpie who came in last night. Fetch it."

Jan stiffened but managed not to react otherwise. Martin had arrived, and she hadn't known? Why the hell had he come in at night? Was he all right?

One of the brownies ran off to do her bidding, short, bowed legs carrying him away, and the queen moved to one of the chairs, settling herself regally. She might be wearing simple clothing, not much different from Jan's own, but when she moved, the sensation of a gown seemed to flow around her.

Without a direct order, Jan moved to the preter's right-hand side, leaning against the wall in case she was called for but staying out of the way until then. She looked around cautiously; she was the only human visible. The others were still asleep or otherwise occupied. None of them were allowed to leave the house, either, all tied by the silver around their necks.

And then suddenly, Martin was there, striding across the yard from out of the tree line. Had he slept out there the night before? Was that why she hadn't known, because he wasn't in the house? There really were tree houses out there, weren't there? Jan almost felt jealous. She'd always wanted a tree house as a kid.

"Ah. My kelpie."

The instinctive rush of fury that hit Jan at the preter's use of a possessive came as an utter surprise. The queen wasn't looking at her, but others might be, so she struggled to control herself before daring to look up again.

Martin had come up onto the deck and gone down on one knee, making a clear obeisance before lifting his head to gaze directly on Nalith's face. "The brownies said you wished to see me. How may I serve you?"

"You asked for a chance to prove yourself," Nalith said, and Jan mistrusted the purr in her voice. It was too close to the sound of the consort's voice back in the court, when he'd tried to finagle their deal. From the way Martin's cheek twitched, just a tick at the left corner, she thought he remembered that, too.

"I did," he agreed, and if you didn't know better, the expression on his face was one of a happy idiot, just waiting for the command to do something gallantly stupid. Jan was too worried to be amused. He hadn't taken any notice of her yet, and she wasn't sure if that was good or bad.

"Are any of the gnomes still in residence?" Nalith asked the lead brownie, the way someone might ask if there was still any cake left after a party. Jan started, unable to help herself. Gnomes?

Turncoats, the creatures that had tried to kill her, twice. Kill and—according to AJ—eat her, trying to prevent her from rescuing Tyler, from stopping the preters from invading. Nalith had gnomes here? The sense of betrayal Jan felt warned her: she was falling under the preter's spell. This creature was not to be trusted, any more than others of her kind. Her hand touched the pocket holding the sachet and carved horse. Elizabeth had said they'd be protection, right?

She hoped to hell that Martin and Tyler were still carrying theirs.

"No, my lady," the brownie said, answering Nalith. "You sent them all out earlier to...take care of matters."

"Did I? Ah. Then find others among your group who will do. I wish to see how kelpies fight."

Martin's expression didn't change. He bowed once and then stepped off the deck into the yard itself. To anyone else, he might have looked almost bored, but Jan had seen Martin bored, and this wasn't it. He was tense, worried. Because of gnomes being here? Or about whatever the preter was up to? Jan cast a glance at the brownies, who were gathered together, clearly choosing up who would be the ones to fight.

Finally, their huddle broke up, and two figures came forward. Like all brownies, they were barely knee-high and scrawny, but Jan was guessing that the scrawniness was over some seriously wiry muscles, and the way they were standing reminded her of wrestlers she'd seen in high school. You might not match them up against a football player, but they could do damage, too. Their tasseled ears twitched, then folded flat against their bald heads the way a cat's did when it was angry or scared. They removed their shoes and stretched their toes, then moved down the stairs to stand across from Martin.

Three feet, max, separated them as they stared at each other. There was no anger, no posturing; they weren't doing this because they wanted to hurt each other, but because the queen had commanded it, to amuse her.

The hatred Jan felt was like champagne in her veins, making her feel light and slightly off-kilter. The preter craved art, desired beauty, and thought that violence was entertainment? She kept gnomes at her beck and call, sent them out to hunt and kill people? She was the same as the others, after all. Not that Jan had doubted it, ever, but...

But for a moment, for a few days, Jan had almost allowed herself to forget and not even realized it.

She'd remember, now.

Jan felt something at her side, a presence, a comforting shadow, and looked sideways to find Tyler next to her. His hair had been trimmed close to the scalp again while they were at the Farm, but he still managed to look sleep tousled. She looked back at Martin, her heart beating too fast for calm, and Tyler's fingers slid into her own, a brief touch against her hand, pressing lightly against the sachet in her pocket, before he was gone.

Jan's fingers clenched against the fabric, but she couldn't look around to see where he'd disappeared to, her gaze as tightly focused on the fight about to happen as anyone else, if for different reasons.

There was no sign, no warning. One instant all three of them were standing there, looking at each other, and the next the two smaller figures launched themselves at Martin, one going for his knees, the other for his shoulders—no, his face, fingers trying to gouge out his eyes. Jan gasped, the faintest noise, and the preter queen turned her head and looked up at the human, a peculiar smile on her face. Jan's heart stopped—had she given away her connection to Martin?

"There is nothing about my courtiers I will not know," the preter queen said, turning back to watch the fight. "And how one fights tells me much."

She couldn't read human emotions, not yet, not well, anyway. Or she was too selfish to even try to learn. Whatever, it didn't matter; she had no idea what Jan was thinking, so her secret was safe.

"They might kill each other," Jan said, feeling as if someone was grasping at her throat. It felt like an asthma attack, but it wasn't; her inhaler wouldn't help this. "What good is he, are they, to you if they're dead?"

The preter queen shrugged; clearly, she did not care.

The two brownies were giving it everything they had, biting and scratching, hissing and throwing themselves at their opponent, putting Martin on the defensive. He moved back, and they followed, tripping him so that he fell backward heavily, coming up smeared with mud and grass.

But he got up, and one of his hands palmed the nearest brownie, getting hold of its ears and yanking like a little boy pulling pigtails. The brownie shrieked, a high-pitched and painful noise, and twisted its neck at an impossible angle, sinking teeth into Martin's hand.

The preter queen was breathing harder, her fingers clenched, and Jan realized with disgust that the bitch was turned on by the violence.

Martin, on his feet again, knocked one of the brownies away, but not before its teeth had torn his pants leg. The other, having escaped his hand, was now trying to do a face-hugger impersonation, clawing at Martin's ears while its legs wrapped around his neck.

His human form could barely keep even with the two supernaturals, giving him no chance to go on the offensive.

"Change," Jan breathed, and it became a chant. "Change change change…"

There was no way he heard her, not over the hooting and cheering of the brownies, who didn't seem to care who won, so long as there was bloodshed, but he tore the second brownie off and stepped back, a shudder running through his body that, even without the sudden intense need to close her eyes, made Jan know he was about to do just that.

The kelpie Jan remembered was a sturdy pony, its hooves glittering black, its coat the red-brown of riverbank mud, its eyes deep brown and mild, with a flicker of mischief.

The beast that appeared before her had the same shape, but beyond that she could not identify it. The coat now gleamed with a sick green sheen, the mane, still thick, was tangled, knotted, and muddy, and the eyes were not golden-brown but a deep, ugly yellow that shone even at this distance.

The hooves were the same sparkling black, until he cracked open one of the brownies' heads, and then they were coated in red.

The creature still tried to attack, grabbing at Martin's mane as though to pull itself onto his back, but let go as soon as it grabbed, crying out and clutching its hand with its other as blood dripped down.

"Saw-grass sharp, that mane, and likely the tail, as well,"

the preter murmured, sounding pleased. "All of it designed for one purpose and yet handsome in execution." She raised her hand and flicked the fingers as though scattering water away. "Two more, aid your kind."

Martin had no more warning than that before two more of the brownies threw themselves into the fight. He backed up, hindquarters bunching as though he were about to run away, then—rather than rearing or screaming the way a normal horse might—he lunged directly into the fight.

And seconds later, there were four small bodies laid out on the grass, one still, the other three moving faintly, either shocked into submission or too injured to get up again.

Jan's eyes forced themselves closed—and did that happen to the preter, too? Impossible to tell, and the bitch would never admit it, if so—and when they opened again, Martin was standing in front of them. His pants leg was ripped to shreds up to his thigh, both of his arms were covered with scratches, his face was bruised, and he looked as though he had at least one black eye.

But the grin on his face was not only triumphant but a little scornful, and the look in his eyes was brilliantly cold, like an icicle on a cold winter morning. There was nothing of the Martin she knew in those eyes. Jan shivered a little, even as the queen leaned forward in her chair.

"I had thought your kind only good for drowning little girls in shallow streams," she said.

"You may find this world surprises you," he replied and then added, almost as an afterthought, "my lady."

Nalith practically purred at his presumption, or how he yoked that presumption into obedience, more likely. Jan choked back her own anger and nausea, remembering their reason for being here. Get into her graces. Find a way to hold her here, see if they could identify a weakness or find a way to use her against the other preters, alert AJ, and let the teams descend.

Nothing else mattered.

# Chapter 10

The Huntsman was old. He remembered when the world was a slower, larger place. He also remembered that it had never been a simpler place. Some things never changed.

The note from the old wolf had come on the heels of the witches' warning. He had needed neither, already aware of the change in the world.

"Haven't seen you in a while," the man across the counter said.

"I've been away." He had been hiding. Spending long afternoons in the Center, the tree-ringed clearing where there was no time, no stress, only peace and calm. The last time he had been there, he had sat all night by a fire, watching the stars wheel and turn, and found no peace, no calm.

Preternaturals stalked this world. AJ had warned him, and the witches had confirmed it. The Huntsman had no beef with supernaturals; how could he, tangled in their hold for all these years? If he sometimes longed for the dust and oblivion that would have been his measure had he not stepped between a wood nymph and a wolf centuries before, that did not mean he did not still love his nymph, and the wolf...

He had called the *lupin* friend for almost as long. Supernaturals did not hold grudges. Not of that sort. And neither could he. But preternaturals did not belong here.

"And now you're back." The human across the counter

finished bagging up his supplies, slow and methodical. "You do nothing without a reason, David."

That was true. The witches—the only of his species who could see what he was, who could understand—had called him to duty.

The grocer was human, but he was human the way the Huntsman himself was: touched by their grace, changed by their magic, able to see the fantastical and, having once seen, unable to live anywhere or any way else.

He had once thought he had paid the price for that, paid in double and in full. He had been wrong.

"There's a storm coming, Jack."

The grocer wasn't fool enough to bother looking at the clear sky outside his shop. "Your lumbago tell you that?"

"No games." He had never been one for games, but Jack had. Once it had been all games and foolishness with the boy, and how long ago that seemed now. Jack hadn't been a boy for decades. "No ache that tells me the fair folk are distressed, that magic is stirring where none should move. The elves are at their tricks again." He was an old-fashioned man, and he would use old-fashioned terms, and to hell with any who mocked him for it.

"Ayup." Jack was no fool, for all that he'd once played one. "And you think we need to do something about it? You?"

"Once a meddler, always a meddler, it seems," the old man said, not without some rue.

Jack put his elbows on the counter, his palms pressed together. He had been a fair-haired boy once, before that hair receded and the bright, clever look in his eye was replaced by a more knowing one. "What do you have in mind?"

"Nothing...yet," the Huntsman said. "But be ready for my call."

When the storm hit, all hands might be needed.

* * *

With his performance against the brownies, Martin became the queen's new favorite, her obsession with art and creativity washed away for the moment by her appreciation for violence. He bowed to her, a shallow thing, but she ate it with a spoon, drawing the kelpie close, her arm tucked through his. She was taller than he but so slender, they made an odd, almost complementary pair.

Jan set her jaw and reminded herself that this was all part of the plan, as much as they had an actual plan, following the pair back into the house like an obedient human. Martin wasn't hers—he was her friend, her colleague, fine, but she didn't *own* him.

This wasn't the same as Tyler and the elf-bitch who'd stolen him. Martin wasn't being abused or brainwashed; they were here for a reason. They were here together, all three of them. Safety in numbers. She wrapped herself around that fact, warmed herself on it.

There was coffee and tea set up in the kitchen and an assortment of warm muffins filled with cheese on a platter. Jan took one, suddenly aware that she was hungry. Whatever else she might think about brownies, they kept house like champions.

The sense of hunger faded once the muffin was gone, and all that was left was an emptiness in her chest. She couldn't identify it at first, then a sudden panic clenched her gut and made her breath come short. She was reaching into her pocket for her inhaler before she realized what it was.

The sense of a clock ticking down a deadline that had moved within her, ever since the bargain she'd made in the court...was gone. No fear, no pressure...but Jan didn't for a moment think that the threat was gone, too. If anything, it was closer than ever before.

"Nothing's changed," she told herself, ignoring the sideways look a *lupin* gave her as it grabbed a muffin for itself. A human talking to herself couldn't be all that off the weird-o-meter, not here. "Just keep going."

There were no clocks or calendars in the house that Jan had seen, and she had a feeling that asking someone what day it was might not be the best way to blend. They were supposed to be here by choice, waiting on Nalith's whim, not waiting on outside forces. The queen's schedule set the day, and everyone seemed to follow along. "So, follow along," she said in the now-empty kitchen and went where everyone else had gone.

The preter queen was settling into her not-quite-a-throne-seat in the main room, Martin standing by her side while she conferred with another one of the supers, a thin, reedy thing with a face like vanilla pudding. Their voices were too low to overhear, but neither of them seemed particularly upset, and Martin's face was still that calm, waiting expression that told her to hold the course and not do anything.

The rest of the room was not crowded, exactly, but filled. Tyler had come back, now dressed and looking more awake, a mug of coffee in his hand. Kerry never woke before midday if he could avoid it, he'd told her, but both Patrick and the unnamed man had joined him, the three of them settled into a corner of the room, watching Nalith's face like dogs might watch their owner, waiting for a command. Jan caught Tyler's eye and was somewhat reassured when his left lid lowered in what might have been a wink. They were still there, still here, still them. For a moment, a strained, dizzy moment, she had doubted that.

"You, Patrick, attend me," Nalith said, dismissing Martin and beckoning for the human, who jumped to his feet as though he had been waiting for her call. He had, of course. Jan watched as he made his way to the preter's side, remembering with a sick twist in her stomach the way Tyler had stood next to the bitch-preter who had captured him, seduced him. How she'd tried to destroy his mind, his will, his personality, turning him into an empty vessel, a tool to be used to open portals.

No. Stjerne had failed. Jan had won. Tyler was here, not safe, no, but *aware*. Human. This wasn't the same. She wouldn't lose him, wouldn't lose either of them.

"I wish to see the progress you have made," the preter said to Patrick. He nodded, almost a bow, really, and left the room, Jan presumed to fetch his current project.

"And there you are. Sing for me, my bird," Nalith said, almost offhandedly, as Patrick came back with a cloth-wrapped object the size of a small child in his arms, his tool kit slung over one shoulder. Tyler didn't bother to ask what she was in the mood for—did he know, did he guess?—but opened his mouth and let sounds come out, a sweet, slightly mournful song that Jan didn't recognize. Not the pop songs he used to sing in the shower, but something older, more suited to this court, about a lady who was locked in a tower and desired more than anything to see the living ocean and be tossed upon its waves.

Nalith didn't seem to be paying any attention, more focused on what Patrick was setting up in front of her, but there was an easing of tension in her shoulders and jaw that gave her away.

With the preter distracted for at least a little while, Jan risked slipping away, moving quietly out of the room. Several of the supers glared at her, as though she were giving offense by leaving, but none of them tried to stop her.

There were maybe two dozen supers that Jan had been able to identify, although it was difficult when so many of them looked alike; there could be ten brownies or thirty, and that was without considering the gnomes.

Jan shuddered as she went into the kitchen. She didn't want to think about the gnomes. They weren't allowed in the house. Let them stay far away, doing whatever errands the preter had sent them on. Let them be someone else's problem, as horrible as that sounded. She had enough to deal with here.

There were three brownies and what looked like a water-sprite of some sort, based on the gills and seaweedy hair, still in the kitchen. They turned to look at her, and while they didn't say anything, she didn't feel particularly welcome, either.

She needed somewhere to think, somewhere she would be left alone with her thoughts but not perceived to be hiding or doing anything wrong that would be carried back to the queen. But this place was almost as bad as the Farm, for privacy.

The basement where most of Nalith's followers gathered, where the most useful gossip could be overheard, was off-limits to humans; that had been made clear their first hour in the court. Going back into the front rooms, having to see Tyler singing like a pet canary for the preter, or Martin standing like some kind of...obedient pet, wasn't going to help her thinking, though.

Jan had the choice of going back upstairs to her room, where anyone could easily find her, or going back out into the yard. She chose the yard.

There was a single super on the deck, its face turned up toward the sun, but it ignored her, and she returned the favor. The grassy area was cleared of any sign of bloodshed or even a battle at all, although she could see the remains of what looked like a campsite at the far end that hadn't quite magically grown over.

In a weird way, the space reminded her a little of the Center, where she'd been taken after her apartment was attacked. The wear marks on the grass there had faded magically, too.

The Center felt utterly different, though; it was calm, steady, instead of the constant upset Jan felt here.

Jan didn't know where the Center actually was—the bansidhe had flown her there, wrapped in its wings, the first time, and Martin had blindfolded her when they'd left so she wouldn't freak out at being dragged into a river, but she wanted to go back rather desperately.

Things had almost made sense in the Center. The thought made her almost smile. She'd been centered in the Center.

No chance of that here. Jan exhaled, trying to force the tension out of her shoulders, through her spine, and out of her body, and rested her hands on the deck railing.

"I'm bored," she said out loud, the first thing that came into her head. "How can I be bored?"

"Because it's boring here."

Jan almost jumped off the porch, then turned to see one of the brownies standing in the doorway, watching her. She couldn't tell them apart, really, except by what clothing they were wearing, but this one seemed almost familiar. Not one of the ones in the kitchen…no, it had been part of the group that had been out here during the fight. Not one of the ones who had attacked, though.

"Excuse me?"

"Boring," the brownie repeated, not seeming to be offended or angry. "This is a dinky little excuse for a town, with nothing to do except dance to her tune, and when she's not playing a tune specifically for you…" The brownie shrugged, skinny shoulders rising and falling with a surprising eloquence. "Boring."

"I had thought…" She wasn't sure what she was going to say.

"What, that we live and die to serve her? That we don't have a life beyond the kitchen and the laundry?"

Jan blushed, feeling the heat in her cheeks, and the brownie laughed, only a little meanly. Cam, that was its name, she remembered now. It was the one that interacted directly with Nalith when needed, and she'd called it by name a few times.

"Yeah, well," the brownie went on, "we're trying to expand our interests. As one does." There seemed to be a joke in there, but Jan couldn't find it. "At least you have the option to wander into town, as boring as it is, once she lengthens your leash a little. We'd raise too many eyebrows, even out here, so she'll probably have you doing the grocery shopping soon enough." The brownie—Cam—thought about it. "Yeah, only woman, she'll send you. She'll want to keep the songbird with her just in case. You won't wander away without him."

They didn't plan to be here long enough to restock the kitchen, Jan thought but didn't say out loud. They didn't *have* time. She couldn't feel the ticking anymore, but if the change of pressure meant the deadline was here, if not today then tomorrow, or maybe it had already happened…

Then the preters would be crossing over again, freed to steal more humans, their plan, whatever it was, back in motion. Probably it wouldn't be an overnight thing, no sudden apocalypse, but Jan felt the ghost of that pressure in her chest again, replacing the fear of an asthma attack with something worse and less easy to predict or control. There was no medication, no inhaler that could stop this. Only them. Somehow.

"Is there an internet café in town?" she asked. "We came here not really sure what was going to happen, and we didn't leave a note because, well, what could we say, 'Off to find the elven queen and offer our services'?"

She had, actually, sent exactly that message. Or she hoped she had, anyway. She needed to talk to Martin, find out if the emails had gone through, and get her damn phone back. If the kelpie had lost or broken it, she was going to kill him.

"Anyway," she went on, trying to be as artless as possible, "the chance to email now would be great, 'cause I'd love to let my friends know I'm fine, that there's no reason to worry about me, before they throw out an APB and the cops show up. Not getting the cops involved is always a better idea."

The brownie's ears twitched once, front to back, and it studied her, as though trying to decide something. Then it smiled, as though it had come to some decision, and shook its head. "No, no cops. They like to poke and prod and cause all sorts of breakage and mess. Definitely do not want them around. They would irritate Her and that would be bad." It shook its head once more, still smiling. "There is a computer in the basement. We use it for… We use it. But you can't go down there."

Humans were not wanted, not allowed, no matter what. Not that it mattered, in this case; any computer in the heart of super territory—supers who had thrown their lot in with the preter queen—was not going to be a good place to get in touch with Glory or AJ.

"I couldn't even just to send email?" she asked anyway, projecting a slightly worried but not-yet-frantic tone into her voice.

"There's Wi-Fi signal over near the campgrounds," the brownie said thoughtfully. "You could go there."

And hope that her cell phone picked up enough signal to work. It wasn't a great plan, but it was the only one she had.

"But don't go until you get permission," the super added. "Herself doesn't like it when her pets wander off."

"I'm not a pet," Jan said, bristling almost automatically.

"Sure you're not," the brownie said, cackling as if she'd just said something unbearably amusing. "You just try going off and see how fast she yanks your chain."

Jan glared at the shorter creature and then marched off the

steps, heading away from both the house and the area where the gnomes had camped, the brownie's mean-spirited cackle following her.

The more supernaturals Jan met, the more she started to think that she really didn't like them.

She did not, however, go beyond the wooded property line that had been pointed out to them their first day. Just in case.

"He's right, you know."

"What?" Jan missed a step and almost tumbled face-first onto the grass when a voice spoke in her ear.

"You can't leave without permission. Or you could, but Herself'd be upset. And she'd either drag you back by the scruff of your neck or not let you back in. And she'd absolutely keep your boy toy, and you'd never see him again."

The speaker danced in front of Jan now, girlish and loose limbed, but the smile on that face was filled with sharp green teeth, and her eyes were pools of solid black that matched the inky hair flowing past her shoulders.

"Jenny Greenteeth," Jan said, more than a little worried as she identified this particular super. There wasn't any water bordering the house or running through the trees that she'd noticed, walking up... No, wait, there was the creek that bordered the town that they'd driven over coming in. It was large enough to have at least one water-sprite, probably more, although Jan would have hoped for one with a...less evil reputation. Surely Martin would have said something? But they hadn't been able to exchange even a word since he'd shown up, and—

"Relax, human," the river spirit said, still grinning, leaning in to sniff at Jan's hair in a way that was deeply disturbing. "I'm no brownie-man, to begrudge you your place in the court. We all come here for our own reasons. She uses us as she will, and we take what she gives."

"And what is she giving you?" Jan asked. They'd known, back at the Farm, there were supers following the preter queen willingly, but not why, not beyond vague guesses and suspicions. The brownie had talked about expanding their interests, whatever that meant, but...

"Entertainment," Greenteeth said, her slim form still dancing around Jan, forcing her to turn in order to keep the super in sight at all times. "I am not of her court, not me, but I watch. It will not be dull while she is here. Allies and enemies, plots and plans, whispers and hisses."

"Your very own reality show?"

"Yesssss..." Those black eyes sparked with something deep in the pupils, and Jan knew she should be disturbed, maybe even frightened, but suddenly Greenteeth seemed less frightening than, somehow, endearing.

"Jenny. Are you englamouring me?" Jan tried to sound stern, but her voice cracked on the last word.

"Heeeee. Human who smells of kelpie and witch-spell knows better. I don't have to try. You're already halfway there." The greenteeth leaned closer and pressed her lips to Jan's, a warm, wet tongue darting out to lick her once quickly, before the super had danced away again.

"That's sexual harassment!" Jan yelled after her, wiping her mouth with the back of her hand, but she was laughing despite herself. The river sprite made her think of Martin again—terribly dangerous and yet charming, disarming.

Like drowning, she thought. A terrible way to die, and yet she'd read somewhere that it was easy, too. All you had to do was let go.

"Not an option," she said and started walking again, keeping the tree line to her left. She could feel Jenny—or something—watching, but she refused to acknowledge it. She hadn't had a chance to walk the borders of the property yet, and it might be something that would be useful later, knowing exactly where, when, and what might come out of those woods. And it kept her out of the house, until she could face the queen again with her besotted mask in place.

The human, Tyler, could sing. Not professionally, no, but he had a good voice, a clear tenor, and apparently an inexhaustible recall for songs, because he hadn't repeated anything yet, and the preter had him singing all morning.

Martin leaned against her chair enough that she was aware of him, but not so much that he was off balance or too far into her personal space in a way that might have appeared to be presumption. It was a constant recalculation and one he was not adept at, but so far she had not reacted badly. The main room was filled: half a dozen of the house-brownies clustered in a group and shooting him dirty looks even now; two fire-wisps that stayed near the fireplace, occasionally ducking in when they got too cool; and a handful of individual supers, most of whom he didn't recognize without AJ there to coach him.

And the humans, of course, the two artists and another he had not been introduced to, on opposite edges of the room as though they did not trust each other and trusted the supers even less.

If so, that was the first wise thought they'd had since falling under the preter's spell.

Jan had slid out of the room much earlier; the queen did not seem to notice that she was gone, but Martin suspected that she had noted and simply did not care to make a fuss about the defection. The queen seemed to have no goal in this morning's gathering, merely enforcing her will on them, reminding them that they were hers, here solely to dance attendance on her. Nalith was flighty, spoiled, bloodthirsty, and casually cruel; exactly what he had expected, after seeing the preter court she had left behind.

And yet, she had left it behind. Not come as the vanguard of an invasion, not even as a conqueror might. She took all sorts into her court and seemed almost, oddly, content in this place, without any significant luxuries or adulation. As queen, she could have commanded an entire world. Here—much less, and she did not seem particularly eager to change that immediately. She had, in fact, run before discovery, rather than striking out in battle.

He still was not fool enough to trust her or dismiss the threat she posed. All preters, in the end, wanted one thing: control.

Supernaturals—and naturals—were not inclined to give that up without a struggle, even under glamour.

"Kelpie." Her hand had lifted gracefully to shoulder height while he was thinking; she was summoning him. Martin dragged his attention back to her, worried that he had missed something, something important. "The gnomes return."

The moment she said that, he could feel it, as though the air rippled against his skin, bringing the feel of thick, sticky fingers, like tree frogs clinging to everything. He scanned the room, catching Tyler's eye and trying to send a warning, but the other man had no experience with turncoats, didn't know what he would be facing. He hoped that wherever Jan was, she was out of their path, could avoid them entirely. They might have no connection to the ones who attacked her, but they couldn't take that risk.

"They have been my weapons, until now," Nalith said. "But now I have you."

Martin didn't pretend to be any sort of champion for morality, but he would rather beat every gnome in existence into the mud with his hooves than work with a single turncoat.

"I am but one," he said, trying to sound honored by her words, rather than nauseated. "And they are many. Together, we will best serve you."

# Chapter 11

Tyler had heard the queen's conversation with Martin, the whispers that followed. His expectations of supernaturals at this point had faded into a wary and weary acceptance: unlike the preters, none of them had tried to hurt him, and some of them had seemed almost decent. Martin...

Martin had helped bring him out of the Other Place. Martin and Jan were friends. Maybe something more than friends, which should have pissed him off, but who was Tyler to judge at this point? He had been dumb enough to go with Stjerne, thinking with his dick instead of either his brain or his heart.

Martin kept Jan safe. That was more than he had been able to do, ever.

The thing was, overall, he didn't mind supernaturals, not back at the Farm and not here. So, while the whispers about the return of the gnomes made him cautious, he wasn't prepared for what came in.

They were not small, not like the brownies. He had thought they would be. Their skin was the greenish-yellow of moss, the kind that probably glowed under black lights, and it looked too slick, too damp, as though they were amphibious. Maybe they were. Their heads were bald, their arms too long, and Tyler thought that he was hallucinating before he realized that, no, their bodies were *changing* as they walked, expanding and contracting, seemingly unrelated pulses, fingers lengthening, bodies hunching, thighs expanding and then contracting down to sticks.

There were four of them, he determined, walking in tight formation, a cadre that seemed to have only one awareness, allowing them to move together that way.

"We are returned," one of them said when they stopped in front of Nalith's chair. Martin had taken a step back, away from the throne, and was watching them the way you might a dog you weren't sure was rabid or not.

"So you have," Nalith said.

"You promised us rewards," the lead gnome said. It stepped in front of the other three and seemed to rise in height—not much, but enough that it could look her in the eye. Its face was more defined now, but that only meant that Tyler was aware of its mouth, oval shaped and filled with too many teeth. Like a suckerfish crossed with a shark, and that thought wasn't at all relaxing. Nor was the next one, driven by way too many hours watching Animal Planet reruns. These things were not just meat eaters; they were carrion eaters. No wonder everyone had taken a step back. He suspected they didn't much care what flesh they gnawed on.

Then one of them slewed its head around and looked directly at him, its eye red–black and glittering, and Tyler amended that. They might not care but clearly thought human was the most tasty. He reached for the sachet the witch had given him, tucked into his pocket. It didn't bring him as much comfort as he'd hoped.

"You were rewarded enough in your actions and the plea-sure you took in them," Nalith said, and while her face was still calm, Tyler heard the warning in her voice. So, too, ap-parently, did the gnomes, because they shifted their feet but did not say anything more.

"Return to your campsite," Nalith told them. "You are not suited for this room, and this room is not suited to you."

There was a pause as everyone tried to figure out who had been insulted the most, and then the cadre of gnomes turned and headed back for the door. The supers who had filled in the space behind, the better to watch the show, now scrambled to get out of their way, as though afraid one of the four might reach out to touch them.

Tyler understood that fear. He had seen more terrifying things. He had been strapped into a chair of thorns and had his will torn from him. He had become nothing but a vessel for another's will—and even he would not willingly suffer one of those creatures to touch him.

There was evil, and it was a sometimes beautiful, bitter thing. But gnomes were not evil, nothing that pure. They were sheer selfish greed, of the sort that could be nothing but ooze and blister.

"You should not let them back, my lady." One of the supers spoke first into the silence after the gnomes left, after the slam of the door said they had gone outside.

"I should not?" Nalith's tone was gentle, almost amused, and Tyler's knees trembled, remembering again the sweet bramble of Stjerne's voice as she told him to give in, to relent, to be nothing but hers. Every nerve, every atom of his body screamed anger, screamed at him to run, to hide, to stay very still and pray that he wasn't noticed. Every nerve and atom except the ones deep inside, in the darkest, coldest place of himself, that told him to give in, to accept what he was, what he would always be.

"My lady." The speaker tried to dig himself out. "I—"

"I will not be defied," she said, her voice still soft, gentle. "Kelpie."

Tyler had seen Martin transform before. Or rather, he hadn't seen it, his eyes forcing themselves shut and opening again only when the man was gone and the beast remained, but he knew the feel of magic pressing on him. He had not realized it could be done so swiftly, though. Nalith had only just given her order when the kelpie struck, gleaming black hooves staving the super's skull in like a pumpkin after frost.

"Fuck me," someone murmured, more awed than horrified, and Tyler swallowed back the bile that had risen in his throat. The show of strength, of indifference, was all that had saved him before. He would not break now. He would not let this preter break him, when others—*Stjerne,* his memory whispered. *Lovely, cruel Stjerne*—had failed.

Martin had not changed back, standing four legged in the cleared center of the room, his victim underneath him, as though waiting for another challenge to appear, another order to be given.

When none came, he snorted, cold amusement clear in the sound, and stepped backward until he paused by Nalith's chair, hooves picking delicately across the hardwood floor. His eyes were bright yellow, his mane caked in blood, and there was nothing gentle or tame about him at all. Even Nalith did not dare to rest her hand on his neck or touch that shoulder. The kelpie killed on her order, but it was no pet, no tool to be picked up without caution.

Tyler exhaled slightly, remembering the Martin who had stolen a car and driven them here, who had gone Under the Hill with Jan to bring him back out. The Martin who held Jan's hand, as if it gave them both comfort. Not tame, no. But not a danger to him here now.

It was just everything *else* he needed to worry about.

The music was loud, the bass thumping deep enough that hearts regulated themselves to its meter, blood pulsed to its rhythm, bodies swaying in unison throughout the club. Despite that, Harry could hear every word the blonde said, as though they were alone in an empty room.

"You are sweet." The woman leaned in, her finger tracing the line of his jaw, her nail short but sharp against his skin. Normally being called "sweet" was the kiss of death to your chances, but the way she said it implied less kittens and teddy bears and more tangled sheets and hot wax. His pupils expanded, and his body leaned toward her, drawn by some unseen thread.

"Yeah, I—"

"Stop playing with him, Erini," a voice interrupted. "Either take him or be done."

"Hey." Harry turned to face the intruder, more upset at another male coming near this hottie than what the man had actually said. "The lady and I were talking."

"My apologies," the guy said, showing too-perfectly-white teeth in something that wasn't really a smile.

Harry blinked, his normal reaction utterly derailed. He wasn't gay, but the guy was seriously hot, too. In fact, he had the same narrow, high-cheekboned face the woman, whatever her name was, had, only on him it didn't look delicate at all. Metrosexual, yeah, that was the word. Same huge eyes, too, greenish, with those same weird pupils.

"Huh." He looked back at the woman, considered the two of them, then shrugged, giving them both his best "I'm a good guy" smile. "Your sister, huh? I promise I'll take good care of her."

"Oh, I'm sure you will," the guy said, and Jesus, that was a creepy-ass smile that made Harry start to reconsider if he wanted to go anywhere with anyone related to this guy, no matter how much his dick was urging him on.

"Indeed," the woman purred, and her finger left his face,

scraping along his chest, lingering just above his belt, an implicit promise of what could happen if she went farther. The fog drifted back into his brain until he forgot everything else, all his concerns.

"Will you come with me?" she asked. "Step away from all this, be mine, and I will be yours? All you need to do is come with me, here and now."

"Yeah. Sure, why not?"

With a triumphant smile, she took his hand and he let her lead him out of the bar, abandoning his buddies, his drink, his jacket, all lost in the musk-scented fog that had engulfed him.

Behind them, the man remained in the bar, casting a jaded look around the room and seeing no human he felt the urge to charm. He fondled the cell phone in his coat pocket, the unfamiliar tech-magic a talisman of sorts, a reminder and a promise that this exile was a temporary one.

Only hours through the portal, and already he wanted to return home. But he could not, not until their mission was completed.

Before they were sent here, the consort had gathered them together, courtiers and their human pets. It had been an honor and a warning: do not fail. They had expected the consort to speak. Instead, it had been Ylster who'd stepped into the moment. The adviser had not spoken in the court since the queen had disappeared, spending all his energies in finding and tracking her, the strongest of them stretched too far and too thin to waste any energies on something as pointless as speech.

*All faith is magic,* Ylster had said, his gaze far beyond what they could see. *Belief is power. The stronger the humans cling to their faith, the more vulnerable they are to us. This has always been so. They have merely changed their focus, and it has taken us a while*

*to catch up. But now they put their faith in tools, in things that may
be manipulated…and controlled.*

*We will use their faith to power ourselves, and they will thank us
for it. Their need for us has always been greater than their desire to
be free. Remember that, and do what you must.*

One human per hunter was enough to bring them to this
world, to open a portal large enough for them to enter and
depart at will. But that was merely a step, not the goal. The
consort had commanded them to enter this realm, to englamour
all they could, to ensure that the portals remain open.

More humans, emptied and bound to the portal-magic,
using their faith and desires to tie them to both realms. That
was their purpose here, so that the queen would be returned,
the consort satisfied. But Erini was hunting because she en-
joyed the hunt, going after difficult targets rather than those
already half-englamoured by their own desires and dreams.

He shook his head, a gesture he had adopted from this
world. He had no interest in human prey; they were soft and
easily distracted. Better to go after the others he could smell,
circling them mere hours after they crossed through the portal. Not human: the otherfolk of this realm, the so-called supernaturals. Lesser creatures, not useful to the consort's plan
but still dangerous. The supernaturals had already interfered
on several occasions, interfering with the acquisition of humans, interfering with portals, and most notably in stealing
a portal-keeper from the very court itself.

He had not been there for that, but hearing of it later had
made him laugh. Stjerne had lost control of her creature and
been punished for it. He would not make that mistake, no
matter how many he took in his string.

More, he would not make the error of thinking of humans
as anything other than tools. No, he would obey the consort
in this as in all things, especially if it hastened their goal, but

not for personal enjoyment. The sooner this was done, the sooner they could go home. Unlike Erini, unlike their missing queen, he did not like this realm. There was too much noise, too much...*fuss* here. The sooner they could subdue it and return, the more pleased he would be.

Seeing two women leaning against the bar, exchanging quips with the man behind it, he smoothed down the leather of his jacket and moved through the crowd. Three at once would at least be a challenge, if he must remain here. Boredom was not to be tolerated.

Cam had taken his queen at her word. The moment the humans had taken their attention away from the two houses they had cleansed, he had directed three each of his pack to take up residence. The computer in the basement of the court kept them connected, although for the most part there was nothing to be communicated. They would establish the houses, set up protective warding, and await instructions. His instructions, not hers.

He checked the email every day, nonetheless. They played a dangerous game, one that could collapse any moment, and his encounter with the human female outside earlier had left him with a vague sense of unease, as though someone had spilled something somewhere and left it there. He might resent the way brownie senses were attuned to whatever house they chose to serve, but he would not ignore those warning signs out of spite. The outer courts needed to remain safe, both for Herself's sake and their own plans.

The preter's decision to claim humans for her court had been unexpected and disturbing. Humans shoved in, took the glory, the greater share of power, every time. And so he had planted the seed in the human's mind, set her to thinking of escape. Nalith needed to depend on them, not humans.

Despite her strength, despite their care, something hovered, crept around the borders. He could not see it, but he felt it. If Nalith did not as well, if she were distracted by her new toys... No. He would not doubt her. He would be ready, and when she had a plan, she would inform him of it.

In the meantime, he would clear the court of these interlopers without any blame for their misfortune falling back on him, and their own plans would go forward. Not to be masters of the world, no, but the whisper in the ear of the mistress of the world. That was always where power lay.

# Chapter 12

Nalith stared at her, those blue eyes hypnotic as a snake's. "You cannot draw."

"No." Jan had no trouble admitting it. She had a reasonable number of skills and strengths, but she'd never been artsy in that regard. Her casualness about that fact seemed to confuse the preter, however.

It was two days after Martin's acceptance into the court. Jan had been summoned to the main room; now the queen was standing in front of her easel, one of the brownies off to her left, not quite hovering, and Jan sat on the footstool she had been directed to when she'd come downstairs, and tried to stay very still.

Jan had determined that none of the court were morning people. She would occasionally see some sprites drifting across the yard in the dawn when she woke up, but they never seemed to come into the house proper, and the gnomes were still banished to their corner campsite. Jan tried not to look in that direction if she could help it. Simply knowing they were there had made it difficult to sleep the past two nights. And Tyler still turned away from her when he came to bed, his body language as stiff and unwelcoming as it had been when he'd first come back, so there was no comfort there, to take or to give.

Ty knew the preters were back. She didn't know if he'd somehow felt portals opening or he'd been keeping track of time better than she had, but he knew. And he knew how they'd have done it: using enthralled humans to hold the connection. Knew that he would have been one of them if Jan hadn't come for him instead. So she had taken to waking with the dawn, leaving him to battle his own demons. It might not have been the right decision, but it was the only one they could manage and still do their job.

Each morning there was the ever-ready pot of coffee and fresh muffins, and a curt, we-have-to-work-together-but-I-don't-like-you-either nod to whatever brownie was working there, before Jan headed into the main room. No matter how early she woke up, the queen was always there first, dressed and alert, already at her easel.

Today the conversation had taken an immediate left turn, with her question about drawing. "You do not seem to care, this lack in yourself."

Jan thought about her answer before giving it. She didn't want to set the preter off, but she saw no reason to lie, either.

"Art is a gift. Pretty much everything we do is a gift. Some make music, some draw, some sing, some dance, some act… and some people's gifts aren't creative. Not that way, anyway. I have a friend, he's an amazing cook. Give him turnips and a bag of flour, and he'll make something amazing. He can't sing a note, though. Believe me, he *really* can't sing." Jan lost herself in the telling, almost forgetting for a moment who she spoke to, that this was not a friend, not even a casual acquaintance you could exchange memories with, without constantly weighing what you were giving away, what you were gaining.

"You have an eye for color, for shape," the preter said, still stuck on her original thought, like a terrier with a rat. "But you cannot perform it."

"Nope." She could design the hell out of someone else's work, though. Jan shrugged, then looked at the preter, unable to help herself. "And it bothers you that it doesn't bother me? Why?"

They hadn't been getting anywhere on figuring out Nalith's weak spot, pussyfooting around and hoping to eavesdrop or trip over a clue. It had been two days since Martin had won his place in the court, four or maybe five since they had left the Farm; the days and nights had blurred together until visiting the witch, sleeping in the truck seemed like memories from last year or stories someone else had told her. And there was no point in waiting on rescue. Martin had left her phone with the truck, the idiot, so she couldn't even check to see if the messages she'd told him to send had gone through. It didn't matter. The deadline had passed. AJ had bigger things to worry about than rescuing them.

At this point, Jan figured she had very little to lose by trying a direct approach.

"I care not what you do or think," Nalith said, oblivious to everything that had gone through Jan's mind. Her head was cocked, but she was staring at the canvas in front of her, not Jan. The piece she had been working on when Jan had arrived had long been abandoned, one of a series of pieces stored in the basement, away from her sight but still cared for in case she called for them later. Now it was a charcoal sketch. It was, Jan thought, supposed to be a tree, maybe the one outside in the front lawn, towering, with half the leaves fallen. But she knew that only as a guess: the preter was no better at drawing than Jan. Even Kerry had tried to tell Nalith that, only to receive a punishing slap and a banishment from her presence for his honesty. He had been sulking outside on the back deck ever since then.

"Why are you here?" Jan asked, deciding to go for broke. "What do you want?"

The preter's entire body stiffened, but she did not look at Jan. "What?"

"Why are you here?" Jan knew that Nalith had smelled preter on Tyler, or something, when they'd first arrived, but not how much she had been able to tell from that. Tyler had not spent any time in Nalith's presence alone to spill any secrets. From what she could tell, he was avoiding getting within reach.

"Tyler and I...we've met your kind before. He's been enthralled." Offer some truth to hide the rest of it? "We *know* that your kind has no particular love for our kind and certainly not for supernaturals." *Careful, Jan. Enough to be real, enough to distract her...* "Your kind comes here and takes what they want, you amuse yourselves and then go back...so why are you here? Why do you stay?"

*Why,* she thought but did not ask, *is your old court so angry with you and so desperate to take you back—by force?*

"You are questioning me?" Nalith sounded as though a chair or rug had just challenged her, less offended than astonished at the improbability.

"My lady, no. Merely trying to understand. You...have a goal. We cannot assist you if we do not have a clear picture of your goal."

Utter and absolute bullshit, honed by too many years of working with clients who expected her to read their minds and deliver whatever was *in* their minds without actually describing it. You weren't supposed to call the clients idiots. Not to their faces, anyway.

And especially not when this particular client would have no hesitation about knocking you into tomorrow.

"Blunt speech, little human."

Jan braced for a blow, but Nalith merely considered her, those odd blue eyes narrowing as she thought. "You would know my mind, little human? You would think to under-stand me?"

"I would try, my lady. To serve you better." The words made Jan's teeth hurt and bile churn in her chest, but she said them easily, without obvious emotion.

The preter put her charcoal stick down and brushed one finger across the easel, smearing the work slightly. "My kind live, move, and breathe in magic. It surrounds us, shapes us. We *are* magic, inherent. You naturals, this realm, whatever you have here you gained from us, stole from us, piece by piece."

That was news to Jan—and she wasn't sure that the witch Elizabeth would agree entirely, although she supposed it would depend on what you called magic. Maybe it was true for the supers, and shape-shifting and portals between realms were just physics and biology after all.

"But for all that," Nalith went on, "for all the glory and beauty of our court, there came a time when I looked out into our world, and..."

Jan waited.

"I did not understand it, the feeling that came to me. Not then, not for some time. I was *bored*." She said the word as though it were a foreign, unfamiliar language and shook her head, the first time Jan had seen her make that gesture. "Nothing moved. Nothing *changed*."

"So...change things?"

This time, the slap did come, but it barely rocked Jan; the preter had put little effort into the blow. "My world does not change."

*Preters hate change,* AJ had said. Jan's mind whirled, trying to fit this new fact into what she had already known, figuring how—if—it changed the shape of the puzzle they had already pieced together. Preters hated change…or *couldn't* change? Was there a difference, or did one rise from the other?

And what did it mean that Nalith…what? What did the preter mean by *bored?* And how did this tie into her being here, to…to drawing or the way she gulped down PBS's *Great Performance,* and every concert Wes could find on DVD or pay-per-view?

"Humans, you change. Constantly. You *create* things to drive away your boredom."

Oh. Jan exhaled. Pieces clicked together a little better, but she still wasn't seeing a complete picture. Her cheek burned from the slap, but she had to risk it. Keep her talking, pray nobody else came in to distract her, try to get more intel…

"Create, my lady?"

"Distractions, interruptions in the sameness of every day. We englamour, enhance, but underneath, it remains the same. Our food, our entertainment, our songs, our views. It began to drive me mad. I could no longer bear it, needed to find a different view, a different *anything.*"

And that had meant fleeing her court. Jan tried to find a way to push, but she didn't need to: Nalith kept talking.

"The humans we brought to us, they had that…but it faded, always faded. As though the very air around us stifled their ability, prevented us. Always, we had to find new sources of entertainment, new *performers.* It was as it had always been, the way it always would be…until something changed. Not in us, not in you, but in the ways between. But I could not see where, could not understand how to make use of it. And then, a storm appeared in the sky, and the way opened, suddenly, unexpectedly. I saw the chance and took it."

Her expression tightened, as though remembering something unpleasant. "I thought… But each thing I put my hand to… I can see, but I cannot *do.*"

There was a layer of irritation, of annoyance, in the preter's voice, a frustration that both despaired and refused to give up. Despite herself, despite knowing how dangerous preters were, Jan felt a moment's real twinge of pity.

"I have never failed."

Jan bit her lip, willing the laughter to stay silent in her throat. Do what was needed, do what would get them information. Do not tell the selfish elf to get the fuck over herself.

"But you do not understand," Nalith said, dismissively. "You see colors wisely, yes, but you cannot create, cannot *perform* even as your leman does. I waste my breath even speaking to you."

Brief moment of pity over, Jan tasted blood as she bit down harder, reminding herself again that she needed to manage this egomaniac, not alienate her. She had come through a gate on impulse, had started all this out of a selfish whim....

"My lady, what do you most desire?"

The preter's words burned under Jan's skin all day, until she was able to round up her companions in as unobtrusive a manner as she could manage and get them outside, where fewer ears might overhear. "She has no idea what she's doing here."

"What do you mean, no idea?"

"I mean, she's here on a whim, winging it, improvising, not a fucking clue."

Martin snorted, running his fingers through his hair as if he was contemplating tearing it out by the roots. "Jan, preters don't do things on a whim."

"Yeah, because all your great gathered wisdom tells you this. Oh, no, wait, you're just as clueless as us humans when it comes to figuring them out, right?"

Martin glared at her but had no comeback. She was right. She knew that she was right. Everything the supers knew was generations out of date, gathered as much from legends as history. AJ had been a cub the last time preters were overtly visiting this world, and he'd admitted that *he* was winging a lot of it, although he'd used better-sounding terms.

"What did she say to you?" Tyler was sitting on the railing, balanced like a cat, seemingly without effort. She had the urge to poke him just to see if he would fall. Had he been that poised before he'd been taken? She couldn't remember.

"I told you already," she said to Martin. "She felt a twitch or an itch or something and followed it here. That she was bored and wants us to somehow make her boo-boo all better. Only, she doesn't know what hurts, and we're supposed to magically gift her with a bandage."

Jan heard her voice rise and tried to modulate it, keeping the sarcastic tone but at a lesser volume, even as Martin made shushing gestures with his hand. Jan made a face at him, to say "Yes, I know, shut up," even as her gaze went through the window to check the scene inside.

Nalith was in the side parlor, meeting with the brownies Jan thought of as her majordomos, the same one who had talked to her on the porch and one other. They were going over a map spread out on the table, the two supers making a case for something, and Nalith listening, neither agreeing nor arguing.

They had been there all evening. Jan and the others had eaten dinner around sunset, filling their plates at the stove and taking them into the dining room. They ate with the other humans and a few of the supers who would join them; most of the others ate later, and Jan was careful not to poke her nose into the kitchen to see if they were given the same food or something else.

Nalith ate alone. Once or twice she had commanded that Tyler sing to her while she ate, but more often she preferred solitude, sitting at the main dining room in lonely splendor. Tonight, though, the two brownies had gone in to join her—not eating, just carrying the maps and waiting until she gestured to them to clear her plates and unroll the sheets of paper. They looked like blueprints and maps, but Jan hadn't been able to see clearly enough to tell of what.

"She wouldn't deign to notice what we do," Jan said even as she knew that that was a lie. Nalith noticed everything, even if she didn't seem to care. Nalith wasn't the only one they had to worry about. Ears were everywhere, and none of them friendly.

"She's been drawn here," Tyler said, finally contributing to the conversation. "I know that much. Something called her, and she can't go back. She'll die inside if she goes back."

Jan paused, then nodded thoughtfully. That fit with what Nalith hadn't said, as much as with what she had. Not that she had taken the route between realms, but that she had been impelled to do so.

"So what?" Martin said. "So what if she has no clue and wants something bright and shiny she didn't have there? Why do we care?"

He, clearly, didn't.

Martin kept his voice low, speaking directly to Jan. "Have you forgotten what she is? What's at risk?"

"No," Jan said, stung. "I haven't. It's only that…" That what? What was digging at her, the splinter in her shoe, the buzz in her ear, that made what had seemed so clear and easy before, now so crowded and complicated? The flash of pity she'd had earlier was back, only it didn't feel like pity anymore. But what, then?

"Huh. 'Bring us your huddled masses yearning to be free.…'"

"What?" Martin and Tyler both looked at her as if she had lost her mind. Maybe she had.

"She's looking for something here. Something she couldn't find at home. Drawn, Tyler had said, and she could see that, clear as if there was a thread pulling in the preter's chest, leading her, half-unwilling and helpless before it. If Ty's right and she'd die if she went back... She's cruel, and selfish, and pretty much horrible in all those ways, but do we really have the right to send her back somewhere she ran from, or use her as a potential hostage, knowing they'll only take her back?"

"Are you shitting me? Seriously, Janny, have you lost your mind? Did she englamour you?" Martin had backed away from her as if she'd suddenly started emitting toxic fumes, and him without a gas mask.

"Jan has always been kind." Tyler said it as if it was a bad thing, the sort of thing that you apologized for.

"I'm not— No, Martin, relax. It's not... It's about being decent," she said defensively. "About being, I don't know, human. Humane. Not being like preters, all selfish and...I don't know."

She'd had a point when she'd started talking. Or not a point maybe but a thought, something important. She couldn't remember what it was now. She had been the one to urge them to come here; why was she arguing against it now? Jan wondered if she would even know if she had been englamoured. She touched her pocket, only then realizing that she'd forgotten to switch the sachet and carved horse into her pocket that morning. Still, surely Martin, if not Tyler, would be able to tell? Or was that what he was telling her, and she couldn't hear him?

"If we can't stop them, there won't be a point to being humane," Martin said. "We'll be cattle, all of us, subject to their whim. All because you felt sorry for a preter queen, who would as soon knock you across the room as look at you."

Jan raised her hand to the side of her face, where a bruise

had risen, purple shadows against her skin. She'd almost forgotten about that.

"Jan." Tyler took her hand in his, his skin cool against her own. "Jan." His voice, the touch of his hand, grounded her, but the not-pity lingered, the sense of something-not-right pressing on her brain.

"Janny, don't do this." Martin's deep brown eyes flickered with those odd golden lights again, reminding her that he wasn't just a slightly odd-looking human. But the sincerity and worry in his voice were entirely real, and all for her. "She likes pretty things, shiny things. But there's a reason she can't draw a picture, can't sing a song, can't do all the things that she's gathered you humans for. There's a reason why they've always taken humans—to entertain them. Because they can't do it themselves. Kindness now, pity now, and you doom us all to a lifetime as slaves, subject to their whim. Nalith seems kind now, but how will she treat us once she's bored, once ennui or whatever kicks in?"

Jan shook her head. That hadn't been what she'd meant... except it had been, too, she guessed. Nalith wanted something she couldn't have, wasn't able to have, and when she realized that...

"You're right. I know you're right. But I don't like this," she said. "There should be some other way."

"Should but isn't," Martin said.

"So, how do we do this?" she asked. "How the hell do you bind a preter queen? Because I haven't found any weakness in her, other than not being able to draw her way out of a wet paper bag."

"That's exactly how. The same way they bind humans," Tyler said, his voice bleak, his hand releasing her own. "With her own obsessions."

★ ★ ★

The deadline had ticked by, leaving everyone on the Farm on edge, expecting something and not knowing what. Shifts and schedules fell by the wayside; everyone was working full-out in the hopes of a breakthrough. AJ had considered issuing some sort of sedative in order to make sure they slept, but he decided it was probably a bad idea.

Midafternoon, two days after the deadline had passed, a scream nearly shattered every eardrum within a square mile, cutting through the stone and timber structure of the Farm like tissue paper. Half the supers dived under tables as though expecting a bomb to hit, while the others did various things with their bodies, expanding wings or pulling up feathers, and in one rather notable case, suddenly being covered with six-inch quills bristling like a porcupine's back. Glory, her hands over her ears in a vain attempt to block out the painful noise, managed to ask, "What the *hell* was that?"

"Bansidhe," someone yelled back at her, barely audible over the noise. And then it was cut off, the echoes still painful inside her brain.

"Ban-what?" she asked, even as her memory and research caught up with her. A Celtic spirit, supposed to foretell death. "Oh. That's not good."

"Double plus ungood," Beth said, sliding to a stop in front of her, feathers fluttering in distress and excitement. "Basement, you."

"But—"

"You're useless in a fight, Glory. Get into the basement, and stay there!"

It hurt, but Beth was right. Glory followed several other supers down the stone-cut stairs into the basement. It was really more of a root cellar, with a solid wooden door between them and the kitchen. It was dark, lit only by the electric lantern one of them carried, but there were blankets and boxes down here among the food supplies, plus what looked like cases of bottled water; someone had thought about the potential need for a bolt-hole, previously. Glory wasn't sure if that made her feel better or worse.

The door slammed above them, and the noise of activity was suddenly cut off, leaving only the sound of six pairs of lungs, breathing.

"So not good," Glory said. Nobody down there with her disagreed.

"Leave everything where it is!" AJ yelled, projecting his growl to carry over the chaos. "If they get through, it won't matter worth a damn what they learn. Leave the barn, forget about everything else, defend the main house!" He strode through the old farmhouse, fighting the urge, the *need,* to change. *Just a few minutes more,* he promised that urge. A few minutes more to make sure everything was in place, everyone was ready. At his left, Meredith paced, already in her four-legged form, teeth bared at the yet-invisible intruders who dared threaten her pack.

"Team A, to the roof," he ordered, trusting that his words would be carried through the crowd. "Team B, go to ground. Come on, you bastards, we trained for this. Get to it!"

They weren't *lupin,* this motley assortment who had come to his call, heeded his warnings about the preternatural threat. But they were fierce and determined, and they knew what was at stake. Now was the time to trust them to do their job and for him to do his.

*Lupin* were guided by the moon's seasons but not bound by them. And he fought better on four legs rather than two. Lifting his face to the ceiling, AJ imagined the moon silver in the sky, hidden now by sunlight, then he let go of his control, opened all of his senses to the magic that hummed inside him, and *changed*.

It wasn't as fast or easy as what he'd seen the kelpie go through, but it didn't hurt, either; more like a fast, surprise orgasm running through his body, twisting him into knots and then pulling him loose almost as quickly. Blood fizzed and his senses roared, and he felt himself drop to all fours, the rightness of this position matching the rightness of his two-legged form. A *lupin* was neither man nor wolf but both equally, and neither.

He snarled and heard his beta echo it as they leaped through the now-open front door and out to defend their chosen pack.

According to plan, the outbuildings should have been emptied and left open. Let the enemy attack those spots if they felt the need; infestations could be dealt with later. Everything of importance was in the house, and it was the house they would defend. The bansidhe's warning had given them enough time to get into place.

AJ hoped that the creature had survived, that it wasn't down in pale blue shreds along the border of the property, but that was all the time he had to give to that thought before the first wave came out of the tree line, flowing toward them in a disturbingly organized fashion.

His mind told him that the sky was pale blue, the trees still holding on to the last of their red-and-gold leaves. His wolf-form eyes saw things not so much in color as motion, the heavy fur on the back of his neck bristling protectively even as his muscles tensed in readiness.

"Got your back, boss" he heard coming from his right, even as Meredith paced at his left, and then something swooped low over his head, cackling madly and soaring up into the sky, three others following. He raised his muzzle and snarled at the owl-headed *splyushka* even as they banked and headed back to the house, taking up aerial cover the way they were supposed to.

When the warehouse had been attacked, the gnomes had tried for a circle-and-press tactic. That had ended badly for them—they had done damage but left themselves too open to counterattack. This time they spread out and kept moving, dashing from tree to rock to fence post, arms and legs elongating and contracting again as needed. It made AJ slightly queasy to watch, but he kept looking, trying to remain aware of the wider field of battle, never letting his gaze rest too long in one place. There was a second line of attackers waiting— he could scent them, the acrid-sweet smell filling his nostrils and making his blood rage with the need to bite, tear, rend. He reined it in. Emotion served thought, not the other way around.

"Left field covered." A report came in, one of the wisps swifting by, barely visible in the morning breeze. "Ready to engage."

"Wait for it…wait for it…." one of the supers to his left muttered, and there was a burst of nervous laughter. Meredith growled, but AJ let them be. Battle nerves were better dealt with by quips, not silence.

A scream and roar came from the north side of the house; a brawl under way, and AJ had his mouth around raw, too-damp skin, his teeth cutting through flesh and down to bone, tearing the elongated arm off his assailant.

A *lupin* pack hunted shoulder to tail, minding each others' flanks, instinctively protecting blind spots. This makeshift pack could not function that way; they had adjusted for it. Overhead, the *splyushka* swirled and dived, less to do damage than to provide distraction, although occasionally AJ saw a gnome snatched up and then dropped from a height, bits of them torn off by heavy claws and dripping down on the combatants.

The smell made him want to throw up; this was not fresh meat, but something tainted, disruptive. Whatever the turncoats had been into, it had rendered them unfit to eat. He spat the arm out and surged forward.

They would take this place over his dead body, and they would pay fiercely for it.

Noise didn't carry through the heavy door and stone walls of the basement. Glory sat on a case of water, her arms wrapped around her, and tried very hard not to panic.

The supers who had come down with her weren't ones she knew. They looked to be two different types, three of them frail boned with narrow heads and long, almost luminescent hair flowing down their backs, the other two normal-ish, but with skin that was dark and rough, like a tree trunk. All five huddled together, occasionally saying something in a soft voice to each other, occasionally glancing in her direction.

"You can't fight?" one of them asked finally.

"Not usefully," Glory admitted. "Not against whatever's out there."

"Turncoats," one of the delicate ones said. "Gnomes. They eat flesh, any flesh they can get. AJ says they threw their lot in with the preternaturals to earn the right to eat whatever they want." She—he, it?—gave a delicate little shudder, hair trembling with the move.

"Huh," Glory said. That didn't match up with the mental image she had of gnomes, which was admittedly formed more by picture books she'd seen in passing than any actual study, but the apprehension in AJ's voice earlier had been real enough for her to accept the super's words as truth. "So, we just sit here and wait for them to hack it out overhead?"

"We can't fight, either," a different super said. "We look and we hear and we heal, but we don't fight." It smiled a little wistfully. "Not usefully."

"My name's Glory," she said, suddenly needing that connection.

"Apple," the super said and nodded to her companion. "That's Oak."

Dryads. At any other time and place, Glory might have been fascinated. Just then, she only nodded at Oak, getting a solemn nod in return.

The three others just huddled together more tightly and didn't speak.

"You live in Europe?" Apple asked, scooting a little closer to Glory.

"London," she said. "England."

"I've never left Connecticut," Apple admitted.

"You never wanted to," Oak said. "Neither have I. We're not meant to wander."

"Neither am I," Glory admitted. "If it were up to me, I'd still be in my flat in London, doing the things I always do, happy in my routine. But when a strange man arrives in your bedroom and tells you you're needed…it's sort of hard to say no."

"They say the Huntsman came for you?" Apple sounded as if she had a bad case of hero worship when she said the name.

"That's what AJ called him, yeah. You know him?"

Apple shook her head, but Oak nodded. "He married an Oak. He comes around sometimes. Human, but old, very old. Older than AJ, maybe. He outwitted AJ once, so he must be wise, too."

"Outwitted AJ?" That sounded like a story she needed to hear. Mentally comparing the dark-eyed, growl-voiced man who had welcomed her to the Farm with the much older human man who had sent her here, Glory decided that she'd probably put even odds on the pair of them.

"They fought over Oak," the first Oak said. "She was going to visit her mother-tree and got caught up in a *lupin* hunt. They were going to eat her and the mother-tree, too. The Huntsman was there, saved Oak, and they fell in love—"

"Wait. Wait a minute." Glory put her hand up to stop the dryad. "Are you seriously telling me that AJ was the wolf in 'Little Red Riding Hood'?"

The dryads both stared at her blankly.

"Right. Never mind." It didn't matter, and it wasn't any crazier than anything else she had seen or learned in the past month. What was it Jan had said—after a while, it all becomes a normal crazy? Yeah. "So, yeah, the Huntsman came and told me Jan needed me. So, I got on a plane, came here, only she's gone and, well, you know the rest."

Somehow, exchanging life stories seemed perfectly natural, as though she were at a tech cocktail party trying to find simpatico mates, rather than sitting in a dark cellar with nonhumans while some kind of fight raged on overhead. It was so quiet, their voices carrying through the still air without any effort, that Glory was reminded of the one storm she'd ever been through, off the coast of North Wales, after the winds had died down and the rain was as steady as your own breathing.

"Did you know Jan?" She had never actually met the other woman in person, only through email and video calls, and there hadn't been time to talk to any of her other team members about anything other than the problem at hand.

Galilia was up there in the fight. And Alon, Beth and Joey, and… Glory closed her eyes, pressing the heels of her palms into her eyelids, trying to make those thoughts shut up.

"We never met her," the dryads said, but one of the other

three raised its face and said, "I did," in a pale, wispy voice that perfectly matched her appearance. "I helped treat Tyler when he had nightmares. She would come sometimes to sit with him."

"Wraiths are healers," Apple said. "Not because they like making people better. They feed on sorrow and pain."

"We are as we are," the wraith that had spoken said. It wasn't defensive, merely a statement of fact.

"If you help someone, no matter your reason, you still helped them. And if you can do it and take care of yourself at the same time…that's aces in my book." Glory still hadn't forgiven Tyler for thinking with his dick and getting Jan— and her!—into this mess in the first place, but that was shit to deal with another time.

"Yes. We are all merely our natures."

"Oh, hey, that's not what I said," Glory objected. "No-body's only their nature, otherwise you wouldn't be able to say, 'Hey, let me help someone who needs pain siphoned off,' rather than just wandering around until you found someone. And AJ wouldn't have become friends with the Huntsman— one of them would have killed the other."

The wraith frowned, her head tilting to the side and pale eyes narrowing. Glory noted with fascination that she didn't have eyelids to close; her eyes actually *narrowed.* "They are predators, both. Each respected the other's strengths, rene-gotiated their territory. That is within their nature. We…we are lazy."

There was a snort from one of the dryads at that.

"We will seek the easiest source of sustenance. A willing source requires less effort to feed from. That is our nature. And it is the nature of those in pain to willingly give it up to another."

"That's the most passive-aggressive excuse I've ever heard.

Are you seriously saying that none of you have any self-empowerment at all?"

"We are bound to our trees," Oak said. "We sway or fall to the winds. Where is there empowerment in that?"

"You're not with your trees now," Glory said. "You came here to the Farm, I presume to help stand against the preters, rather than just waiting to see what wind would prevail. So, why not see how far you can take it?"

Rather than the immediate reaction Glory would have expected, there was silence. All five of them seemed to be considering her words. The wraiths were dubious, she thought—their expressions were subtle and hard to read. Apple seemed uncertain. Oak, though, she had a faint smile on her face, as though she liked what she was thinking.

Oaks were a hard wood, Glory remembered. Apparently, that carried through to their dryads. But while they seemed content to wait, passive, Glory couldn't. She got up off her crate and started to pace the confines of the cellar, stepping out of the warm glow of the lantern, poking her nose into the shadows. The cellar was dry enough and warm enough, all things considered. It would have been filled with dried fruits and root vegetables, she supposed, back when the house was first built and it was actually in use by humans. Or maybe they had used it to store cider or…

She circled back through the light and out into the shadows again, skirting the narrow wooden staircase. The urge to go up the steps, to see what was happening, itched in her, but she beat it down.

And that image triggered another, sending her back into the center again, looking intently.

"We need something to use as a weapon," she said.

"A what?"

"In case…well, you know. In case someone comes down

here." Every horror movie she had ever unwillingly watched reappeared in her brain, all the ways something could pop out and take off your head or stab you in the gut.

They stared at her, not uncomprehendingly, but with an odd sort of pity or grim humor.

"If they come down here, we're dead," Apple said.

Glory snorted and kept looking for something she could use as a club.

"Fall back." AJ's muzzle was sore, and his gums itched from the gnome-blood caked around his teeth, but his gaze was still alert and his thoughts were clear. Meredith, still at his side, made an interrogative whine, not questioning but requiring more explicit instructions.

"They've paused, when they should be pressing us. That means they're about to try something else. If the house falls, we need to be ready to evacuate. You have to get the human and her team out of here."

She might have argued, but here and now, he was alpha, and his word ruled. She ducked her head and loped away.

One of the *kiyakii* slid into position where she had been, covering his flank. AJ nodded his thanks, then refocused his attention on the field in front of him. There were more gnome bodies there than anything else, ripped apart until they could no longer re-form and regroup. But nearly a third of the defenders had paid the cost, and he could only assume that it was the same where he could not see. He scanned the field, seeing numbers, not faces, not names. He couldn't think about the friends who had doubtless gone down. There would be time to mourn individuals when this was done. If they lived long enough to mourn. The line had not broken, but it was ragged and weary. If the turncoats had aid...

So far, the others he had scented had hung back, not taken

part in the battle. But they would; he knew that. It was how he would have played it out, sending in the shock troops first, then the smarter, savvier fighters to mop up—and search the buildings.

Preters, in *his* den.

AJ bared his muzzle in a defiant grin, even though the enemy was too far away to see. They might find the scent, but there were other scents laid down, too, trails leading to dead ends and pitfalls, tangled in with the truth. He, AJ, could untangle them, but no one else.

"They're moving forward," one of the *splyushka* told him, fluttering down to land a few feet away. It was young; its hard, narrow mouth clacked nervously, and its feathers fluttered, but it stood its ground. Feathered, yes, but not flighty. AJ felt a surge of pride.

"Then let's shove them back," he said.

The sharp, cracking noise was a shock, after what seemed like hours of muffled silence. Glory got to her feet, the two-foot-long piece of planking she had found clutched in her hands like a baseball bat. Odds were it would splinter the moment she brought it down on anything hard; at least she'd have that one chance.

Oak stood up when she heard the sound, and reached down to scoop up some of the dirt from the hard-packed floor, cupping it in her hands. Glory nodded approval.

"You blind 'em and I'll bash 'em," she said in a low whisper and then glanced at the remaining four. "And you guys just sit there. Or you can run, if you get a chance."

The door swung open, and there was the sound of surprisingly heavy steps on the stairs. Glory tensed, but the voice that came out of the dark was a familiar one.

"Come on."

"Elsa?" Apple practically flew up the stairs. "Did we win?"

"No." The *jötunndotter* wasn't any grimmer than usual, but the exhaustion in her voice came through clearly. "But we haven't lost yet, either. Gloriana, you need to go."

"What?" First she had to hide, then she had to run…. Her pacifistic tendencies be damned, caution boiled over into frustration, and she gripped the piece of wood more tightly. "I want to—"

There was a yelp and a growl at the top of the stairs, then the sound of something heavy being knocked over. Elsa swore in some language Glory didn't know, and suddenly Apple was falling back down the stairs as though she'd been pushed, landing on her backside with an expression of shock on her round face.

And then something leaped from the shadows of the stairway, something not-Elsa, moving too fast to be the troll, too fast and too sleek, arms reaching, elongated fingers grabbing at the air, and Glory didn't think, didn't ask, but stepped forward and rather than swinging with her makeshift weapon, stabbed straight ahead with it, the broken tip meeting a sudden resistance, then giving way, sliding *into* something, the weight on the end heavy enough to bring Glory's arms down in shock.

She pulled back, and something came back with the club, something that looked like an oversize frog with a human head and smelled like… She gagged and dropped the wood, backing away.

"Gnome," one of the wraiths said, its voice even more fading away.

"And more coming." Elsa took another step down, dropping another gnome to the ground, its neck clearly broken. "No humans can be taken here, not with the knowledge you have. You need to get out another way. Apple. Take her."

"What?" Apple was still on the dirt floor, although she had scuttled back away from the two gnome bodies.

"I'll do it." Oak raised her hand to volunteer. "Come, human. See how the other half grows."

"What?" Glory had a moment, much like when she woke up to a strange man in her bedroom watching her, that something was about to happen that she wasn't expecting, that she wasn't going to like, and she was about to say no when Oak took her by the hand and put the other one over her mouth, and they stepped *into* the dirt wall.

There was no air, only pressure on all sides, and the stink of wet dirt and mold and cold against her skin, pressure building in her lungs and against her bones, fingers stretching, toes stretching, seeking nourishment, air water food survival, and then there was air in her lungs and Glory inhaled and coughed, almost dropping to her knees in relief. Oak's hands fell away, and she opened her eyes…and then wished that she hadn't. They were away from the main building, within reach of the tree line, but around them were torn and bloodied bodies, all still, all dead. Most of them looked like the gnomes that had attacked them, but in the face of so much death, Glory couldn't bring herself to be pleased.

And not all of them were gnomes. Her mind tried to sort them out, looking, against its will, for a familiar face, something that might identify the bodies as someone she had known.

"Don't look," the dryad said, her voice stricken with pain. "Don't look. Come."

"I can't…."

"I know. But you must come."

Glory closed her eyes and thought about Jan, who had gone into another world because she had to. About Tyler, who had escaped what sounded like an utter horror of brainwashing, taking it one step at a time. Because the only way to survive and not lose your mind was to go forward, not back.

"All right." She lifted her gaze from the ground, shaking off the dirt that still clung to her skin—*don't think about it, don't think about what you've done*—and walked on, heading for the trees.

"Gone." It was a faint whisper, but a familiar one. One of the wraiths. He had told them to go to the basement; they would be more useful after the battle, if there was anyone to succor. Gone where? Who had gone? Where? There was no clarification, and AJ snarled, picking his way through the bodies, his gaze never wavering from his goal.

It stood there in the middle of the field, standing as if it didn't even notice the corpses around it. It probably didn't. Between one step and the next, AJ changed, spine elongating, fur sloughing off, claws retracting and pads forming into fingers. He stood in front of the preter, skin naked in the cold air, and did not flinch.

"You are not welcome here," he told it. "Your pawns are dead, your game revealed, and the next move will put you into check. Concede and retreat."

The preter probably didn't have a clue about chess, but since AJ didn't expect they would give in, either, it didn't matter. His tone sent the message.

"We have no grief with you, creature," the preter said. Its voice was smooth and sweet, its expression composed of a mix of curiosity and compassion. It was an excellent presentation, but AJ was old, bitter, and not falling for it.

"No grief, no," he agreed. "You barely notice us, save to swat us out of your way. But the obstruction bit back this time, didn't it? And we have more teeth and claw, waiting for you. Concede and retreat."

"Where are the humans?"

AJ held himself perfectly still, save a slight cock of his head, as though he were wondering if he'd heard correctly. "Humans?"

"The humans. They belong to us. Give them back, and we will leave your enclave be."

So that was what this was all about. AJ wasn't sure if he should be insulted or not.

"The human male was won from your court, by means your consort agreed to. There is no claim to him, nor the woman."

AJ mostly didn't care about humans. He would have handed the male over without blinking if he thought it would win them anything. But the thought of giving them Jan made a growl form in his chest. She had become pack, and he would not give her up.

He couldn't, anyway. They weren't on the Farm. But this preter didn't seem to know that. Good.

"You will give the humans to us. Or you will all die."

AJ had heard more impressive threats before. He didn't discount this one for being issued in a bland monotone, though. Far from it.

There was only one human on the Farm. The Huntsman, who was his friend, had sent him Glory, who was Jan's friend. That meant that she, too, was pack.

"I am *lupin*," AJ said, smiling. "You have forgotten what that means. Let me teach you."

The woods were thicker than Glory had thought, not just a border line but an actual thicket, the trees taller and wider than any she'd ever been close to.

"I'm to take you to the Center," Oak said. "But I've never gone from here. It's going to take me a minute to find my bearings."

"All right," Glory said. She wasn't really in a position to say anything else. She had no idea what the Center was, but anywhere was better than here. Leaning against one of the trees, she watched the dryad turn slowly, her eyes closed. There was noise coming from behind them, where she thought the farmhouse was, but within the copse it was almost silent, just the occasional creak or rustle to indicate that they weren't alone. Glory, used to the noises of a major city, would have been nervous—all right, she would have been terrified, after everything that had happened—but instead all she felt was a numb sort of calmness. It was less shock, she decided, than a weird sense of the inevitable. She was in shock, and no fucking wonder. She'd never seen anything die in front of her before. Not even a pet. She had only ever killed spiders before, and even then reluctantly. The fact that those *things* back in the basement had been trying to kill her, that she had only been defending herself...it made no difference, she realized. They were still dead, and she couldn't be pleased.

*Pacifists get killed in wartime,* her dad used to say. But so did warriors.

She had known when she'd gotten that frantic phone call from Jan and heard about what had really happened to Tyler, when she'd agreed to help rather than hanging up or trying to get her friend sectioned, that life was never going to be the same. She just wondered now if there was going to be a life at all, however changed.

"All right. This way." Oak still had her eyes closed, but she was facing Glory, and the expression on her face was calm, almost happy, if she was reading it right. She might not have been; supernaturals were a few degrees off the norm to her still.

"Where are we going?"

"I told you. To the Center."

"Oh." *All right, then.*

When Oak held out her hand, Glory took it, even as there was a larger, louder rustle in the trees and a smooth, even-toned voice, dripping with malice, said, "There you are, human."

## Chapter 13

"They're not coming," Jan said, chewing at the cuticle of her thumb. "If they were, they would be here by now. AJ wouldn't leave us hanging. Something went wrong. Maybe the messages didn't go through or…"

Or the Farm wasn't under AJ's control anymore.

It was late at night, the three of them in Jan and Tyler's room, the first time they'd been able to gather. Today had been the worst day yet; the queen agitated, and the brownies had been everywhere, their ears twitching, snapping orders at everyone else. Patrick's wooden sculpture had been shattered during a fight, and the human had disappeared; nobody had asked after him, either not caring or too afraid. They'd escaped as soon as possible, hoping the chaos would keep Nalith from noticing they'd gone.

Jan sat on the bed with her arms around her knees, Tyler in the single chair, while Martin paced, hemmed in by the size of the room. They were both making her dizzy, in different ways: Martin with his movement and Tyler with his too-tight stillness. She felt the tension in her chest that usually heralded another asthma attack and scanned the room until she found her inhaler, sitting on the dresser.

Something in the house itself seemed to inhibit her asthma attacks, the same way she'd felt Under the Hill, in the preter court. But the sensation remained, like something pressing at her lungs, trying to steal her ability to breathe. Between that and the dizziness, it was hard to concentrate. She wanted to kick them both out of the room, crawl back under the covers, and go to sleep. Maybe forever.

Jan was pretty sure it was just depression talking, depression and maybe a touch of Nalith's glamour weighing on her. Today had been the worst, but ever since she had questioned the queen, the preter had kept her close at hand, nearly two days of constant attendance, from early in the morning to late at night. It had created a situation where the three of them had not been able to talk freely or even at all. When Tyler finished singing, the queen sent him off to work with Wes, the technician. They were setting up the entire house with cabling that didn't seem to be connected to anything in particular but had to be set just so, matching one of the blueprints Jan had seen her going over with the brownies. Outer courts, Nalith called them. Homes, emptied, ready to be filled with more supers, more humans sworn to the queen. Homes...oh, god, homes where the murders had happened? That moment in the witch's living room seemed impossibly far away now, but Jan could remember the woman's face when she'd talked about the dead. Entire families.

And Martin...

Nalith kept making Martin fight. Never to the death, always calling them back before anyone was permanently damaged, but each time Jan felt her stomach twist a little harder, her lungs squeeze a little tighter. Worse, Martin seemed to enjoy it. He never said anything, but he didn't hold back when she summoned him, either. Jan wanted to believe that it was just playing the role, making the queen believe that he was a willing subject but...she knew him too well. He *liked* hurting...well, she was having trouble calling them *people,* and the time Nalith had set him to fight the pack of gnomes en masse, Jan had quietly cheered him on as well, but still. It was a side of Martin she didn't like.

*You can't know us.*

*Martin is…dangerous.*

Words of advice from people who knew the kelpie better than she ever could. Words she needed to remember. But Martin was her only lifeline here, Martin and Tyler, and she was afraid that she was losing both of them.

She wanted to ask them what they thought had happened to Patrick. She didn't want them to answer.

"Do you have any idea what all those cables are for?" she asked Tyler, trying to stay focused and practical.

"No, and neither does Wes. She gave us the schematic, told us to get the equipment and do it."

Wes was allowed off the property. Tyler wasn't. None of them were. And Wes was so deep in thrall, he would cut off his own hand if Nalith asked it of him. They could not trust him, even a bit. They couldn't trust anyone.

"She does nothing without a purpose," Martin said. "Those cables have to do with her protections, somehow. Something tied to the new form of magic. The more she fortifies this house, the harder it will be to get her out of it, like a spider in its lair. We can't stay here any longer, not without being trapped ourselves."

Jan licked her lips, tried to force her heartbeat to slow down. "We still have no idea how to bind her."

"I told you," Tyler said, impatient. "We need to use her obsessions, her desires, her weaknesses. They're as weak as we are. Maybe weaker, because they see no reason to deny themselves, expect no cost to their indulgences."

Jan flicked a glance at Martin, who had finally stopped pacing, staring out the room's single window, his hand on the curtain. The fabric was a deep blue, and his hand seemed to almost disappear against it, the pale brown skin overwhelmed by the weight of the drape.

"You're not as useless as you look, human," the kelpie said, still looking out the window, and Jan bristled on Tyler's behalf.

Her boyfriend—was he still? They had never broken up, but he hadn't touched her since they'd gotten back, had barely acknowledged what they'd had before—grinned tiredly, his face for a moment again the familiar, mocking Tyler she had fallen in love with. "Not entirely, no."

"So, we know why it would work, but not how to actually spring the trap," she said, focusing on what she could do something about, not what was out of her control. "What do we have to offer them?"

"The Farm."

"What?" She couldn't have heard Martin correctly. Even Ty looked surprised.

"We offer her the Farm. Everyone in it. An entire enclave of supers, already trained to work together, turned to her purposes. We came from there, so she will think she can take them as easily as she took us. And if we tell her we were fighting against the ones who are trying to take her back…"

"The enemy of my enemy is my friend?" Tyler was running over the possibilities in his head; she knew that look.

"More like the enemy of my enemy is my tool," Jan said drily, but she was already running through the possibilities herself, mocking up a diagram in her brain. She would kill for one of the whiteboards they'd left behind, but putting anything down in writing was too dangerous in a house filled with spies.

"Telling her would be too obvious. One of us has to let something slip, get her to draw it from us, maybe—" She didn't want to say it, but she did anyway. "Maybe seduce it from us."

"It would have to be Tyler," Martin said. "Preters find humans acceptable as mates, but to them we're, well, you heard. Humans may be lesser creatures, but shifters are even lower than that."

"Sexist pony," Jan said. "What about me?"

Both men blinked at that, and Tyler smirked a little. "We could sell tickets to that."

"Mind out of the gutter, boy. Seduction isn't fucking. It's a tease, an enticement, a promise—that's half the fun, seeing how far that promise goes. She thinks she owns Martin already, and Ty..."

Her voice trailed off, unsure how much she wanted to—could safely—say.

"And you don't think I could promise and not deliver. Because she's a preter, and I'm damaged goods."

"Could you?" She met his gaze squarely, not blinking away from the topic. "Could you go this far and no further, and stay focused on the task?"

He looked back at her, the familiar lean lines of his face no longer as softened as they'd been when he was still confused about who he was or where he was. "I don't know."

Tyler used to bluff his way through card games and conference calls without hesitation, but he'd never lied to her in the months they'd been together. Not directly, at least. Jan frowned. She didn't think he had, anyway, and it didn't matter now. The point was, he was being honest here, and that meant that she was right; it was up to her.

The thought made her want to crawl under the bed and never come out. Except there were probably dust bunnies under there, and she'd have an asthma attack and never be able to stop. Somehow, facing down a preter queen was less worrisome than an asthma attack.

And that was probably proof positive that she'd lost her mind somewhere along the way.

"All right. So I'll do it. What then?"

"Then we get her to AJ," Martin said. "He's the mastermind. Let him figure the rest out."

Jan thought about pointing out that they hadn't heard back from AJ, that they had no idea what was going on back at the Farm, that they might not be able to reach him, to tell the *lupin* what was going on. She didn't say any of that. None of them really believed they were going to pull off the first half of the plan, so why worry about the second part?

"I need to go," Martin said suddenly. "She's calling for me."

Jan hadn't heard anything, but human ears missed a lot, and it would not surprise her a bit to learn that kelpies had hearing at a different range than humans *or* that Nalith had the equivalent of a kelpie whistle. "So? Go."

And that left her and Tyler in the room together. For the first time since they'd arrived, it didn't feel awkward, as though somehow this discussion had opened a door that had been locked between them.

"I can't be part of this."

"What?" She felt her jaw, honest-to-god, drop at his statement.

"I can't be part of this. I can't help you. Jan, I... Even with the protection the witch gave us, every time she looks at me, I have this urge to throw myself at her feet, beg her to...to *heal* me. To fill me, the space inside that's so empty and cold. And I know she can't, don't even go there, I know it's just... going back to the addiction. But every time she tells me to sing, every time she touches me, something inside breaks a little more. You were right. I thought putting myself against her would prove I was stronger, that I could do this, but I can't. I'm sorry. I'm failing you again, but Martin is here. Martin will take care of you."

"Take care of me?" Of all the things to fasten on to, that was the only thing she could see, her mind filled with red fumes. "Take care of *me?* Who the hell do you think has been taking care of everyone else? Who the hell do you think has been *doing* things, while you sat in your shack and shook with fear?" God, that was a low blow, but it wasn't an untrue one, and she couldn't bring herself to regret it. "I'm not some little girl to be petted and protected, Tyler Wash."

Tyler was staring at her. She shut her mouth with a snap and stared back at him, aware that even when she was yelling, she had been doing it in a harsh whisper, worried that someone would overhear. She knew it was wrong, she was latching on to the wrong thing, but Jan couldn't help it.

He had been the one to protect her, once. He had reassured her that she was strong, that she was pretty, that the things that had hurt her once couldn't do so again. She had curled into him like a teddy bear and let his words convince her she was someone else entirely.

She had tried to return that, tried to be the person he could believe, and failed utterly. How could she believe in herself, in their ability to pull this off, if she couldn't even do that?

Tyler clenched his hands, then forced them to relax. She'd seen him do that before, back at the Farm. "You still need someone at your back. Someone you can rely on. You can't rely on me."

If she listened to his voice, she would think that he didn't care, that none of this meant anything to him. But they were still looking at each other, and the pain in his eyes, the drawn lines of his face, nearly broke her.

Once, she'd been needed to hold on to him, no matter what. Now the only thing she could do was let him go.

"If you leave without permission..." Her voice trailed off. He knew, better than anyone, what a scorned preter might, could, do.

"I'm not going anywhere," he said. "I need to stay. There's something I need to do. I just can't help you, can't be useful to the plan, until it's done."

There was something he wasn't telling her, something he had in mind. Jan wanted him to trust her enough to share everything, wanted to be that person for him, but probably, just then, that person didn't exist.

Too much pain. Too much damage. They couldn't be the people they had been before.

"All right." She paused and then stood, slipping on her shoes and reaching for a heavier sweater—the house was drafty in places. So many things to say, and none of them... This wasn't the place. "Be careful."

He didn't promise anything, just watched as she left the room, intent on her as if she was the last thing he would ever see.

Jan went down the stairs carefully, feeling as though her bones might shatter if she stepped too firmly or made undue noise. Martin was already down in the kitchen, loitering with casual intent, a mug of tea in his hand that he wasn't drinking. There were a handful of supers around the kitchen table, but conversation was muted. Herself must be in a bad mood, then.

None of the other humans and no brownies were visible. Jan exhaled, trying to make her chest unclench. *Focus.* If she was going to match wit against Nalith, then she needed to actually *have* some wit, not be fluttering apart like a schoolgirl with her first broken heart.

"Everything all right?" Martin had moved across the room on the pretext of freshening his tea, standing close enough to her that they could speak without being overheard, but not so close that they looked, well, close. Jan wasn't sure when they'd gotten so good at this; she supposed necessity kicked your ass into shape.

"No. But when has that ever stopped us?"

They were about to take on a preter queen with the prep equivalent of a paper clip and a USB cable, and down a man. What was there to be worried about?

"Ty can't do it." She didn't clarify "it"; she didn't have to. "He's too close to breaking."

Martin snorted. "He's already broken."

"You were the one who said he should come."

"I said he *needed* to come. And he did. And you needed to let him."

"I told you to stay away from those self-help pop-psych websites," she said. "You're crap at human emotions."

Martin didn't deny it. "So, he's going to flit? Are we going to have to cover for him, or do we use that as a distraction, get you up close and personal with Herself?"

"No. He said he was going to stay, that there was something he needed to do. What? Why are you looking like that?" His eyes, normally a deep brown when he was in human form, were doing that weird sparking, not-human thing again.

"Humans," he said, and it wasn't an endearment.

"Hey. What?" He'd thought of something or figured something out, and he wasn't sharing.

"Your leman is an idiot. This is not news. At least he's smart enough to know he can't dissemble enough to fool her. When this is over, we need to get him to the Center. We should have done that before, but AJ did not think it would be safe."

Jan thought of the weird peacefulness she had felt there in the grassy clearing somewhere outside this world, surrounded by ancient trees, sleeping under unfamiliar stars. Centered at the Center. She thought about Tyler there and nodded. "Yeah. When this is over."

Assuming they survived. Assuming the preter court didn't overrun the world. Assuming a whole hell of a lot.

Jan rubbed at her chest, aware that the tightness had eased but not entirely disappeared. Stress. Just a little bit. "I need coffee. And a chocolate doughnut. And a hot shower and a decent internet connection with a thirty-six-inch monitor, while I'm wishing."

"There's a fresh pot of coffee over there," Martin said. She nodded, getting a cup down from the counter and pouring herself some; then she reached over to grab a still-warm scone from the platter left on the counter and went back upstairs to take her shower. Tyler was nowhere to be seen.

The attack that threw him against the wall was not entirely unexpected, but the quarter it came from was. Tyler blinked at Martin, acutely aware of the muscled forearm against his throat, too close to cutting off his oxygen, if not crushing his windpipe entirely.

The person Tyler had been would have struggled, fought, asked what the hell was going on. But the preters had done their work well, and when confronted with an angry non-human, its eyes wide and the pupils carrying more yellow than brown, Tyler's new instincts took over and dropped him into as submissive a pose as possible, his muscles slack and his own gaze cast downward, presenting no challenge at all.

"Whatever you're thinking, whatever you think you're thinking, *don't*." The supernatural's breath, this close, smelled stale and musty, with flickers of sulfur. Even if he had wanted to respond, he couldn't; the grip on his throat prevented speech. "You're angry and you're scared, I get that. You tried to face the bitch down, face them all down, get back some of your manhood, and you couldn't, and now you want to blast them all out of existence, don't you? Starting with this one, oh, so close to hand?"

The words were hard and cold, enunciated with a cold precision, and Tyler managed to swallow, despite the pressure against his throat. The wall at his back somehow seemed softer than those words or the creature in front of him.

"I don't know what you have in mind or how you think you're going to manage that. Knife in the back, send nukes through a portal, whatever. But it's not going to do the job. It's not going to suddenly make you all better. In fact, it'll make it a whole lot worse."

The arm eased, and Tyler slid down the wall until his feet touched the ground again. He didn't move, uncertain if he could stay upright without the wall behind him.

"You don't understand." His voice was raw, as if he'd been screaming for hours. He shuddered, the memory of doing just that coming back to him, less a flashback than an undertow of emotion dragging him under.

"You're right," Martin agreed. "I don't. I don't understand the pain, the fear you went through. I don't understand the hold that elf-bitch had on you. I don't understand what brought you back. I want to, I *envy* you it, but I don't understand it."

The super made a visible effort to rein in his anger and— Tyler thought, suddenly—his jealousy. "I do know this—you can't destroy them. Neither of us can destroy the other. There's a balance. We can't unbalance it without consequences any more than they can."

Tyler frowned at him, momentarily distracted from his own trauma. "What consequences are they facing?"

"I don't know. But I think, the way their world is, so

empty? That's part of it. I think they had a Center, too, but it's gone askew. Probably a long time ago."

Martin wasn't making any sense, but at least his eyes were all brown again.

Tyler stared up at the ceiling, suddenly feeling the urge to explain himself. Jan couldn't understand, but maybe the supernatural would. "Jan thinks I miss it, that I crave *her*— Stjerne. I don't. Not like that. Not even like I crave shit that's bad for me, like cigarettes." And, god, he missed cigarettes, would always miss them to his dying day, even though he hadn't thought of them once when he was There. "It's not like that. But it still has its claws in me, thorns digging into my skin, and I need to get them *out*."

"Yeah. I get it. But you can't go off crazy, and you can't do whatever it was you were thinking."

"Yeah, well, maybe I'm tired of your rules," Tyler said, finally finding the ability to push away from the wall. He wobbled a little but didn't crash over, and the kelpie didn't insult him by offering help. He'd tried to explain, and all he got in return was a lecture. Screw that. "Your rules also make humans into tools, pawns, like we're not able to decide our own fate." He thought about saying more, but no words fell out. With a curt nod, he ordered his body to move and walked away.

"You're the only ones who can," Martin said behind him, just loud enough to be heard.

He kept walking.


"Idiot humans," Martin muttered, and a passing kobold shot him a surprised but appreciative look. If there was one thing in this house the non-humans could agree on, it seemed, it was that humans were more trouble than they were worth.

But without them…would any of this work? Supernaturals,

preternaturals…all predicated on the base existence of *naturals*. Theory and philosophy made Martin's head hurt, but since he had answered AJ's call, since he had become Jan's guardian, those thoughts came up occasionally and wouldn't go away.

Super. Preter. Natural. They were less powerful, on the obvious scale, but they were also the most numerous, the most adaptable.

Martin flexed his fingers, not wanting to think and unable to prevent it. A kelpie existed. Occasionally, it killed, not out of malice but because that was what it did. *Lupin* hunted. Dryads were timid. Bansidhe warned of impending death. *Jötunndotter…* He wasn't sure what the *jötunndotter* did, actually. Moved slowly, he supposed.

But what they were was not what they did. Not always. Not forever. He had, twice now, not killed Jan when she entered the water on his back. AJ had turned away from hunting when he did not kill the Huntsman, had turned instead into a protector. Gnomes had gotten aggressive. The bansidhe had warned of death—but also acted to *prevent* it. Preters…preters did not change their ways, did not come into this world out of season, except now they *did*.

They had all changed. Of their own will or something else influencing them. So what else wasn't true?

No. He couldn't risk it, couldn't think about maybes. The realms existed and needed to remain so. The queen needed to return to her court, the controlled portals needed to be closed, the means of control shut down. Tyler could not get in the way of that, either by killing the queen or whatever else he had in mind.

The kelpie wondered briefly if he should have killed Tyler now, to keep him from doing anything foolish or causing problems later.

No, he decided. It was unlikely the human had the ability

to influence anything, and his death would distress Jan. But it might become a thing later.

"Come on, AJ. You're the one with all the plans. I'm just the swishtail, remember? Give us a sign. Tell us what the hell to do."

The oddly mannered chaos of battle ended with a sudden howl that echoed over the entire property. As though it were a signal, those still fighting waded in with increased fervor, berserkers with wings and claws and hooves. Nothing was held back; none of them expected to leave the field of battle save as carrion.

"Come on, you bastards," Elsa growled, her voice deep enough to push through the sounds of fighting, loud enough to carry across fields without any other amplification but her lungs. The *jötunndotter* could not move quickly, but she moved steadily, and gnomes learned to avoid her if they could. To either side, behind and in front of her, the Farm's defenders lashed out, but they were bruised and bloody, tired from too long without a break. They would fall soon.

Elsa turned her head stiffly and looked at the slender, beak-faced being beside her. *Splyushka* and *jötunndotter*, air and rock, side by side. There was something funny, and fitting, and utterly improbably perfect about it. "Where are the preters? Why aren't they showing themselves?"

"They will," Andy said. "But we need to be done by then."

She nodded. "We will be. Just hold them back a little longer."

The sun dropped below the tree line behind the Farm, the sky bloodier than the now-muddy, trampled ground. The last glitterings of light caught the corner of the wooden bridge on the far side of the property, playing along the creek that flowed below it. The water was oddly still, even the current subdued, as though the life had gone from it. In the fields behind it, the grass moved only under wind, and even the birds and squirrels had abandoned the trees. In the ponds, fish stayed deep, avoiding the surface.

Gnomes moved through the main building, their forms compact again, checking every room intently. Their fingers touched everything, restlessly sorting through the piles of paper, ghosting over the whiteboards without smudging the dry-erase markers. Their eyes caught everything, sorting and filing. Occasionally one of them would catch up a sheet of paper or an object and tuck it away, carrying it to the preter lord waiting in the main room.

The preter was looking into the air somewhere over their heads, his eyes bright and focused. "Yes," he said to no one they could see. "We have secured the location. It was not as clean as we might have preferred, but they resisted so strongly, we had no other option. So far, there has been nothing that would indicate they had any knowledge of where she hides, nor any ability to stop us."

The air seemed to tell him something, and his mouth pursed up in disapproval, but he did not argue. "Yes. Agreed."

The preters plotted and schemed and gave orders. The gnomes took those orders and carried them out, but they were not the tools these elf-folk thought. They looked and thought and plotted on their own behalf, as well. Other races scrambled and sparred; they worked together, one goal in mind, one purpose.

Gnomes took orders from many but served none but themselves. Soon, soon, all the other races would learn that. And then the destruction would begin.

They thought that, holding it close to themselves, and

waited for the preter to finish his conversation and notice them again.

Done with his conversation, the preter stalked out to the back porch, looking out into the darkness. Under the glow of kerosene lamps and lights strung from the main house on extension cords, a ditch had been dug past the barn, and bodies were being tossed into it unceremoniously, attackers and defenders alike.

The gnomes muttered to themselves as they worked, discontent boiling under their skin; whatever they had fought for, the results had not pleased them.

Every now and again, one of them would look over their shoulder, but never up into the moonlit sky, where the last remaining defender floated on outstretched wings, silently watching the mass burials. When the last spade of dirt landed, filling in the ditch, the watcher wrapped its pale blue arms around itself and keened into the darkness, a lament and warning that raised the hackles of humans for miles, without their understanding why.

The preter lord smiled finally, a cold, bloodless smirk. "You thought cracking your machines and burning your papers, secreting your humans away would be enough. But none of it matters now. We can do it on our own."

The new moon slid into the sky, a rising arc, and the preter inhaled as though he had caught scent of home.

And from West Virginia to New Hampshire, power lines crackled and the air swirled and filled with mist as portals opened…

…and overnight, one by one, a handful more humans disappeared.

## Chapter 14

Voices were raised in argument, escaping the building and spilling out into the night. A preternatural might choose to disguise itself, to drape a glamour around its form to appear human, harmless, to moderate its voice into something flat and dull. When it did not choose to do so, there was no mistaking it.

"Sheer dumb luck." The voice rang out into the room, silencing the other voices—but only for a breath of time.

"Luck that is recognized and acted on cannot, by definition, be dumb. Unless you mean to say that it is mute."

"I mean to say that we stumbled into this world at exactly the right time, not because we planned it but because of sheer dumb luck."

"Enough, the two of you!" Another voice, fierce and hot, dominating even them. "The consort bound us to the terms of the truce. Those terms, bound by magic, brought us here at the moment the dark moon would rise and our own strength would be at its greatest. Is that luck or destiny?"

It would have been unwise to doubt the consort's wisdom or destiny, even here, far from his reach. Particularly since they were about to extend his reach so significantly.

There were eleven preters gathered, of the seventeen currently in this realm. Nine had come over in the original batch, the nine remaining of the ten who had been first set to this task, plus two more, of the five sent once the first had succeeded. Once the consort determined where Nalith had gone, and how, it had been a simple enough matter to do the same. But simply following would not have been enough: the court's pride had been pricked, and they must do more to regain what had been lost.

Thus, this gathering. It was not enough to simply reclaim their errant queen, no. They needed to make this world their own, use it to punish both her and this realm, to ensure that none ever challenged them again.

The preter court was wise and dangerous, and if they gave mercy it was of their own whim. They did not feel inclined, this night, to mercy.

They were gathered in a hall, in the darkened basement of a building filled with relics of the human religions, gilded and pretty but otherwise meaningless to them. They had chosen this place not for its decor but its space and its location: the magic, what their pets called "signal," flared most brightly here.

Brightly, but not so brightly as Under the Hill, where it had sparked like lightning, filling the sky with the crackle of power. Too many drew upon it here, interfered with it. That was not acceptable and would, like so much, be changed.

Behind them, their pets waited. Blank eyed and obedient, they were weighted with silver chains around their necks, draping down over to rest against their hearts. Twenty-two humans, cross-legged on the carpet. It had been attempted to hold three at once, but the results had been unpleasant: one human longed and needed reassurance, two were content, but three seemed to tip them into rebellion.

Rebellion was not permitted.

"Enough." A new voice spoke. The original nine had been courtiers, set to their task by command. Those who had come later were lords, higher in the consort's regard, and expected obedience in return. If the original nine resented that, resented this latecomer giving orders, they gave no sign. "Luck and destiny are mortal conceits, designed to ease the sting of their failures. I will have no more such spoken in my hearing."

They fell silent, but the undercurrent of nerves remained. For all their arrogance and pride, they knew themselves to be creatures of tradition, not comfortable with the new, the untried. And this, all of this, was new, uncertain, a thing that had once been considered impossible. Only the change in their world, the shift in the alignment of things, allowed them to even dare it, moving on some strange, strong instinct that swirled the magic and re-formed it, court guiding and humans carrying the weight.

A Great Portal. More, a Great Portal that was stable, that did not move and fade with the seasons or disappear if something harmed the human who carried it.

A Great Portal *they* would control entirely.

The old ways, dependent on tide and turn, would not have been enough to hold it steady. The new ways, the binding of human souls to hold the portal, was limited in scope. But eleven here, in the dark of the moon, a high magic time, with twice eleven soul-spaces for them to use...

Change came slowly to them, but they were not fools to refuse it.

The consort had commanded them, *challenged* them to come here, and their pride demanded that they answer. And then— then they would take their queen home and leave only devastation behind.

Seduction, Jan was discovering, was all in the mind.

"Where we were, before, there is a bridge." Jan had been juggling how to start in her head, and every idea seemed worse than the other, either lame or too obvious or nothing she could actually do or say without falling into hysterical giggles, which wouldn't help at all. Sitting on a pile of cushions in the path of the late-afternoon sunlight while Nalith sketched her, a brownie sitting stiffly at her knee unhappy to be there but unable to refuse the queen's command, Jan found the words had risen without thought or plan.

"Hhhmmm?" So long as Jan did not move, Nalith allowed her to speak, but that did not mean she was listening. Yet.

"It arches over a creek, and if you were to see it, in the course of the day, it would be only a wooden bridge, small and meaningless. But in the afternoon, when the sun hits it just so, the light catches red and gold in the grain of the planks, and it is almost as though it is made of flame, caught in form, arcing over running water."

Jan had actually only seen the light do that once, walking the borders of the Farm with Martin. But she had stopped and watched, as the light had flickered and then moved on, and thought it was one of the most beautiful things she had ever seen.

Martin, of course, hadn't noticed a thing. But she thought Nalith, with her small obsession with light, might have.

"Not that the light here isn't nice—" and she put all the doubtfulness she had into the word *nice* "—but there, it seems as though there's a special quality, a life to it, somehow. I think that's why so many artists live there."

There were, as far as she knew, no artists anywhere near the Farm, although it wouldn't have surprised her to find a high-priced gallery down the road, catering to the CEOs and retired sports stars who had second homes up there. But her words seemed to set a hook, because Nalith paused in her sketching, her hand hesitating just a bit before making the next stroke.

Jan tried not to look toward the other side of the room,

where Tyler was sitting, talking with Kerry. She hadn't spoken to him since that morning, when he'd disappeared from their room. He wasn't cold, just distant, deep inside his own thoughts, and she had decided it was better to leave him there.

"Tell me of this place."

It was a command, her voice as coolly bored as ever, save when she discussed her own attempts at creating, but Jan cheered inwardly. Outwardly, she remained still, the perfect model.

"It is similar to here, but different, too. South of here, a small community, but connected to the major cities, Boston and New York. It's on the grid, so you lack for nothing, but there is quiet, too. Time to think, to create."

She paused and then let a hint of surprise and excitement come into her voice, as though she had only just thought of it. "My lady, I would take you there, if I could. It would be a setting worthy of you."

"And this House is not?"

*Careful, Jan,* she warned herself. *Seduce, don't bludgeon.* This was too important to screw up. Suddenly every panic attack she had ever had over dating, over flirting, over making a mistake in public, came back and tried to whammy her.

The brownie on her knee, as though sensing her unrest, or maybe just responding to the warning tone in Nalith's voice, sniggered. Jan kept her face calm, but the hand that had been placed on the brownie's neck, as though cupping it to her, tightened enough to leave marks in the super's flesh, and it fell silent, warned. If it broke form, distracted the preter from her sketching, Nalith's ire would be focused on both of them, not merely Jan.

The faintest scuffle of noise drew her attention, but she knew even without looking that Martin had entered the room. He did not come far inside, lingering by the doorway, and there was nothing he could do to help anyway, but knowing he was there gave her the courage to continue. She might not be useful in a fight, but this was a battle of a different sort, using words and images rather than weapons or claws. And words and images, she knew.

"This place, it is lovely, but it is too small, too isolated to properly showcase you, what you will become. My lady should have outposts, yes, throughout the land, but she should not reside in one. She deserves a hub, a center, where all would circle around *her*."

"A center, yes."

Jan hadn't chosen the word intentionally, but the moment Nalith repeated it, she could feel the hook catch the preter and knew all she had to do now was reel her in. "The houses are spread at a distance, but not isolated, and artists and dancers and singers would come to you, a proper patron and student of their arts." Her eyes settled on Tyler, and she remembered what he had said about the cables and how fascinated Nalith seemed with the project. The preters had used the internet to connect with humans in the first place, had somehow hooked their magic into the network. *That's the final carrot, the thing that will get her...*

"And of course, the entire complex is already on the grid. I helped set the system up myself." Utter truth, that. "Full digital, top speed—the entire internet, all the power of human technology at your command."

"And all of it merely waiting for me to walk in?"

"My lady." Jan risked looking directly at Nalith then. "They simply do not know they are waiting for you."

The preter's narrow lips quirked, and that flash of humor, rarely seen but irresistible, transformed her for just an instant before it was gone. Jan's breath was taken away, even as her brain was calculating the effects, judging her work the way she used to judge a website that had just gone live. Part of Nalith knew that Jan's words were only the very best butter, but Ty had been right; she couldn't resist. Even if only half of what Jan had said was true, the preter would have to follow through. Her ego would demand it.

"And you would take me to this place?"

"My lady." One of the other brownies—of course it was Cam, Jan thought, able to pick them out now—stepped forward. "My lady, this house is safe for you, a defended location. We know there are others coming, have sensed them. It would not be wise—" He heard the words coming out of his mouth and tried to stuff them back, too late. You did not question Nalith's wisdom, ever.

"You would take me to this place?" Nalith asked Jan again, ignoring the brownie.

"My lady. It would be my pleasure."

The two figures entered the café and looked around cautiously, clearly ill at ease in the surroundings.

"Sit wherever ya want," a woman called out from behind the counter, indicating the dozen or so tables, half of which were empty. A few of the diners looked up to see who had arrived but quickly returned their attention to their food. The newcomers did not invite close observation. "Someone'll get to you right away."

They chose a table away from the window, as isolated as they could manage, and sat down. The menus were in front of them, and they studied the offerings rather than talking to each other or looking around.

"Horrible place," one said, a quiet under-breath mutter. "I cannot imagine that she would deem this locale acceptable."

"I cannot imagine what she thinks at all," the female said, "but she is here. The sooner we settle this, the sooner we can leave." They had left their human pets with the others while they scouted, each of them feeling uncomfortable with their portal-holders so far away.

"Hey. What can I get'cha?" The waitress was young, naturally cheerful, and had clearly summed them up and decided they had the potential to be decent tippers.

"The breakfast special," the man said, putting down the menu, and his companion held up two fingers, indicating that she would go with that, as well.

"Sure thing. Coffee?"

"Please."

The waitress tapped a tablet in her hand and entered their order. She scurried away, returning a few minutes later with their waffles.

"Nice town," one of the strangers said awkwardly.

"It's little but it's ours. You want real syrup with that?"

"Of course." There was a pause as the waitress brought over a small brown pitcher and placed it on the table. Her customers both nodded, almost regally, she thought, and picked up their forks, looking around the restaurant as though wondering what to do next. The waitress dismissed that thought—of course everyone knew how to eat waffles!—and went back to refilling coffee mugs.

"We need to wait," the first preter said, cutting into the food and lifting a piece to his mouth. He chewed automatically, the best waffles this side of Belgium, according to the sign out front, consumed the same way he did all the food in this realm, without pleasure. "We cannot simply march up and demand that she return with us."

"We could," his companion said, "but it would be noisy. And likely fruitless, yes." They had spent the dawn hours walking around the structure Nalith had hidden herself in; there was magic wrapped around it, the new kind of magic she had discovered and tried to keep for herself. More, there were other creatures there, including the stink of gnomes. The preters might accept the homage of such creatures here, as they were useful, but to allow them to den so close? Nalith had forgotten herself utterly.

"We will remind her," the preter said out loud, and her companion nodded, knowing her thoughts easily. As they had reminded Stjerne when she'd overstepped her place one time too many, had lost them one of the mortal portal-holders, and the consort's protection had been dropped.

"We will. But that act is not for us to do so, not alone." They burned to confront her, force her to recant her abandonment, take up her proper role and put things back to order. The court should not be without its queen, consorts should not give orders, they should not be relying so heavily on *humans* to accomplish their goals. But it was the consort's right to rebuke his queen, not theirs. They were here only to find her, track her, and keep her in one place until he could arrive.

Soon. The others would complete the first part of their task soon. All they had to do was hold her here until then.

And if they did violence to her would-be courtiers and guards in the process? No one would chide them for that.

The sound of footsteps on the floor approached their table and then stopped. They both looked up, expecting their waitress to have returned with the coffee.

"You folks traveling through or here for some leaf peeping?"

The human stood by their table, his head cocked to the side, indicating that he expected them to respond. Unlike the others around them, who wore a seemingly random choice of colors and clothing, he was dressed all in one shade of blue, blouse and trousers matched by a leather utility belt like a workman. But he carried himself proudly, with an edge of caution that both preters quickly identified. A guard of some sort, aware in ways the other humans were not that they did not belong here. And the scar across his face, a still-raw slash, said he was not a human who was easily cowed.

The term he used, "leaf peeping," was unfamiliar, but the intent behind the question was clear. He was challenging them.

The female preter rested her hands on the table, her eyes bright. There was a temptation to englamour this one, but capturing him would cause more problems than it would solve; a guard would be expected to report in, and his going missing might raise alarms they had no wish to deal with just then. Likewise, they could not simply kill him.

"We are visiting a friend who lives in the area," the male said, placing his fork down on the table and folding his hands in an attempt to look harmless. "Is there something wrong?" His voice soothed and eased: *There is nothing wrong here, nothing at all.* A risk; if the human was sensitive to magics, as some were, he would know he was being manipulated, raising more questions.

The human studied him carefully, too closely, and then, finally, shook his head, dismissing them from whatever suspicions he had brought. "We've had some trouble the past few weeks," he said. "Your friend will fill you in, no doubt. It's been all the gossip. So we're careful with faces we don't recognize. I'm sure you understand."

"Of course. Such diligence is to be commended. Might I ask as to the nature of the trouble?"

"The murder kind," the guard said bluntly, the faint englamouring cast on his perception not affecting him so much that he lost track of his duty. "Two local families, and two cops went missing looking for them." He studied them, searching for some reaction. When they merely looked back at him, he smiled briefly, grimly, and touched the brim of his hat. "You folks enjoy your breakfast."

"Herself?" the male murmured as the human moved away, leaving them to their discussion again.

"Or the creatures she has gathered around her," his companion said. "You saw the scar on his face—that is the work of one the lower sorts. How she chooses to amuse herself is no concern of ours. Finish your food. The others will be finishing soon. When they are done...then we will be able to go home."

"Hmm," the other preter said, casting a glance around the restaurant. "We should look up that guard before we go. He lacked the spark of some others, but there was an intelligence there that might be useful."

"We can come back for him later," she agreed. *"Later."*

What one gnome knew, they all knew. They knew about the human female, who had evaded them not once but twice, who had gone into the otherland and come out again. When she had appeared at Herself's court, they had known, and they had waited and watched. Herself might be fooled into thinking this human was tame like the others, but gnomes knew better.

They were not so foolish as to choose a single side or to trust the promises of anyone, super or preternatural. Both sides lied. Both sides used. But if they broke each other, gnomes would remain.

They would play the game and win.

So when the *lupin,* the Wolf, called a warning against the preternatural threat, they heard but did not heed, waiting for a better offer. And it came, as they knew it would. When their preter lords called, they responded. When Herself commanded, they obeyed. They did the dirty work, the bloody work. But always, always, they watched and waited.

Eventually, the time would come for them. If they could survive.

"We cannot go. They will slaughter us. Have you forgotten what happened the last time, and the time before that?"

They had attempted to stop the Wolf's pack twice before, on the preters' orders, and most had been slaughtered. *Gēnomos* stalked and they rended and they disappeared, that was what they did, not this open frontal warfare.

"This is not the Wolf."

"This is *worse!*"

"A risk. A risk we knew and counted for."

"A risk that fails is not a good risk."

"The cost is high but the reward sweet."

"Enough!" One voice cut across the many, where they were huddled in a tent at the far edges of the property, as far from Herself as they could manage without raising her ire. "There is no other choice. Not now. Not yet. We die, to live."

"We die, to live," the other voices muttered, agreement reluctant but inevitable. What one knew, they all knew, and what one won, they all won.

## Chapter 15

Jan knew that something was wrong first, because she was watching Tyler. He didn't say anything, kept singing some old love song Jan vaguely remembered from the oldies station, but she knew that his mood had changed. He didn't look at anyone when he sang, letting his gaze float off somewhere, his thoughts entirely within his head. He used to look like that when he was working, too, not so much thinking as letting thoughts come to him. It was almost reassuring, that familiarity in the middle of so much that was strange. But halfway through, that cracked a little, and he was back, entirely present in his eyes. And the look wasn't scared or worried: it was broken.

Jan studied her lover cautiously, from under lowered lids. She had been released from her posing duties, the brownie that had been perched on her knee scrambling off, shooting her a dirty look as though arranging their positions had been *her* idea. She had hoped to escape as well, needing time to recover from the stress of trying to woo the preter over to the idea of the Farm as a potential site for her court, as well as the stress of holding her position for so long, but Nalith had gestured for her to come close, then indicated that the human was to stay by her.

Exhausted but outwardly obedient, Jan had squatted on her heels by the preter's chair. Occasionally, the preter lifted one of Jan's hands to look closely at some detail or tilted her face to check the line of her jaw, then turned back to check her drawing, but otherwise she ignored her. The preter had her fingers on Jan's chin just then, angling her to one side, so Jan had a clear view of the moment Ty's expression changed. Her heart raced, a shot of adrenaline wracking her body, similar to an asthma attack but without the constriction. It was anticipation, fear, stress, all shaped into a bullet and slammed into her heart.

*What?* She asked him silently. *What is it?*

Then the fingers on her skin dug in too hard, the preter having somehow sensed that her attention had wandered, and Jan yelped, wrenching her head away instinctively. She hunched over, anticipating a blow, but none came. The mix of conversations, previously a low hum in the room, died, and Jan risked looking up.

Nalith had risen to her feet, the sketch in front of her forgotten. Her narrow, elegant face was pulled even tighter, making her cheekbones and chin seem even sharper, and her eyes...

Her eyes, when she looked around the room, were filled with an unholy gleam, the deep red of a candle flame obliterating any trace of blue. The atavistic response that had dulled in Jan over months of dealing with non-humans, the week of constant exposure to a preter, rose again suddenly newly urgent, urging her to *get the hell away.*

"Call in the gnomes," Nalith ordered, her voice sharp and thin as shattered glass. "Deploy them at the borders of the property. All others, inside. Deploy internal defenses. Now."

She did not raise her voice: she did not have to. All the supernaturals within the range—the entire main floor of the house, from the sound of things—moved immediately, following whatever plans she had established. Jan waited, still half-crouched on the polished wooden floor, until the main room had emptied of all but Nalith and the four humans, all in various stages of confusion.

"My lady?" Her voice shook, but Jan told herself that it *should* be shaking in the role she was playing. Anything that upset her queen should upset her. "What troubles you?"

The preter's hand dropped back to Jan's head, stroking her hair as though she were a cat. Jan managed to restrain a shudder, although across the room Tyler's body shook once in revulsion. He was revisiting his own memories again, Jan suspected, and her heart ached for him, even as her brain was racing to get on top of this new development. "My lady?"

"It is nothing," Nalith said, her voice still splinter sharp. "Merely an intrusion on my territory by those I do not wish to see."

Hope rose that it was AJ and his crew, finally coming to their aid, and then was dashed again. Tyler wouldn't look like that if it were supernaturals, certainly not supernaturals he knew. And Nalith would not treat AJ and his crew as such a threat, even if she knew about them, which she didn't…did she? Jan's head hurt as much as her chest, trying to parse that, so she let it go. If it was AJ, they'd roll with it. If not…if not, they were in danger, too.

The other two humans were looking at Nalith not with fear or concern but utter befuddlement. The idea that there might be something that could upset her, much less challenge her, was beyond their comprehension. Jan had a sudden unkind thought that they looked like dogs who'd just been told all the bacon was gone.

"Others of your kind, my lady?" Ty had stood up, although he stayed safely across the room from Nalith. He wasn't asking, really; he knew.

"Perhaps even your former mistress," Nalith said, intentionally cruel, and Tyler's jaw clenched, his shoulders hunching over slightly, but he didn't otherwise react to the blow. Before either one of them could react, or Jan could figure out how to deal with this, there was the sound of loud voices and running feet outside, and one of the brownies came racing in, weirdly flushed. It wasn't one she could identify, which meant that it was lower in their pack rankings, or however they figured it. Odd: normally they didn't come in to speak directly to Nalith.

"M-my lady, my lady, they are gone."

"Who are gone?" Those fire-red eyes turned on the brownie, and it gulped but did not flee.

"The gnomes, my lady. They are not in their compound, and they do not respond to the call."

Turncoats, AJ had named them, changing sides and abandoning their fellow supers to work for a preter lord—or lady, as it had turned out. Jan didn't know why she was surprised that they had abandoned Nalith, as well. Gnomes, it seemed, played no side but their own.

Nalith was not surprised. Nalith was furious. Jan fell back, scuttling on her knees without shame until she felt the reassuring bulk of a wall behind her, and wondered if getting behind the sofa would help. Tyler held still, as though hoping that Nalith would forget he was there, and the other two humans, although clueless, weren't dumb, keeping their mouths shut and their gazes elsewhere.

"All gone?"

"All, my lady."

There was more noise in the hallway, and some of the supers came back in, clearly waiting for new orders. Martin, Jan saw, was among them, although toward the back of the small crowd. She did a quick mental count. Without the gnomes and minus the supers Nalith had sent to the new houses, they were down to less than thirty, and that included the four humans.

"I will deal with them later," Nalith said. Jan thought the preter might believe her own words, or she might be whistling, trying to save face in front of the others. Most of them looked as if they *wanted* to believe her, wanted to believe that whatever was coming, she could handle it without the gnomes' defense.

"There are weapons in the shed. Cam and Alia, distribute them. Tell my winged guardians to take the roof, make sure nothing attempts to land there." She looked around the room, and this time she saw the humans, clearly.

"And you, my pets. Will you fight for me?" It wasn't a question. "Serve me, in this, as you have in other ways."

Wes and Kerry stepped forward as if they were volunteering to go on a picnic. Idiots. They might have muscles, but she would bet that neither of them had so much as made a fist since they were in grade school. In a fight against foes Nalith feared? They would be cannon fodder. But they weren't her responsibility. Jan held her breath, and Tyler shook his head roughly, running a hand over his scalp, leaving it resting on the back of his neck, hesitating.

"You would rather chew out your eyes than fight for me, would you not, my singer?" She was using that voice again, the one that hinted at glamour, promised it, making you ask rather than forcing it on you. Jan hated that voice.

"Yes. My lady."

Nalith smiled, and for once—for once—there seemed to be nothing cruel about it. "Then think of it thus. You would be fighting not for me but to inflict harm on others of my kind, who intend less well to your world. You would strike a blow against those who hurt you."

Jan bit her lip. She didn't want Tyler in harm's way, but if he could take real action, finally *hurt* the preters, in some way close to how they had hurt him, at least a little...maybe that would be the healing he needed.

Finally, after an agonizing wait, Tyler nodded once.

"And you, my little guide, my useless one?" The preter queen was looking at her, that awful gaze focused on her, pulling her in no matter what she might wish, might fear. If she would only give in to that fire, let herself be consumed by it, then all the worry, all the pain and fear, would be gone, and she would be warm and cared for, all the rest of her life....

Jan resisted. She drew on the memories of facing down Nalith's consort, of walking into—and out of—the preter court, holding on to the knowledge of what a preter's care was like, the sound of Tyler's nightmares and the look in his eyes when he finally came back to this world, all of it bricks in a wall she built, slowly, painfully, between herself and that demanding gaze.

When she felt safe enough, she looked not at Nalith but at Tyler. He was looking at her, waiting. When she nodded once, the tension in his face eased at her assent. Whatever had been going on before in his head, it didn't matter now. He wasn't alone. She wasn't alone. Whatever happened, they would face it together this time.

Nalith either missed the subtext or, more likely, Jan thought, chose to ignore it, so long as she got what she wanted.

"Martin."

Martin pushed through the crowd, putting himself front and center. "My lady."

"You will lead the defense."

"No."

The silence in the room previously was nothing to the utter dead air that filled the room at that.

"You would prefer to guard your lady?"

"No." Martin's voice was flat, unemotional, and final.

"No." It wasn't phrased as a question, but she was clearly waiting for an explanation. Jan stared at him, wondering what the hell was going on in his head.

His expression gave nothing away, his eyes flat brown, not showing any of the supernatural spark *or* human-recognizable emotion.

"You are here in this world, and I recognize you," he said slowly. "But this pitting of forces against each other, the violence that is filling our world, it solves nothing. You know this. We cannot destroy each other, or the balance between the realms will shift. You *know* this."

"I know nothing of the sort." Nalith's voice was tight, angry, and her entire body screamed danger, at least to Jan. Martin kept speaking, seemingly oblivious to the threat.

"You do not belong here. They will bloody the very bones of the earth, tear apart our Center, to reclaim you. Sending more violence against that will not save you, nor earn you a place here."

It wasn't Martin's voice, Jan realized suddenly. Or it was his voice, but he wasn't *in* it.

"Upstart creature." And now Nalith let loose her anger, lashing out with one hand. She was nowhere near him, and yet Martin staggered back, his limbs jerking as though he'd receive an electric shock, a high-voltage one. His eyes widened, and Jan felt her eyes try to close, indicating that he was about to change form. Then the impulse apparently passed, and he went to one knee, lowering his head.

"My lady. I will guard your house." The words were grudging, but Nalith took them at face value, that whatever had spoken before had been cowed into obedience.

"Go. Take these humans with you. Make them useful."

"What the hell was that?" The moment they were outside the main room, Tyler rounded on Martin, his voice low but furious. "Were you trying to get killed? Were you trying to get all of us killed?"

Martin held up his hand, black nails glinting in the overhead light, drawing Jan's eye to them. She had gotten used to his looks, the fine dark hairs scattered over his skin, the narrow face and too-wide-set eyes, but the nails always reminded her: they were hooves in another form.

"You two. Kerry, go to the shed. There are weapons there. Find something you think you can wield. Wes, go find Patrick's supplies, all of them, and bring them down. His chisels might be the right size for some of our cohort to use. They were in good enough shape to be deadly."

Both humans looked vaguely ill, but nodded and went off to follow his instructions, still driven by their obedience to the preter queen.

"What happened in there?" Jan asked. "What you said…"

"He told me the same bullshit," Tyler said, still furious. "That violence solves nothing, yak yak yak. Which, coming from him, is nice, isn't it?"

"It wasn't him."

"What?"

"It wasn't him," Jan said again. And then she said to Martin, "That wasn't you talking in there, was it?" Jan needed him to answer that. It probably wouldn't be one she wanted to hear, but she was getting used to that.

Martin merely shrugged. "Does it matter?"

"Yes!" There were days, she swore, she wanted to hold the kelpie's head underwater. Not that it would do much other than amuse him.

"What, something is beaming its words into your head, working your jaw?"

"No." Martin was certain about that, Jan less so. "It wasn't words. It was just like this…knowing. Like when you're trying to understand something and then all of a sudden it's all there in your head?"

Tyler shook his head, but Jan nodded.

"There is a balance to this world, to both realms," Martin said, putting a hand on each of their shoulders and pushing them into the now-empty and abandoned kitchen. "We have always known this, and you humans, too, when you think about it. The Center remains, and we balance around it. Occasionally it tilts one way or the other, but over time, it recalibrates, remains steady. If the portals hadn't changed, that would have remained. Now...the preters may have lost their center, and we've done something that...filled the gap?" Martin's long face scrunched together, as if he was giving himself a headache. "The magic changed, and they were vulnerable to it, changed by it. If we kill them all, here, we may damage our Center, as well." He frowned. "I think. This is more Elsa's thing, not mine."

"Yeah, you're just the dumb blond. We got that," Jan said with more than a touch of sarcasm. "So, if the balance is thrown off," she asked, "then what? What happens?"

"I don't know. I don't want to know. Change may not always be a bad thing, but that does not automatically make it a good thing."

"You said that before, about maintaining a balance." Tyler caught Jan's glance at him and shrugged. "He was trying to talk me out of being an idiot."

"Hmm," she said and then decided that they didn't have time to dig into that, not without knowing what was about to happen. "And about the Center and earning a place here?"

"That...wasn't me. I think it *was* the Center."

Somehow, that was the only thing in all this that made sense to Jan, that the oasis of calm and recovery would be able to reach out and speak through Martin's voice. In fact, when she thought about it, it all made perfect sense. She had lost her mind.

"My life is insane," she said. "All right, so we're supposed to help with the defense?"

"I can't," Martin said. "But I needed to agree, to get you two out of there."

"I'm staying," Tyler said. "I have to."

"You're going to die, human," Martin said, as if he'd said it before, and Tyler shrugged, looking unhappy. "Maybe."

There was a sharp rap of something hitting glass, and all three of them turned to look at the kitchen's single window. A hand pressed against it, palm down, and then made a point ing gesture toward the door.

It wasn't a gnome's hand, so Jan moved to unlatch the lock. A slender figure with dark, mica-glittery skin slipped in, its clothing rumpled, shoes covered in mud and its face splat- tered with what Jan was pretty sure was blood. Not its own: it seemed unharmed, if exhausted.

"Seth." The lizardlike super had been one of AJ's lieuten- ants back at the Farm. "Are you all right? What happened? Did AJ send you?" The questions tumbled out of her mouth, even as she reached out to brush at the smudge on its cheek. "Is everyone okay? Did you get my email?"

Seth shook his head, not saying no but rather indicating that there was no time to answer questions. "We've been looking for you. AJ's orders. The witch told us where you were. You need to come. Now. AJ needs you."

That was all Martin had to hear. He half turned, opening the refrigerator to grab three bottles of water, handing one to Jan. "All right," he said. "But we have to hurry—the preters have found their missing queen, and they're coming, fast."

Seth blinked at them, double eyelids making the effect seem even more surprised. "Preters, here?"

"And we don't want to be here when they get here," Martin said.

"Right. No. Right." Seth blinked his underlids again and then slid back out the door, clearly expecting them to follow. Martin was barely a step behind, while Jan, the water still in her hand, was staring dumbly, trying to catch up to what had just happened.

"Wait, how are we going to—" she started to say, but they were already gone. "Damn it," she swore, checking to make sure that she had her inhaler in her pocket, the witch's sachet and the carved horse in the other. There wasn't anything still upstairs that was hers, really.

"Come on. Let's go," she said to Ty.

"I can't."

"What?" Her first thought was that she'd misheard.

"I can't. I won't."

"Ty..." She looked at the door, then back to her boyfriend, feeling helpless. "You've got to!"

"I don't got to do anything except what feels right. Zan said so, back at the Farm. And it feels right to stay."

"Jesus Christ, Tyler." Jan almost hurled her water bottle at him. "You— I can't—"

"Go. You don't need to be here." Before she had time to parse that, either, she was in his arms, a rough and unexpected hug. It was the first time he had initiated contact, and certainly the most intimate contact, since...since before he had gone to meet Stjerne, the preter who had stolen him. "I love you," he said, almost a confession. "I always have. I always will. But I can't *be* like this. I can't let go, and that means I can't be with you, either. Let me do this."

And then he shoved her away, out the door, and closed it roughly behind her.

The backyard was quiet. The area where the gnomes had

been camping was a mess of abandoned bedrolls and tents, but nothing moved, not even a squirrel or bird. She could hear traffic from down the road, the sound of an occasional car, and voices shouting to each other, but if there were a dozen or more supernaturals gathering, preparing for battle, she could neither see nor hear them.

Somehow that was worse than if she'd walked out into an armed camp.

Martin and Seth were nowhere to be seen, either. Jan felt abandoned by both her companions, a hot splice of self-pity mixed with panic. Should she go back into the house, throw herself onto Nalith's nonexistent mercy, fight and hope that whatever had spoken through Martin's voice was wrong, that battle wouldn't doom them all?

No. Whatever happened, whatever Tyler decided, Jan knew she could no more go back into that house than she could fly. Martin had told her where he'd left that car; she didn't have GPS or a map, but maybe she could find that and…then she'd worry about where to go next.

Uncapping the water bottle she only now just realized she was holding, Jan stepped off the back deck and started walking as casually as she could. The yard was large enough, but it seemed twice as wide when you were hoping not to be noticed.

"You, human."

"Yes?" Her voice didn't crack, not even when hard, thin fingers latched on to her arm, halting her midstep.

"You're not armed."

*No,* she thought, half-crazed, *you took them all.* She hadn't encountered a multi-limbed super before, much less one shaped vaguely and disturbingly like a praying mantis. "I… No. I was supposed to go out to the shed to find a weapon."

The super snorted, impressive considering it didn't seem to

have a nose, only a wide mouth set *over* its eyes. "Nothing out there you could use, bitty thing like you. Here." It reached out with a lower limb, and she took the serrated blade offered almost automatically. "Go low and stab," it told her. "You'll do more damage that way than trying to go overhand."

"Oh. Okay. I'll... I'm going to walk the perimeter. One thing I'm really good at is screaming loud, if I see something I don't like."

Jan was pretty sure the super grinned at her, and the grip on her arm turned into a pat on the shoulder. "Not bad for a human," it said and then went on its way in the opposite direction.

Jan finally remembered to breathe and, with the knife in one hand and the water bottle in the other, kept heading for the far edge of the property, where a break in the fence suggested she might be able to slip through unnoticed. It took sliding sideways to manage, and the splintered wood dug into her legs, but she got through.

When another hand grabbed at her from behind, tugging the sleeve of her blouse, she swung instinctively, the point of the blade digging up until it met resistance, and she heard a startled yelp.

"Woman, what?"

"Oh." Jan let the blade drop back a little, looking into Seth's startled face. "Sorry?"

"Good reflexes" was all he said, although he winced a little as he flexed the arm she'd hit. "We're going to need that. Now, put that away and come *on*."

Martin was waiting across the driveway on the other side, looking impatient but also relieved. Out of the frying pan and into the fire, she suspected. But Tyler wasn't the only one who went with his gut. This, crazy as it was, felt right.

They made it on foot to the bridge that led into town.

A girl with pale green hair sat on the stone-lined bank and kicked her feet absently, looking up when they approached. Not Jenny Greenteeth, but another water-sprite. "I guarded the car like you said," she told Seth. "Good luck."

It was the truck they had taken from the Farm. That unexpected bit of familiarity hit Jan harder than expected. This had been the truck that had taken her from New Haven originally, sandwiched between AJ and Martin, having no idea how her world had already changed....

"What happened?" she asked. "Why did it take you so long to find us? Why didn't anyone else come? Is AJ pissed we took off?"

"Farm's gone," Seth said bluntly. "Preters are here."

The ritual had followed the rise of the new moon. Although they could not see it, deep in the basement room, the gathered preters could *feel* it. As it reached the apex of its nightly cycle, the humans waiting patiently were gathered in the center of the room, their masters placing a hand on their chests, under the silver chain, and commanded each to take up the others' hands, creating an outward-facing circle, their masters a looser ring around them.

There was an unearthly silence, the sound of their breathing the only sound, softly echoed in the dark corners of the room before fading. Then their fingers curved inward, nails digging into the flesh underneath like bloodied thorns, and the humans cried out in a blend of agony and joy, the pain their masters inflicted welcomed as proof of their affection. The sound filled the room, driving out the silence, creating the bond that tied human to preter, giving the magic a bridge to move over, united preternatural with natural.

One-to-one, such a bridge created and opened a single portal. Combined and focused, matched to the natural bridge of the new moon, and that single portal expanded, deepened, until the mist filled the entire church, and the painted concrete walls were replaced with the cold stone walls of the Court Under the Hill.

Above them, on the streets of this town, and the one next to it, and the ones surrounding it, computer screens and cell phones flickered as the universes twisted into each other, the logic behind them hijacked to another cause.

And there in the basement, on a dais that had not been there a moment ago, presided the consort, regal, cold, and filled with rage. He stood, and his advisers stood with him, watching as he strode off the dais and into the natural world.

Behind him, at a respectful distance, came a dozen more of the court, the greater lords and lesser ones, until only the consort's advisers and a score of lesser preters remained, to hold the court until they returned. They watched through the Grand Portal but said no word, made no gesture of greeting or farewell.

The consort had put aside his robes, replacing them with trousers and a close-fitting shirt and vest, low boots on his feet, his long, chestnut-brown curls tied back instead of flowing around his shoulders. His gaze raked over the humans, then lingered over the preters who had opened the way for him.

"Well done," he said. "It will hold?"

"It will." The proper response would have been *It will, my prince.* The dropped honorific did not go unnoticed, and the consort's lips pressed into an even thinner line, but he did not challenge the courtier. And that, too, did not go unnoticed. The consort had held the court together in crisis, but he would not be able to maintain that hold forever; if the queen did not return, if they failed here, his reign would have no legitimacy. She had bred no heir, and without a queen, the court itself would fail, the courtiers turning on each other until there was nothing left. They all knew it.

"Then let us reclaim my lady," the consort said. "And then we will claim this realm, once and for all, so that it will bother us no more."

"'Fraid I can't let you do that."

A human stepped out of the shadows. He was older, his hair silvered, his long leather coat open to show a crisp white shirt and dark slacks. He could have been any corporate manager, heading home after a long day, except for the small, sharp ax he held in his hands.

One of the preters snarled at the intruder, who merely raised an eyebrow at it, then turned to the consort. "There are rules. You're breaking them."

"The rules have been rewritten," the consort said. "And your people are the ones who rewrote them."

"Maybe so," the human said. "We do a lot of dumb things, mostly without thinking. Sometimes it turns out okay, sometimes it doesn't. But that's why we look out for each other, fix the stuff that's gone wrong. Find the source of the noise and shut it down."

"Noise?" The consort was almost amused.

"Noise. Static. Clamor. The natural realm objects to your intrusion. Every witch on the East Coast knew where you were the moment this thing opened—did you really think you could *sneak* in?" The human, too, sounded amused.

"Does this look like *sneaking?*"

The human looked around, making a performance of it. "Under the cover of dark, in a deserted building, coming without invite? Yes, my lord preter, it looks much like sneaking."

"Stand aside, human," another of the preters said, almost growling.

"Can't."

The consort was still not taking the threat seriously. "Just you, to turn back time? Do you seek to challenge me, to win another truce? That will not happen."

"No truce," the Huntsman said. "Die."

He swung the ax as though he were aiming at a tree, a low sweep that any of the preters could have easily dodged, but when they did, another form came from the shadows as well, lower to the ground, teeth glinting white and red just before they fastened into flesh and hauled their prey to the floor.

And the shadows came apart, revealing the battered, blood-ied remnants of what had fled the Farm, mixed with a hand-ful of humans, most of them female, each carrying an ax or sword or, in at least one instance, an athame.

"Glad you made it," the Huntsman said, dodging a preter's lunge. He stepped to the side, and the ax bit into preternatu-ral flesh and bone, taking it down as easily as a sapling. But even on the ground, it struck back, long fingers curling into the Huntsman's clothing, burning through to the flesh like a living brand, and the human cursed, trying to yank free.

"You doubted me?" Jack said, a green-wire garrote in his hands, stopping to finish off the Huntsman's opponent. "I'm hurt."

"Kill, don't flirt," one of the supernaturals growled at the both of them, and then they were too busy to spare breath for talking.

## Chapter 16

Once they were in the truck and out of Little Creek, Seth started to talk. From the first warning of danger to the flight from the Farm, the tattered, bloodied survivors of the battle heading each to different, predetermined points.

"And then the witches found us. Which is one for the history books, mate. Witches finding *us*." He was hyper, twitching with energy he didn't seem to know how to use.

"I should have been there."

"Yeah." Seth didn't cut Martin any slack. "You should have. But your job was to keep this one safe, and you did that. So don't try feeling around for the guilt or regret. You're not good at it, and anyway, AJ would have sent you two out the moment things got iffy, same as he did the other human."

"What other human?" Jan put a hand on the dashboard, bracing herself as she turned to look at Seth. "What other human?" she asked again, her voice rising. She and Tyler had been the only humans at the Farm. The only other humans who knew about it, as far as she knew, had been members of her team. Her friends.

"The Huntsman sent her, so don't yell at me."

"Who?" But she knew, a hollow, heavy feeling in her stomach. "Glory. Why the fuck was Glory there? Is she all right?" Her friend was tough and fierce and smart, but she was supposed to be safe in London, not in the middle of all this.

"Why is the Huntsman involved?" Martin asked.

"I don't know, and how the hell should I know?" Seth answered them both, guiding the truck onto the highway and putting on speed until he was going a few miles over the limit, letting other cars pass him on the left. "The Huntsman and witches and it's cats and dogs living together, man, we're living *history*. Anyway, when the attack hit, AJ sent the human and the dryads into the basement. Elsa said she got them out when the defenses fell, but I don't know anything more than that. I'm sorry."

Jan stared out the window at the road passing by and instinctively reached for her inhaler, safe in her pocket. She didn't need it, and it wouldn't help relieve worry, but at this point it was almost a talisman. So long as she didn't lose it, everything would be okay. Eventually. "The preters are here."

"Yeah. And the turncoats their dogs, like that's any surprise. Nobody else, though, not that we saw."

"That's good. Right?" When neither of them answered her, she went on, "So, what's a Huntsman?"

"Old friend of AJ's," Martin said. "Human, or he was, long time ago. Got tangled up in a dryad's roots and stayed. If he's rousting other humans... Huh."

"Yah, like I said. Interesting times." Seth was starting to come down off his jittering high, slumping a little in the seat.

"And we're going to where AJ is?"

"Plans were, if everything went to hell, we split up, scatter, and do what damage we could until either we got an all clear or it all went south for good. AJ sent me to get you, bring you to where he was. Don't know more than that."

"So, where—" Jan started to ask, when Martin put a hand over hers. His skin was cooler than usual and slightly clammy, and the black nails were ragged at the edges. "Doesn't matter," he said. "Get some sleep. Whatever we're going into, if AJ needs us, we're going to need to be alert."

There was no way she was going to be able to sleep, torn between worry about what they were driving into and worry for Tyler, left behind to face whatever was coming for Nalith. But there wasn't any point in arguing, either. Jan let her head fall back against the seat back, stretched her legs out in front of her as best she could, and closed her eyes, hoping that would satisfy the kelpie.

He squeezed her hand once and tucked his thumb under her palm, the gesture as comforting as a hug.

"Once more, dear friends, once more," she murmured and was rewarded by Seth's soft laugh.

The street outside was silent, any humans who might have been out having trusted their instincts and taken another route that evening. A few cars were parked along the curb, but their engines were cold. Overhead, the dark moon hung in place like an evil eye, unblinking.

There was blood in the air. They could smell it, standing outside the building where the preter lords had told them to come. Nearly fifty of them, all that was left of the hundreds when this started, all that could make their way to this place at this time. And if some of them kept looking over their shoulder, convinced that Herself would be there, ready to flay them alive for abandoning her, none broke ranks.

They were supposed to join the preter lords as they came through the Grand Portal, form shock troops to their preternatural grand purpose, do all the things minion armies did. Supposed to serve and die, if needed, so their betters could live and rule.

"Screw that shit," one of them said and stepped up onto the stone steps, the others close behind.

Inside the church, the noise of battle came from elsewhere, curses and the clank and crack of weapons. Their attention was drawn not to the wide staircase leading downstairs, however, but to the faint glow rising through the floor. A misty blue arc, barely three feet high and a dozen feet wide, filling the nave.

A collective sigh escaped them, relief, fear, and anticipation.

"Is it enough?"

"It has to be."

The Grand Portal itself was out of reach; to go downstairs would be to be drawn into the fighting, where both sides had no reason to care for them. This was their chance, while all other attention was distracted.

"Make sure your body stays inside the band," the one who had spoken before said. "Anything that goes outside might not come with."

A running start, steps matched to prevent anyone from tripping over an unwary limb, and they ducked and slid under the glowing arc, into the portal.

Gnomes were no strangers to change: their bodies shifted and contorted naturally, elongating or contracting to fit the space. But going through a portal pulled and shoved them in ways outside their own control, turning them sideways and upside down into screaming winds and bitter cold before dropping them abruptly onto cold, hard stone.

They rolled and got to their feet, hands shaping into claws, eyes alert to danger even before they focused enough to see the tall—armed—forms circling them.

Preters. Armed, alert preters.

"Well, well," a voice said from the crowd, dry and eager. "Maybe it won't be so boring staying here, after all."

"Oh, fuck," one of the gnomes muttered.

The plan had depended on the elves being distracted by the portal, by whatever it was they wanted to do to the other realm. But gnomes were used to things going wrong.

"Will you yield, live, and serve?" another of those dry voices asked. The preters had already drawn weapons, edged blades glinting in the pale lights of the cavern, so the question wasn't so much a query as a suggestion.

They had answered that question before and lied. There was no room now for prevarication or treachery.

"Die here, or die there," the lead gnome said, speaking for them all. "It doesn't matter."

# Chapter 17

"Come on," Seth said urgently.

They had abandoned the truck a few blocks away, Seth practically dragging them down the street. Jan had no idea what city they were in, or even what state, although she thought it might be Hartford, from the not-quite-gentrified feel. The air was cold, and the streetlights cast more shadows than light as they passed underneath. Caught up in her own half-awake thoughts, Jan crashed to a stop on a corner, when both Seth and Martin both halted abruptly.

"We're too late," Seth said, his face up, sniffing at the air.

"Never too late," Martin said. "Not until everyone's dead." With that uncomfortably cryptic comment, he started moving again, running not for the building itself—a church, Jan finally realized—but the wrought-iron gate behind the building. Her eyelids flickered in a now-familiar urge to close, and when she opened them again, a dark, four-legged form was soaring over the gate.

"Show-off," Seth muttered and headed for the gate's swinging door, unhooking the latch and slipping inside like just another shadow in the night.

"Too late for what?" Jan asked, caught between confusion and a sort of undefined rage that had apparently been building in her while she slept, and Martin, it seemed, got information she didn't have.

*"Supers,"* she said with disgust and then, for better measure, *"men."*

Wishing she still had the blade they had found in the preter realm, or a Taser, or something that could qualify as a weapon, Jan touched the fabric of her pocket over the inhaler once for reassurance and followed the super through the gate.

On the other side, there was a narrow verge of grass and then low, thin shapes that she identified as tombstones. They were in the graveyard. An old church, then, and as her eyes adjusted, she saw that it filled the entire city block, a low scape of headstones broken by the occasional mausoleum or statue.

Scattered and moving through that stonescape were other shadows, breaking apart and coming together, over and over again. And while on the other side of the gate there had been silence, here the night was filled by the grunts and low-pitched screams of bodies being thrown against each other, and an occasional, nerve-rattling sound like metal being scraped against stone and bone.

"Oh, god." As her eyes adjusted, she was able to make out more detail, seeing that the fighting filled the graveyard, still more forms emerging from the double doors at the side of the building, occasionally falling back inside the building as though going back for seconds. She scanned the entire scene, instinctively looking for and then finding Martin. He was surrounded on all sides, hooves striking out. One hit a preter, another clashed off a tombstone, creating hot blue sparks and sending the abused stone tumbling over to the ground.

Another set of bodies flew past her—literally—as a winged super went by carrying an elongated form that could only be a preter. A third, unidentified figure ran alongside, hacking at the preter with a blade. A wet splatter of something hit Jan, and she raised her hand instinctively to wipe it away. Her hand came away glistening with something dark and heavy, strands dangling from her finger.

She heaved, and her chest caught, fingers squeezing her lungs until all the air left and none could get in, panic starting even as she fumbled for her inhaler, pulling it out of her jeans pocket and fitting it to her mouth, breathing in. It took real force to move her hand away long enough to exhale, and when she tried to breathe again, her lungs unclenched only long enough for her to toss the contents of her stomach onto the grass in front of her.

She stayed down on her knees, some part of her brain telling her that she was less of a target that way, and forced herself to watch the battle raging in front of her. It was brutal, the sounds vicious, and she couldn't tell which side, if either, was winning.

Her lungs still felt like something was pressing against them, and her mouth and throat felt awful from throwing up, but she could breathe, could move. The smell of the sachet in her pocket came to her faintly, and she breathed in, openmouthed. The panic receded a little more, and she could think again. *I need to do something.* But the thought of moving, of doing anything, was beyond comprehension. Nalith had been right; she was useless.

A body came out of the shadows at her—it was flying backward, she realized, even as she reacted, ducking out of the way and grabbing at it as it went past, yanking down hard until it hit the ground.

"Nice!" A supernatural grinned at her from out of the gloom, its face streaked with what might've been mud or blood and was probably both. Its teeth were very white, and then it was gone, back into the melee.

At her feet, the preternatural groaned and tried to get up, and Jan put her foot on its face, pressing it back down to the ground. "Stay put," she told it. It would be smarter to break its neck or something. The knife the supernatural had given her in the yard was tucked inside her jacket—she hadn't wanted to be walking on the street with it visible. She could pull it out, stab it…but she didn't know where a killing blow would be, and if it broke free and grabbed her, then *it* would have the knife. She was wearing boots—maybe a heavy stomp would do it, and…

The faint sting of the splatter was still tingling on her face, and the acrid taste of vomit in her mouth was too real, the thuds and low screams around her too insistent. Not even a preter. She couldn't.

Jan's eyes had adjusted enough to the lighting, or lack thereof, to see the battle better now. She didn't want to see it better, didn't want to see it at all, but that was Martin in there, and Seth, and somewhere AJ, too. They were fighting for their lives—and hers. Jan had no illusions about that. The preter lying restless but still under her foot would destroy her, given a chance. Maybe not kill her, but something worse than that—would take her will away, turn her into something that served out of some kind of twisted love/fear/masochism thing.

"I know it wasn't you who did that to Tyler," she said to it, almost conversationally, "but you did it to someone else to be here, didn't you?" That was how they held the portals open, with humans. Human slaves. Human "pets," tortured emotionally and physically until they would do anything for the preter who held their leash. Until Ty, broken free and healing, still couldn't return to his old life, couldn't accept love or hope, but stayed behind so he could wash the pain off with blood….

The preter looked up at her, its face pale and beautiful, even half-coated in its own blood. "And they loved me for it," it agreed, its voice too beautiful, too melodic, to come from such a creature. "As will you."

Everyone had their breaking point. Jan knew that, rationally. She knew that there was provocation that caused someone to bend down and pick up a stone, to hurl it with such force that it became a weapon, a killing tool.

When blood splattered up her arms, across her torso, the metallic grit of something on her tongue, and she wasn't sure if it was her blood or not, Jan dropped the rock in her hands, her fingers clenching convulsively.

Too many friends had died. Too many things had been destroyed. Jan couldn't feel regret at her actions. She couldn't feel anything at all.

If the preters won here, they would do terrible things. They'd admitted it in their own words. By the time anyone else realized what had happened, tried to resist, it would be too late.

But if they killed all the preters, every last one of them who was here, then the magic tying them to the humans and holding open the portal would also die. Wouldn't it? Wouldn't that stop them, if not for always, then at least for now, until they could find a way to shut the portals forever?

Where were the humans? Jan thought suddenly. Where were the ones holding *open* the portal? Indecision pushed aside the numbness, indecision and fear not for herself but for the others. Others like Ty, who hadn't had someone like her and Martin to get them out, get them home safe. Where were they?

*Worry about them later,* a small, cold part of her brain said. *As long as the preters need them, they're safe, physically.*

*Mostly,* another part of her brain said, remembering Tyler in the first moments. *Only mostly.*

Mostly had to be enough. The preters were the real threat.

Jan reached inside her jacket and pulled out the knife. She didn't know how to fight with it, but if someone fell on her, she could probably manage to stab them. She could take out one or two....

*We cannot destroy each other, or the balance between the realms will shift. You* know *this.*

Martin's voice, but not Martin shaping the words. Jan didn't believe in god, or gods, or fate...but she believed in the Center. She had to; she'd *been* there.

This wasn't what the words had meant, Jan told herself, taking a firmer grip on the fabric-wrapped hilt, trying to rub off the sweat on her palm. That had been about all-out war, about destroying realms, not—

Balance. About maintaining balance. How no matter who tried to change the balance or for what reasons, imbalance would only make things worse in the long run.

Jan wasn't sure she wanted to know what "worse" might be. But she couldn't just stand there and let people—more people—she called friend, die. Her fingers curling around the hilt of the knife, Jan tried to find that place she'd been in before, that numb space where killing had become the only possible reaction. Her nostrils flared, and for a moment—just a moment—she could almost smell what Martin and Seth had reacted to. Blood, yeah, and fear, and a particular cold taint that she had come to recognize was the scent of a preter.

And it was coming from *behind* her.

Somehow, impossibly, she wasn't surprised to see Nalith or the shadow lurking just behind her. If even she, Jan, could smell the bloodshed here, there was no way the preter queen could resist it, even if it meant abandoning her own court.

She had done it once before, after all, hadn't she?

"You got here fast," she said almost idly, letting the blade rest obviously in her hand. If Nalith tried to aid the preters, Jan was pretty sure that she would be able to thrust the blade into the queen's side. Pretty sure.

What she wasn't sure about was if Tyler would try to stop her or not.

"I killed the one who brought me here," Nalith said, her gaze on the battlefield, not acknowledging Jan's words or even her existence. "So that they could not open that portal again, could not find me, to bring me back. When their scouts came close, I merely moved, keeping a pace ahead of them at all times. I did not think that they would go to such lengths, to bring so many over at once."

She sounded almost pleased by those lengths, by the carnage. Apparently, Jan thought with cold amusement, even unwanted attention fed her preternatural ego.

*Like Stjerne,* she thought. *Like the consort. All me-me-me.*

"It's not only about you anymore," Jan said. "You paid too much attention to this realm, so now they want it. Not to keep it, though. If they win, they'll destroy everything you desire about us. They will take you back like a spoiled child being sent to her room, and lay waste to the things you value. It will destroy the spark you were chasing, grind it into ash, and laugh when it goes out forever. The Center *warned* you."

The Center didn't speak to her, a mere mortal human, but she was good at looking at the pieces, putting them together and finding the pattern that made it all work. Logic. It wasn't just for breakfast anymore.

"They will not succeed," Nalith said, still not looking at her. Preternatural eyesight must be better than human, the way she was almost eating the scene in front of her, her face rapt with…something. "I am stronger than them, in any configuration they attempt. I will not go back."

"Yeah." Jan pulled up as much sarcasm and irony and doubt

and all the other tones she'd ever used to cut someone down, and loaded that one word with it. It was enough to make Nalith turn and look at her. "But they're not going to stop trying, are they? You preters, you don't change. You don't *want* to change, most of you, and the fact that you did, that scares the ever-living whatever out of them."

There was a slight brush of something against her hand and then the familiar feeling of fingers sliding against her palm, clasping it. A human hand, slightly sweaty but *real*. She squeezed once briefly and kept talking. "And they will keep coming, to either take you or destroy you, and you will keep—what? Moving? Throwing your new court in front of you like some kind of living wall? Think about this, then, when you're contemplating that future. You're using our tech to enhance your own magic. I don't know how, but I know you are. Only thing is, our tech? It's fragile. A single power outage and you'll be just as helpless as we are."

Maybe. A theory, on the spur of the moment. *Don't show doubt,* Jan thought. *Be ruthless, go for the kill.*

"No, you'll be even more, because you'll be dependent on your court. And how well will those leashed dogs be loyal, if you show them weakness?"

Nalith straightened her shoulders, her pale blue eyes not showing the spark that supers did, but unnerving enough in the night. "They will give up. Eventually. Especially if your people kill enough of them."

"So long as you are here, they will return." Tyler spoke up now, his voice small but clear, even when Nalith turned to stare at him, as though her lapdog had just bitten her. "They could let me go—I didn't matter. But you are part of them. They could have chosen a new queen, pretended you were dead or had never existed, but they couldn't."

"It's not in their nature," Jan said. "They won't change."

Nalith lifted her chin proudly, refuting them. "I changed."

"No, you didn't," Jan said, sure now that she was on the right track. "Not inside, where it matters. You saw something you wanted, something you didn't have, and you tried to take it, demanded it as your right. But it doesn't work that way." Jan took a breath to say something else, something scathing, but Tyler squeezed her hand harder, a clear warning. Push her too far, and she would kill them.

A shape came over the far-right line of tombstones, kicking a preter in the face and sliding under the blade of another. Jan's breath caught: Martin. She couldn't see if he was injured, but he was moving awkwardly, without his usual horse-form grace. And then a third form came out of the gloom just as he dealt with the first two, trying to cut Martin's legs out from under him. Jan forgot Nalith, forgot everything but the danger in front of her. She dropped Tyler's hand and moved forward, her other hand gripping the small blade the super had given her. Off balance on the gore-slick grass, she was still able to jab the blade up, catching the preter in what she thought was either his thigh or ass. Either way, it was enough to distract him away from Martin.

Another figure swooped in from above and finished him off, even as Jan scurried back to relative safety, her breath harsh in her throat and the insane desire to let loose with a whoop curling in her chest.

"Are you insane?" Tyler hissed, grabbing her elbow and pulling her close to him. She might have been; it almost didn't matter.

Nobody seemed to have realized that the preter queen was among them. She had wrapped herself in thicker shadows, and even knowing she was there, Jan had trouble finding her again.

"I've tried." Nalith continued their conversation as though

nothing had happened, her gaze seemingly caught by a tombstone off to their left, waist high and deeply carved with rosettes. "I've tried everything. It comes so easily to you all, even you. Everything in this world has some spark, some thing, that lets you create. Even the meanest, dullest child draws, dances, sings, and there is a spark. I want that."

Jan stared up at the preter. All this—for that? Because she wanted to be an artist? But it made sense, in a weird sort of way. Preters were cold, hard—all the things that the fairy tales said about elves. But they loved arts, and poetry, and all that, and maybe for one of them, being a patron, however twisted, hadn't been enough.

The queen had wanted it enough to give up everything. Would destroy everything if she couldn't have it. She didn't understand that you couldn't force that, either, couldn't *demand* it and make it happen.

But preters had honor, too. The consort had honored their bargain, had let them walk away. Nalith had asked for their fealty, not forced it. They had been the ones fooling her, not the other way around.

Oh, this was going to *suck*.

"You don't have it." It was hard—Jan had never been good at letting anyone down, gently or otherwise. She was more likely to encourage beyond reasonable limits than tell them their heart's desire was out of reach. But the stakes were too high, and the body count was mounting. Soon, they'd notice the three of them, and…and Jan wasn't sure they could run fast enough, even if they started now. "Wanting isn't enough. You could work the rest of your life—" however long that was "—and you still wouldn't be anything more than technically adept."

"Where is it? Where do you hide that skill?" It was a demand rather than a question, but now Jan could almost hear the panic underneath it.

"Nobody knows. I told you that. Nobody knows why one person gets it and another doesn't, or why this person can sing and that person can draw, or... It just happens."

"I want it," Nalith said again, a touch of fire in her voice.

Jan tensed but didn't back down. Cruel to be kind; hell, cruel to survive. She'd learned that lesson better than Nalith had learned hers. "Yeah, well, life sucks that way. Here, at least. Probably there, too, from what you've said."

The preter drew herself up—and then stopped. Her attention had been caught by something, but Jan didn't risk looking away to see what it was.

"Nalith." The voice was silver-bright and familiar. Next to her, Tyler shuddered once but said nothing. A preter limped toward them, barely sparing the humans a glance. It wasn't the consort, nor were the two moving with him. The fighting slowed, shadow-figures moving to surround them. Jan swallowed, feeling sweat on her face and down her back, despite the chill.

"Damn it, Seth, I told you to get them safe, not to bring them here." AJ's growl, unpretty but far more welcoming, as the *lupin* matched the consort's pace, carefully and almost subtly preventing him from coming closer to the two humans.

Around them, the fighting slowed as the survivors realized that their leaders were distracted, and why.

"Under your own accord, or theirs," Jan said in a low voice, playing a hunch. Preters were cold, proud, selfish. But they had their own honor. And Nalith had been—was—a queen.

"I am...fond of this place," Nalith said. "The sunlight, the colors. I wanted to...to possess it. To make it part of me. But you are not wrong. It resists, refuses me." Her smile was sharp, but for once, there was little cruelty in it, and Jan thought what there was might have been directed inward, not out. "I am not accustomed to being refused."

"Humans," Tyler said. "We're obnoxious that way, sometimes."

"I would have been a benevolent queen," she said, and Jan was pretty sure that she believed that, which was a whole new kind of terrifying.

"You can be," Jan said. "Just not here."

After a major project was finished, Jan always felt wound up, jittery—until the realization that they were done set in, at which point she felt the urge to crawl into bed, pull the covers over her head, and lie there like a lump, exhausted by the anticlimax. That same urge hit her now, looking at the portal shimmering in the basement of the old church.

"What about…them?" She lifted one index finger and pointed at the humans, lining the wall and staring at the portal as if it was the best reality show on TV ever.

"We take them with us," the consort said matter-of-factly.

"The hell you do."

"Jan." Tyler stopped her from saying more. "Wait."

She glared at him, then Martin touched her hand, and she dropped her gaze. Ty had been one of those, once. He knew, better than she, what they were feeling, thinking. "What, then? Let them go back, as…pets?"

"Humans have been doing it for centuries," AJ said. His face was bruised, as if someone had taken a two-by-four to the left side of his head—for all she knew, someone *had*—and he was listing slightly, but there was no doubt that he was in control of the moment. Jan would be annoyed at being replaced if she weren't so grateful for it.

"If they were treated the same way you were…"

"They were." He had no hesitation on that score.

"So, don't you think maybe they have someone who wants them home?" *Like you did,* she didn't say. He'd either know that or not, but this wasn't the place or time.

"I think maybe it doesn't matter. They're broken. Unless the supers are willing to spend six months trying to glue the pieces back for all of them... How the hell are they supposed to recover, when nobody will believe where they've been or what happened to them?"

And there was no one here to hold them went unspoken. It took true love, a true heart, to break a preter's glamour.

"They are ours," the consort repeated.

"My lady," Jan said with exaggerated politeness to Nalith. "Please tell your consort to shut the hell up."

"Shut up," she said to him. Then "Your leman is correct. Whatever damage was done to them in our care, your people cannot cure. It was ever thus." Her smile was both sad and weirdly proud. "What Under the Hill takes, it keeps."

"She's not wrong, Jan," AJ said, his voice harsh but not entirely unkind. "You were able to save Tyler because, well, you had a stronger bond. Love trumps everything else. But you don't have that here. We can't even know these people *have* a true love to make the attempt."

She slid her hand into her pocket and pulled out the remains of some dried herbs and cotton. The sachet had worn through during the fight. The little horse was cool and smooth under her fingertips. A healing fetish. "We have to try!"

"Why?"

Jan exhaled hard and reminded herself that she wasn't arguing with humans. AJ and Martin and the others were... well, not human. They didn't feel the same way she did. It was getting harder to remember that, until they reminded her.

"Jan." It was the first time Nalith had ever used her name. "I will ensure that they are cared for. They will lack for no comfort in my court. And if ever any wish their freedom or a leman comes to find them, they will be released."

It took a true heart to break the glamour, reclaim a human who was taken. Maybe—maybe, and Jan wasn't placing any bets on it—a true heart could keep them safe there, too.

It was as good a deal as she was going to be able to make, without giving something in return. Jan nodded once, still reluctant. "They're your art," she said softly. "Care for them."

Nalith made a gesture, and the remaining preternaturals—far the worse for wear and war—went to the humans, tapping them on the shoulder and summoning them back to awareness. Slowly, they moved toward the mistily glowing arch of the portal and disappeared through it.

Jan remembered her own travels through the portals and swallowed hard, the sensation of tumbling through an airless void still number two in her nightmare hit list, right after being attacked by gnomes.

"Oh. The gnomes…" she said, horrified that she had forgotten, even for a moment.

"Gone to ground. Literally, it seems." AJ was grimly satisfied by that. "The few who were still around have disappeared. Hopefully they'll be licking their wounds for a long time, because we're not going to forget anytime soon."

"Nor will I," Nalith said, equally grim, and the two exchanged looks that made Jan stop worrying about the turncoats. As tough as she liked to think she'd become, she didn't have a patch on either one of those two.

"Fare thee well, Janet," Nalith said. "You were a terrible servant, and I am well rid of you."

"Go home, my lady," Jan replied. "Put your house in order and take care of your remaining servants. I pray I never see you or your kind again."

Not a win, not a loss. Stalemate. Or maybe, Jan thought bitterly, balance.

A few minutes later, the mist pulled into the portal's frame and disappeared, leaving the basement empty of all save a dozen supernaturals, two humans, and a few scorch marks on the floor and ceiling where the portal had been.

"So," Martin said, having changed back into human shape at some point during the negotiations with the preter queen. Jan hadn't even noticed her eyes closing; she'd been so focused. "What now?"

"We need to break the portals, make it so they can never come back again," Tyler said. He was holding Jan's hand so tightly her fingers had gone numb, but she couldn't bring herself to care or try to get loose. "The only way we'll ever be safe is to break the portals."

Jan shook her head, even as AJ said, "We can't. We can't even stop them from using humans again to force a portal."

"But—" Tyler's voice was pure pain. Whatever healing he'd hoped to find, whatever protection the sachet had given him, it hadn't been enough, and Jan's heart ached for him.

"We can't stop them *yet*," AJ amended. "We'll keep working on it."

A woman who had stayed on the outskirts with the other combatants now inserted herself into their loose huddle. She was human, Jan realized, and her face was covered with splatters of blood. "Whatever happened, the world has changed. We can't go back. Magic can be lost, forgotten…but it can't be unmade." She looked at them each in turn, her eyes cold but not unfriendly. "We will always be at risk."

A witch, like Elizabeth. How many others had been out there, in the fight? How many had died? Jan wasn't sure she wanted to know, but knew she would have to, eventually.

"We've always been at risk," Jan said. "Right now, our best hope is that Nalith, once she regains control of the court, remembers how badly she failed here, how badly they need her there—and that we know how to find her, how to hurt them, if they overstep again."

"So, our survival is dependent on the wounded ego of a preter?" AJ was too dignified, even now, to roll his eyes, but they could hear the disbelieving exasperation in his voice.

"Yeah," Martin said. "Funny, huh?"

"You have a sick sense of humor, swishtail."

"You're not the first to say that." He leaned against Jan slightly, and she realized that he was bleeding. "It's nothing," he said, hearing her gasp. "I'm fine."

"You're an idiot," she said and looked up to see Tyler watching both of them. He had a strange expression on his face, one she couldn't read.

"We're all idiots," he said, getting closer to look at Martin's arm. The kelpie snorted but let the humans guide him to a chair while they fussed over him.

Her best friend. Her leman. Both alive. Not right, not well, not healthy, but alive. Right then, that was all she could focus on.

"So, what now?" Martin asked again, looking over at AJ. The *lupin* raised his brow and shrugged. "I don't know about the rest of you," he said, turning briefly to look at where the portal had been, "and it may be the worst cliché in history, but I need a drink."

## Chapter 18

Three days later, the exhaustion had faded, and Jan had almost stopped jumping at shadows in the night. Almost.

She was actually quite proud of the fact that when a deep
voice came out of the darkness, she only clenched the mug
between her hands more tightly and kept her ass planted on
the log she was sitting on.

"So, you are Jan," that voice said.

She almost smiled at that. "I think so. I'm not really sure
right now."

It had been three days since Martin had brought her to the
Center and left her there. For rest, he had said. But he had
left her alone, with nothing to do but think. She was good at
thinking. Less so, it seemed, at resting. Even without the tick-
tick-tick of the deadline in her chest, even without the manic
anxiety, once the deadline had passed, she still felt…odd.

The others at the Center left her alone, mostly. She was fed,
and if she wanted to talk to someone, they didn't exactly run
away, but…these weren't the supers she knew, the people she
knew, and Jan suspected that she smelled of preter to them.

Sometimes, she thought she smelled of preter to herself,
too. Preter and super and blood and dust, and not much of
Jan left at all.

She went to bed each night with the carved horse pressed
against her palm, wishing she were home, curled on the sofa
with Tyler. Or sitting on the grass with Martin, watching

niskies splash in the pond. But the Farm wasn't home, and her apartment and Tyler's were gone, someone else living in them now.

And Glory, who was supposed to be here, was supposed to be *here, safe,* and wasn't.

If Jan couldn't find peace here, then how could she find it anywhere?

The source of that deep voice sat on the log next to her, groaning a little as he stretched his legs out in front of him and got comfortable.

There were other campfires, all of them more social than hers, and she should have resented being approached, but she knew who the old man was.

"Once the off-natural touches you, you are never the same," the Huntsman agreed, seemingly responding to both what she'd said and what she'd been thinking. "But that does not change who you are."

"No. No, I guess it doesn't." But it changed everything else.

He didn't seem to want to talk, so Jan went back to staring at the fire. Even though it was late autumn back home, it never seemed to get cold in the Center, just enough of a temperature drop to make it good sleeping weather. For her, anyway; she didn't know what the various supers thought about it, but most of them had fur or scales to deal with, not bare flesh.

She missed Martin. She missed Tyler. She wondered if Nalith had anyone she missed, or if she was pleased to be reunited with her consort.

Somehow, Jan didn't think she did, or was. Something burned in the preter, something fierce and determined, but it wasn't a heart.

"You're very brave," the Huntsman said out of nowhere.

That not only made her smile but laugh. "What, you mean

the 'terrified but going forward anyway' thing? Yeah. I got that. It's the picking up after that's got me stumped."

"Ah." It was an intensely irritating noise, the kind a teacher made when you couldn't answer a question they thought you should know cold.

She stared into the fire, taking the little horse out of her pocket. For healing, the witch had said. And had given it to her, not the others. Jan rubbed her fingers over the dots in the horse's flank, along the arched mane, and then put it back in her pocket. Maybe it wasn't magic at all. Maybe it was just…comfort.

Tyler had been invited to the Center, too. Martin would have taken them both. He had declined. She understood that, a little. He wanted to get distance, find himself in the real world, the human world.

She wasn't ready for that. Not yet. She might not have changed, but she wasn't the same, either. And unlike Ty, she'd chosen it. Most of it. And…they weren't all bad memories.

Except, of course, for the ones that were really bad.

Jan let out a sigh and heard the Huntsman echo it, with something that might have been a chuckle, too, as if he knew what she was thinking. He probably did.

How did you go back to an ordinary life when you'd been, however briefly, extra-ordinary? Except that was exactly what you did, apparently. The dead were buried or burned. AJ's pack was back to stealing cars, Elsa was returning to her mountain—she was from the Appalachians, not Norway or whatever, Jan had learned with a shock—and the others were doing whatever it was they'd done before. The threat was over, life resumed.

Jan seemed to be the only one who didn't know where she was or what to do.

"I found this," the Huntsman said. "In the crook of a tree,

in the copse of trees on the Farm when we were cleaning up."
He handed her a black plastic bag, folded flat, with something
inside. She took it, opened it.

A notebook, slightly stained with coffee rings on its red
cover. Inside, notes scrawled in blank ink, in handwriting
she didn't recognize, but turns of phrase and little scrawled
doodles that she did.

Her breath caught a little. Glory's notes. Everything they
had learned, everything she was working on when the Farm
was overrun, put somewhere safe, so someone could find them
later. Jan's throat tightened, and she wished it was an asthma
attack, that there was something that would ease the pain.
Glory wasn't here, wasn't anywhere. They hadn't found anything to bury, AJ said. Nothing at all, just…gone.

It was her fault that Glory had gotten caught up in this.
Hers—and the Huntsman's, for bringing her to the Farm, but
Jan's at the very start.

Because it was there, because Glory had written it, Jan tried
to make out the words, squinting in the firelight. At the top
of one page, chosen randomly: "Not multiple universes: one
overlapping over and over again?" There were other com-
ments about strings and theology, and strings of code Jan
couldn't decipher, and the letters *LHC* over and over again,
often underlined. And then one word: *cool*.

Jan stared at it. Strings. Large Hadron Collider. Multiple
universes. She wasn't a scientist, but she was a geek, and she
had *New Scientist* and NASA on her Twitter feed, once upon
a time, just like every other geek. *Cool*. "Seriously, Glor?"

She could almost hear her friend's laughter, her face alive
with an imp of mischief, ready to leap into some new rabbit
hole, just because it was there.

Jan's responsibility for bringing her into it, but Glory would
have been pissed as hell if she'd been kept out of this, all this,

the exciting and the terrifying. Maybe the Huntsman had known that somehow. And that she would have gone down swinging, to the very end.

Jan set her jaw and flipped to the last pages with writing on them. "Binary thinking. Set patterns. Zero is the key? Sixteen could be scary. Do not let them form sixteen. Or, bloody hell, anything higher." There were more formulas, crosshatched and scribbled out, and then, the last thing Glory had written: "We need a damned physicist, not code monkeys. Put that on shopping list for when Jan gets back: one damned physicist."

"So, that's what happened," Jan said quietly, almost to herself, caught between wonder and fear. "We poked at the universe, and poked all the way damn through, somehow. And Nalith caught at the threads and rewove them."

"Does it make sense to you now?" the Huntsman asked

"No. But I don't think it's supposed to." She closed the notebook, rested it on her lap, thought about the sixteen humans in a circle around the portal, sixteen given to the uncertain mercies of the preter queen.

Even a lab of actual rocket scientists might not be enough to fix this. You couldn't undo, undiscover science, any more than you could undo magic. Like getting on Martin's back, you had to ride or die.

"What do you think happened to her?" she asked out of the blue. "To them?" Glory and the dryad who'd tried to save her.

The fire snapped and sparked, barely enough to read by, but didn't do much to illuminate the shape next to her, his face still in shadow. "What do you think?"

"I think she's okay," Jan said, still hearing that faint laughter in her ears. "I don't know why, but I think she's somewhere safe. That she grabbed a thread, somehow, and... It's foolish, wish-fulfillment thinking, but—"

"The universe is a funny, tricky thing," he said, his voice thoughtful. "If there's no body, there's…chance."

Jan let her hand rest on the notebook, looked up at the unknown star formations that wheeled and shone over the Center, and nodded. She had seen too much to discount chance.

"So, what now?" she asked. "I've got no job, no home, no—" she started to say *no friends,* but that wasn't true. That wasn't true at all.

The Huntsman chuckled, as though hearing her thoughts. You couldn't undiscover. You could only keep discovering.

"I think I'd like to go home now," she said.

"Back where it all started, are you?"

Jan scattered the rest of her muffin on the ground, watching the pigeons peck at it. She didn't look up when AJ sat down on the bench next to her.

"You can't go back. You can only go forward. Isn't that right?"

It had been this bench, in the Green, where AJ and Martin had first broken the news to her, about Tyler being elf-napped, about supernaturals and preternaturals, about what it would take to get him home. Everything that had happened had started here.

"If I'd known then…" The *lupin* hesitated.

"You'd have done exactly the same."

"Yeah. I would have."

She wanted to hate him, blame him. Instead, she wiped her hands on her jeans and watched the pigeons.

A hand touched her shoulder, fingers cool, bringing just the hint of green water and brine to her nose. She reached up and let her fingers cover Martin's, acknowledging him there without turning to look.

Her best friend was a homicidal serial killer who occasionally had another form, and her other best friend was...missing, presumed having an adventure.

"Tyler's left," she said. "Taken a job in California."

"I'm sorry."

She wanted to say that it was okay, but it wasn't. There was a gaping hole inside her heart, worse even than the first time, when she'd thought he'd walked out on her, that he'd run off with another woman. Knowing that the man she loved, loved her but couldn't *be* with her...that was an entirely different kind of pain. She wasn't strong enough to wish him well, either.

"I'll survive," she said instead.

"Yes." AJ was smiling, she thought, although she didn't look sideways to check. "Yes, you will."

★ ★ ★ ★ ★

# C.E. MURPHY

## YOU CAN NEVER GO HOME AGAIN

Joanne Walker has survived an encounter with the master at great personal cost, but now her father is missing—stolen from the timeline. She must finally return to North Carolina to find him—and to meet Aidan, the son she left behind long ago.

That would be enough for any shaman to face, but Joanne's beloved Appalachians are being torn apart by an evil reaching forward from the distant past. Anything that gets in its way becomes tainted—or worse.

And Aidan has gotten in the way.

Only by calling on every aspect of her shamanic powers can Joanne pull the past apart and weave a better future. It will take everything she has—and more.

Unless she can turn back time....

### Available wherever books are sold!

### Be sure to connect with us at:
Harlequin.com/Newsletters
Facebook.com/HarlequinBooks
Twitter.com/HarlequinBooks

# Discover The Portals series by

# LAURA ANNE GILMAN

*He has been taken, and you are his only chance.*

All of humanity is at risk when a portal between worlds opens. A preternatural force has entered the natural world and seeks to make humans its slaves. Now humans and shape-shifters must unite against a shared enemy. When Jan's boyfriend is dragged across the portal, she must take up arms or risk losing Tyler—and the world she knows—forever.

## Available wherever books are sold!

## www.LauraAnneGilman.net

NEW YORK TIMES BESTSELLING AUTHOR

# MICHELLE SAGARA

## THE END OF HER JOURNEY IS
## ONLY THE BEGINNING...

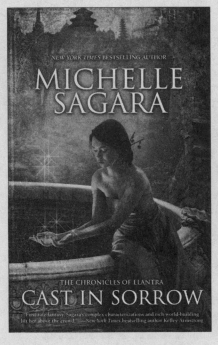

The Barrani would be happy to see her die. So Kaylin Neya is a bit surprised by her safe arrival in the West March. Especially when enemies new and old surround her and those she would call friends are equally dangerous....

And then the real trouble starts. Kaylin's assignment is to be a "harmoniste"—one who helps tell the truth behind a Barrani Recitation. But in a land where words are more effective than weapons, Kaylin's duties are deadly. With the wrong phrase she could tear a people further asunder. And with the right ones... well, then she might be able to heal a blight on a race.

If only she understood the story....

## Available wherever books are sold!

### Be sure to connect with us at:

Harlequin.com/Newsletters
Facebook.com/HarlequinBooks
Twitter.com/HarlequinBooks

SMS356TR